GONE

Helena Echlin grew up in north London and now lives in San Francisco, where she works as a freelance writer.

Helena Echlin

GONE

VINTAGE

Published by Vintage 2003

2 4 6 8 10 9 7 5 3 1

Grateful acknowledgement for permission to reprint song
lyrics is made to the following: the Warner/Chappell Corpo-
ration for 'Honey I'm Home' by Shania Twain and Robert
John Lange, and 'If I Ain't Got You' by Trisha Yearwood;
EMI Music Publishing for 'Daddy's Hands' by Holly Dunn;
Sony Music Publishing for 'A Little Gasoline' by Tammy
Rogers and Dean Miller; and Acuff-Rose Music Publishing
for 'All My Exes Live in Texas' by George Strait.

First published in Great Britain in 2002 by
Secker & Warburg

Addresses for companies within The Random House Group Limited can be found at:
www.randomhouse.co.uk/offices.htm

The Random House Group Limited supports The Forest Stewardship
Council (FSC®), the leading international forest certification organisation.
Our books carrying the FSC label are printed on FSC® certified paper.
FSC is the only forest certification scheme endorsed by the leading
environmental organisations, including Greenpeace. Our
paper procurement policy can be found at
www.randomhouse.co.uk/environment

MIX
Paper | Supporting
responsible forestry
FSC® C018179

The Random House Group Limited Reg. No. 954009
www.randomhouse.co.uk

A CIP catalogue record for this book
is available from the British Library

ISBN 0 099 43768 6

Printed and bound in Great Britain by Clays Ltd, St Ives PLC

For Jordan

I would like to thank the friends whose advice reshaped drafts, especially Ben Rice, Diana Sabot and David Shelley, as well as my agent, Laura Susijn, who believed in this book from the beginning, and my editor, Geoff Mulligan, whose insight brought it to completion.

Contents

1

Tough Guy

'WOULD YOU STILL LOVE me if I lost both my arms and legs?' Elizabeth asks. Spencer squeezes her thigh. Then he moves his fingers higher.

'I'll always love you,' he replies.

'Would you still love me if I was just my brain? Sitting in a jar and kept alive artificially?'

'You wouldn't be you if you were just a brain.' Spencer strokes her thigh with the back of his fingers and she leans back in her seat and opens her legs. When she has her eyes closed, she begins to remember. But when she opens her eyes, England vanishes.

So while his hand works, she gazes down the taut road and across the desert. The plain is covered with smoke-coloured sage, dotted with flowers she does not know the name of. Their petals are red, their stamens are burned wicks. This place is like something razed to the ground; nothing left but tough shrubs, a fine dust like ash. And that is why she likes it, its emptiness and space. She can be whoever she wants here.

When they stop at a Dairy Queen, the man behind the counter says, 'Hi, how are you?' For a moment, Elizabeth wonders if she might have met him before, but of course, his greeting is customary in America. Sex is turning her into an amnesiac. She is dazed and speechless. Her long dark hair is wild as a cavewoman's from the wind, her lipstick kissed away. Spencer's stubble has grazed her fair skin with hundreds of minute scratches, giving her a sunburned glow. They spent the day at one of the lakes that lie among the rust-coloured hills, swimming naked in the cool water and making love among the thorn bushes. Now they are on their way home.

'Why don't you try your luck at that?' asks Spencer. He squeezes her waist. On the counter there is a glass jar filled with water, assorted small change pebbled on the bottom. In the centre, a nickel sits on a small plastic pedestal. A sign says: *Drop a quarter directly on the nickel and win a Sixteen-Ounce Blizzard.* When she leans closer, she sees that the glass is bent so that the view of the coins is distorted. The nickel on its pedestal isn't in the centre of the jar at all. She pauses, and Spencer says, 'Do you want me to do it for you?' He drops the coin and they watch it turn over and over until it lands gently on top of the nickel.

'That's a kid's game,' says the man behind the counter, who has been watching them. 'Kids are supposed to win prizes. You both look like over-twelves to me.'

'It doesn't say that anywhere,' Spencer points out.

'Well, I don't make the rules,' says the man.

'Don't force us to report this incident to the manager,' Spencer says reasonably.

'I am the manager,' says the man.

'No, you're not.' Spencer nods at the badge on the man's uniform, adorned with a row of gold stars. *Dean Packer, Cashier. Four-Star Employee.*

'Are you calling me a liar?'

'Whoa there,' says Spencer, as if talking to a frisky racehorse. He pauses. 'Let me ask you something. How much is that Blizzard worth?'

'Couple dollars,' says Dean, sulkily.

'A couple of dollars,' Spencer repeats. 'Now, I eat a lot of burgers and I drink a lot of shakes. And if you don't give me that Blizzard, you'll lose a lot more than a couple of dollars. You'll lose my business. You'll lose her business.' He puts an arm around Elizabeth and pauses. 'Alternatively, you could get yourself a pair of loyal customers.'

Dean hesitates. Then he squeezes a nozzle until it oozes white milk shake into a paper cup. Spencer grins.

Elizabeth is disappointed. She had somehow been fooled by the word 'blizzard' into thinking it would be enormous. She saw the two of them sharing it out like manna, to happy children. In the car, the sweet sticky white stuff drips into her lap.

When Spencer asked her to join him in America, Elizabeth didn't stop to think about whether she knew him well enough or what she would do there. She said yes, in love with his blue-green eyes and his gold pirate's earring, his hot hard body and his close-shaved scalp that feels as rough as a cat's tongue. They met when she was an undergraduate studying music and he was at Oxford on a medical fellowship. That was just six months ago. Now he is doing his residency at a hospital on the edge of a desert town, and she is looking for work, living in a house made out of bottles, thousands of sweet miles away from home.

Each morning at dawn, Spencer pulls on his scrubs and leaves for the hospital. It is an hour's drive down the highway. Elizabeth does not have a job yet, so she sprawls in bed until late. The bed is made from two single mattresses pushed together and held tight in a frame made from nailed planks. They couldn't find anything big enough second-hand, so instead Spencer built them the Love Raft. So far, the Love Raft is the only thing in the bedroom, except for an old-fashioned brass lamp with a green glass shade that Spencer brought from his father's house. Her clothes lie in a tangle in her open suitcase.

3

Spencer rented the bottle house when she agreed to move out here. Its distance from the town makes it cheap. An architect with a passion for recycling built the place from used bottles and cans and anything he could lay his hands on. The walls are concrete, the roof is corrugated iron. Beer bottles and wine bottles are set in the concrete. From outside, the house is a great magpie's heap of junk glass and glinting metal. On the roof, a bent TV antenna rotates in the breeze, an old car wreck lies in the yard. The architect was a visionary who had no eye for detail. But inside, the sun streams through the green and brown glass and fills their four rooms with church-like mossy light.

Today Elizabeth sleeps later than usual. Finally, she gets up and goes to the kitchen, sets out a cup and a tea bag, and puts their one pan on the stove. The air is so thin here that water takes a long time to boil. Maybe it's the altitude that has been making her feel so tired. Her days are wasted. She makes shopping trips into town, which means walking to the end of their dirt road to wait for a bus which comes once an hour, since Spencer needs the truck to get to the hospital. She gets off the bus in a vast parking lot, then wanders across to the air-conditioned and hygienic mall, where yellow signs warn customers not to slip on the freshly mopped floor and in the bathrooms disposable seat covers protect against germs. Elizabeth makes small purchases for the bottle house, clothes hangers or pillowcases. Then she sits in the coffee shop and drinks iced coffees as strong as petrol. When she has to drop a few coins or a note into the tips jar labelled 'Thanks a Latte', she always fumbles with the money, trying to remember what each coin is worth.

She is ashamed of her inertia. When Spencer gets home from the hospital, he builds shelves and hammers up hooks, singing Willie Nelson songs as he works. Elizabeth just sits, or sometimes she makes a show of searching through the classifieds in the paper. The local high school needs a music teacher, and she circled the ad, but hasn't applied.

Elizabeth once saw a documentary that showed how the world looked to a snail, and how it looked to a fly. The snail paused at the edge of a quiet country lane, terrified as cars rushed by in a blur. The fly saw everything in slow motion. For the fly, the world was a graceful ballet, and it easily avoided the hand gliding to swat it. Spencer seems to live in the fly's time and she in the snail's.

Elizabeth uses some of the hot water to make Raisin 'n' Spice Instant Oatmeal, then goes outside. She wanders past the scrap car and along the dusty path across the plain. But she doesn't see the rocks or the cacti with their paddle-shaped branches or the lizard darting past her feet. She is walking through the house again, running her finger along a dusty dado, over the cold marble of the mantelpiece, pressing her cheek against the red bird flying in the stained-glass window. She came here to forget, but instead she keeps remembering. In the mall coffee shop, in walks on the plain, while she prepares their simple meals, places and people appear again. And instead of resisting, she slavishly assists, detail by luxurious detail. It is as if she is cleaning the grime from a vast masterpiece. As if she hopes to find something lost, to identify some long-blurred object.

*

Her mother was sitting on the sofa. 'Mum, I've been calling you for ages,' Elizabeth said.

'I didn't hear you,' her mother replied. She was still, staring ahead. Elizabeth longed to know what her mother was thinking about, what it was that could absorb her so completely that she didn't hear her children's voices. Elizabeth's father had made sea trout with *sauce bercy*, a tempting invalid's meal. Its savour floated up the stairs, but

Elizabeth's mother didn't smell it. However hard her father tried, he couldn't make her mother feel better. 'I'm *coming*,' said her mother, but she didn't move. Elizabeth waited. For her mother, time was a sewing machine that stopped, then juddered into life again. For hours sometimes, her mother didn't move or speak. But Elizabeth had never found out why.

★

Elizabeth is worried. She has been living here for nearly a month, and in all that time, her parents have not called her, have not replied to any of her messages. When Elizabeth left England, her mother sulked and wept by turns, but her father kept on making jokes, the way he always did, and she is surprised that he, at least, hasn't called by now. She does not expect to hear from her brother. Duncan has probably never written a letter in his life.

'How long has this been going on for?' asks Spencer. He has just got home from work to discover that the toilet isn't working. It doesn't flush properly and something keeps trickling.

'I'm not really sure,' says Elizabeth. 'I was out taking a walk.' Spencer puts his beer down on the edge of the bath, opens the cistern.

'I can't fix this. I need all sorts of stuff I don't have.' So they get in the truck and drive across the dusky plain and down the highway to Home Depot.

The store is the size of a cathedral, draped with orange banners reading 'Roofs', 'Gutters', 'Doors'. Shelves reaching to the ceiling are stacked with sheets of glass and lengths of guttering. There are rows of bins filled with nails and screws. Men with tape measures clipped to their jeans stroll up and down the aisles, chewing on meatball subs from the concession stand.

Spencer marches off, whistling a little under his breath. He grew up on a ranch that is a four-hour drive away, but sits in a landscape exactly like this one. The desert plains stretch unchanged for hundreds of miles in every direction. His mother died when he was a child. His father had the money to spoil him, but instead he insisted that his son take a fair share of the chores and learn young how to do things for himself. Spencer rode his horse bareback around the fields, and his father taught him how to use a gun to shoot grouse and how to choke the pesky prairie dogs with scattered bubble gum. He showed Spencer how to put up a tent, how to change a tyre, how to mend a roof, how to construct a wall. Elizabeth wishes she had learned about bricks and plaster, nails and screws, so that she too could build and mend things, so that she too could stride down the aisle knowing exactly what to look for. Trailing after him, she comes to a halt in front of the shower curtains. White, pink, patterned with conch shells or sailboats. She tries to imagine what would go with the bottles.

It amazes her how many things are needed to fill and furnish a house. They have bought a frayed green couch from the Salvation Army and a blue-and-red Mexican rug from a stall by the side of the road. They purchased an unpleasant but extensive floral dinner set from a man who had spread the plates and dishes on the meagre lawn in front of his house. They saw his felt-tipped sign, 'Everything Dirt Cheap', as they were driving by. The man let the dinner set go for a few dollars because, he told them, his wife had left him and he didn't want any reminders of her. But despite all these recent acquisitions, their rooms still feel bare.

'You gotta commit,' Spencer says. He has come back, having found what he needed, a pair of needlenose pliers. He shifts restlessly on his feet, ready to go.

'I'll just be one minute.' Maybe these things matter to her more because she's the one who spends the day in the house. 'That one would soon start looking dirty,' she says pointing to the white curtain. 'And that one looks like a sticking plaster,' she says, pointing to the pink one. 'Maybe we should go somewhere else.'

'Jesus,' says Spencer.

'What? What's your problem?'

'Don't snap at me.' Today he removed a piece of metal from a man's penis. The man had inserted it to increase his sexual pleasure, but it got infected. The operation was extremely fiddly. Spencer's T-shirt is sticking to his clammy back and there are threadlike veins in the whites of his eyes. 'It's just – that's what there is, sweetheart. We're not even here for a shower curtain. And it's late. Sometimes you gotta focus.'

'I thought since we were here anyway, we should just get one. Look, this will be decadent,' she tells him, dragging out a swathe of dark red, trying to be cheerful. He frowns.

'I don't like it when you brush things away. You snap at me, then suddenly everything's back to normal again. You're like a comic strip with some of the squares missing.'

On the way home, they see a pink neon cowboy hat with the words 'Rodeo Nites' beneath it, and Spencer pulls into the parking lot. 'Why are we stopping?' Elizabeth asks.

'I'm going to teach you how to dance,' he says. 'This'll make us feel better. It's what I grew up on.' They enter a makeshift building of concrete blocks and have their hands stamped. Inside, the pillars have been thoughtfully decorated with strings of lights in the shape of little beer bottles. Men in skin-tight Wrangler's and block-heeled cowboy boots are dancing, picking their feet up as daintily as marsh birds. They twirl women round and round without looking at them.

'It's quite simple,' says Spencer. 'Two long, two short.

And don't bounce.' He puts one hand on her waist and the other in hers and launches her out on to the floor. After a few minutes, he whispers, 'You're not following, sweetheart.'

'I am following,' she hisses back. 'I'm doing exactly what you showed me.'

'Two long, two short,' he repeats, tapping the beat on her shoulder. Her violin teacher used to do that when she could not get the rhythm right.

'Why can't we do turns like everybody else?' she asks. 'I want to *move*.'

'You're not ready for that yet.'

'But it's boring just doing the same thing over and over.'

'Dancing isn't about getting a workout in,' Spencer replies. He stops and waits for her to answer. But Elizabeth cannot stand to argue with him. She wishes he would lose his temper, but he remains calm, reasonable. Minutiae don't bother him. The shower curtain, the magpie house, even the broken toilet. In arguments with him, her usual ability to think logically dissolves, and instead she longs for a conflagration. When she doesn't say anything, he sighs.

'Maybe we should just take a break,' he says.

While Spencer makes his way to the bar, Elizabeth retreats to watch the other dancers. She catches the eye of a whip-thin man, dipping a dark-haired woman with careless grace. He winks. His partner looks around at Elizabeth, then pulls him closer, laughing at something he is saying. Elizabeth has seen these men filling their trucks at the gas station or waiting for coffee in diners. While they wait, they drum their fingers on the counter. She's seen them spitting from their truck windows at traffic lights, the whine of country music on the radio. They are the last cowboys, she thinks.

The man's partner disappears in the direction of the bathroom. She is wearing a ruffled skirt that swings out when she moves, and too much lipgloss. The man moves towards Elizabeth, then stops near her at the edge of the dance floor. He leans against a pillar and taps his foot. He is watching her out of the corner of his eye. He's very thin. Mr Whip, she thinks. Then someone pushes roughly round the pillar and bumps into Mr Whip, splashing him with beer. Mr Whip stands absolutely still. Beer drips from his wrist, soaks his sleeve. He stares at the man who bumped into him, and the man stares back.

'What's your problem?' Mr Whip drawls.

'You're the one with the problem, tough guy,' begins the man. Mr Whip draws himself up, and at that the man raises his hands placatingly. 'Look, take it easy. I said I'm sorry.' He has not said he's sorry. Mr Whip snorts and turns on his heel.

> Daddy's hands were soft and kind when I was cryin'.
> Daddy's hands were hard as steel when I'd done wrong.
> Daddy's hands weren't always gentle but I've come to
>   understand
> There was always love in Daddy's hands.

The music is coming from a truck's radio, a blue Ford pickup. Elizabeth smiles at the words. Her father almost never lost his temper. He probably did not even know how to throw a punch. He said he wanted them to write on his tombstone, *As Skilled On the Battlefield As In Conversation*. But he was not skilled on the battlefield.

Elizabeth sees the silhouette of the dark-haired woman sitting inside the truck. She is fluffing her hair in the mirror. Then on the other side of the truck someone says, 'Bullshit, you cocksucking motherfucker.' There is a muffled gasping and some thuds. She watches as Mr Whip climbs into the truck and reverses out. On the bumper there is a sticker reading *Gun Control Is Being Able To Hit Your Target*. As the truck drives away a dark shape picks itself up from the ground.

'Hey,' calls Spencer. 'You all right, man?'

'Forget about it,' the man calls, waving his hand in disgust.

On the way home, she asks Spencer: 'Have you ever been in a fight?'

'Only at school.'

'Are you good at it? Do you know how to punch?'

'Why? Do you?'

'Just wondering.' Her boyfriend Dax taught her, years ago. How to punch, how to kick, how to bite and draw blood.

'I could defend myself,' says Spencer. 'I've got a few tricks up my sleeve my father taught me.'

'Like what?'

'I'm driving.'

'Pull over and show me.'

Spencer sighs. He stops the truck on the dirt shoulder. The sky is littered with stars and a rabbit bolts into the stubby bushes. 'Come here,' he says. She stands in front of him. 'Now try and grab me,' he commands her. She reaches out, feels his finger boring into her wrist, and her arm drops. 'Try again,' he says. She lunges for him and this time his finger is behind her ear and she crumples to the ground. 'It's just a matter of knowing your opponent's weak spots,' he tells her, helping her up. 'Their pressure points, which are the places where a nerve travels close to the skin. Everyone has them. One in each arm, one in the neck, one behind the ears. Press down hard enough and they won't be able to take it.'

'Could you hurt someone that way?'

'You shouldn't have to hurt them,' Spencer says, 'but you could. There's a spot in your neck called the jugular notch, and if I pressed down hard enough there, first you'd gag, then if I kept going, you wouldn't be able to breathe and you'd suffocate.'

'Show me.' She knows she is being childish, but can't help it, slightly dizzy with vodka tonics. She wants to measure his strength.

'What's the matter with you?' says Spencer. 'I'm not going to *show* you.' He jumps back in the truck and slams his door, waiting for her to get in.

'I suppose if it was my funeral, you wouldn't come home for it.' It is her mother, finally, stung into calling by Elizabeth's announcement that she won't be home for Christmas. Elizabeth plans to accompany Spencer to his father's place instead, since she has never met him and besides, plane tickets to England are at their most expensive over Christmas. Because her parents weren't answering the phone, Elizabeth was forced to explain this in a message. Now she thinks if she had chosen one reason instead of two, she might have sounded more believable.

'Or if you came,' her mother continues, 'you'd just invite all those freeloading friends of yours.'

'Of course I'd come home if it were your funeral,' says Elizabeth.

'So you're saying you *can* come home for Christmas, but you don't want to,' says her mother.

'I want to but I can't.' She *doesn't* want to. It is because she wants to escape the person she was. It is because she has decided to stop trying to make her mother happy. It is because she is afraid of Duncan.

'I know you,' says her mother. 'Spend, spend, spend. That's why you can't afford it. When Dad and I moved in together, we had two plates, one set of cutlery and a card table. We didn't have enough money for curtains, so the neighbours could look in and watch us having dinner, taking turns with the knife and fork.'

'I know,' says Elizabeth, ignoring the exaggeration. There is a long pause. Her mother sighs. Then in a rush of unapologetic generosity, she says, 'Dad and I could help you with your plane fare. I don't want you to be worried about money.'

'I'll think about it,' says Elizabeth, hating herself for not standing firm. 'I'll let you know.' She waits until her mother hangs up, then slams the receiver back into the cradle.

Then she goes to the bathroom and discovers that the toilet isn't working at all now. When she flushes, the water just swills uneasily in the bowl. So she crouches behind the car wreck and pees in the dust. Like a true pioneer, she thinks. Afterwards, she hoists herself on to the rusty hood and practises spitting as far as she can. She wants to be able to spit like a cowboy, with nonchalant force. 'Cocksucking motherfucker,' she mutters until she feels better.

'What are these for?' she says. Poking about, she has discovered a pair of soft cuffs, closed with Velcro, in the bag that Spencer takes to the hospital. Each cuff is attached to a white cloth strap with a metal buckle.

'For holding down difficult patients.'

'Difficult?'

'If they're drunk, or violent, or mentally disturbed. Those buckles go round the bedposts. It's for their own good.'

'Oh.' She pauses. 'Tie me up.'

'What?'

'It's not going to be very exciting if I have to ask you again.'

'Why don't you tie *me* up?' Spencer says playfully.

'Because I want to be tied up. I want you to grab me and throw me on the bed.'

'Are you sure?'

'"Every woman adores a Fascist,"' she quotes at him with a coquettish look. He reaches out and pulls her into his arms and kisses her hard, then forces her down on to their bed. She wriggles and kicks, and her foot catches the lamp next to their bed and knocks it over. Its glass shade smashes and it goes out.

'What the hell were you doing?' asks Spencer.

'Struggling.'

'I thought you wanted me to be forceful.'

She sighs. 'But it's no fun if I don't resist.' She knows perfectly well that her idea of love is not gentle enough. But she just can't get over it. This nagging craving for brute strength.

Spencer stands up and turns on the main light. 'I don't feel comfortable with this,' he says. 'Anyway, I've got to call a plumber and see if he can come by tomorrow. I can't fix the toilet. At the very least, I'd need a closet snake.'

'I was just playing,' she says. 'Anyway, it's not about what's right and what's wrong. Why can't you forget about being the enlightened modern male for once? You're so bloody rigid.' She gets up, wraps herself in the sheet and stalks away.

'Don't walk off when I'm talking to you!' His voice cracks. She carries on walking, goes into the bathroom and locks the door. When she comes out, he's gone.

Elizabeth sits on the couch, pulls her knees up to her chest and wraps her arms around them. Her knees dig into her eye sockets until she sees jags of violet.

Then a voice in her head says, 'Come on, tough guy.' The words make her think of a dark bar. She imagines herself with an elbow on the wet counter, locked in an arm wrestle with a faceless opponent. 'Come on, tough guy,' calls the audience, cheering her on. 'Come on, tough guy. You can do it.' And she slams her opponent's forearm down.

She realises that what she should do is mend the toilet herself. Then, when Spencer comes back, everything will be fixed. 'Come on, tough guy, can't you mend a toilet?' All she needs to do is imagine an audience of sweaty rednecks yelling encouragement. It could be a creative visualisation, a self-help book, a motivational seminar! She will tell Spencer about it, and they'll laugh at the idea of her travelling round the country urging the timid to envision themselves in their Inner Bar. Elizabeth gets up and goes outside. The truck is still there. Spencer must have gone for a walk. *Come on, tough guy, let's go to Home Depot,* she tells herself. *Let's nail this sucker.*

She strides down the aisle trying to look as if she knows where she's going, like the kind of a person who would recognise a closet snake if she saw one. 'Watch out, darlin',' drawls a voice. She has just bumped into a denim-clad chest. She looks up and sees Mr Whip.

'You lookin' for somethin'?'

'A closet snake,' she says sheepishly. *A closet snake: someone who is secretly a reptile.*

'What would you be needing one of those for?'

'My toilet's blocked,' she tells him, noticing that she did not say *our.*

'I don't like to leave a lady in distress,' he says, his eyes crinkling up at the edges. 'Come right this way.' And there it is, under the orange banner saying 'Bathrooms', a black length of rubber tubing, a metal handle to pump with. He presents it to her ceremoniously, draped across his fingers like a medal on a ribbon. 'I like a girl who's good with her hands.'

'That's me.' She smiles and turns to go. Mr Whip does a few graceful steps and skates in front of her.

'Haven't I seen you before?'

'I don't think so.'

'Where you from?'

'Somewhere else.'

'And what are you doing in this part of the world? Coming to see if there's any cowboys left?'

'You got it,' she replies, smiling, attempting to sling the closet snake over her shoulder.

'We're a dyin' breed,' he tells her.

'Are you a real cowboy?' she asks, slightly doubtful. His hips are slim as a girl's, his waist cinched with a silver-clasped belt. But he walks with a bow-legged stride.

'The genuine McCoy.' He draws out the last syllable of 'genuine' to make it sound like 'wine'. 'Listen, I was going to git myself something to eat. Why don't you join me?' He grins.

'Why not?' she says.

She tails his truck down the highway. The clouds are black streaks in a violet sky. She could eat a bloody steak with him, drink beer, shoot pool. Then they would have sex on his truck bed. Mr Whip would fight any man who laid eyes on her, kicking him with his sharp-toed boots. She and Mr Whip would fight too, and in the morning she would have black eyes and Mr Whip would have crusted scratch marks. She remembers what it was like to feel that way, the dizzy fairground thrill of it.

But the voice singing from her radio is sad.

> Oh, it's like a honeymoon without champagne,
> A shiny set of rails without a train.
> I've got a doublewide heart with room for two,
> But it don't mean nothing
> If I ain't got you.

She snaps it off. Mr Whip turns into the parking lot of *Charlies Steak House*. No one seems to bother with apostrophes here. In front of the restaurant, there's a life-size brown plastic bull, horns lowered, one paw frozen above the concrete. At the last moment, instead of turning off, she accelerates down the road without looking back.

At the bottle house, the light is on, but Spencer is standing in the driveway. 'I'm back,' Elizabeth shouts out the window. She climbs out of the truck and kisses him, and

16

he kisses her back. He never holds grudges. His love for her is so simple and pure. Next to him, she is a lady from a Renaissance court, used to a life of biting pleasantries and weighted silences. She tries not to think about what nearly happened and what has happened, all the things she will never tell him. 'I bought a closet snake,' she says. Then she realises that water is seeping into her shoes, a slow dark continent spilling over the doorstep.

'It's a bit late for that now,' he replies. She sees that his jeans are wet to the knees. Inside, their cheap red-and-blue Mexican rug with the mistake in the pattern is dark and soaked. Water is gushing forth from the toilet. Spencer sloshes after her and picks up a bucket. Then he starts to laugh.

'Let's worry about all this in the morning. We'll sleep in the back of the truck. Let's just go get a drink.'

Rodeo Nites is packed this evening, a new band called Refried Dreams is playing. After the argument, Elizabeth feels tender and calm. In the illuminated ads up on the walls, the bottles of beer set against backgrounds of desert rocks or mountain meadows are great amber pillars like religious monuments. Then a voice sings softly in her ear.

> *Honey, I'm back, my head's killing me,*
> *I need to relax and watch TV.*
> *Get off the phone – give the dog a bone,*
> *Hey! Hey! Honey, I'm home.*

She starts and sees Mr Whip. There are two red spots on his cheeks. 'Where'd you run off to tonight?' he asks, very quietly. She'd forgotten all about him, forgotten they might see him at Rodeo Nites. 'I'm going to the bathroom,' he says, 'and while I'm gone you can work on your explanation.' He is standing so close that when she looks down she can see the tiny pinpricks in an ornamental feather pattern on his boots.

As soon as he leaves, a dark-haired woman marches up, the same one she saw him dancing with a few nights ago. She is wearing a denim skirt and ankle-high red boots. Her dark hair has been teased and sprayed into an improbable abundance. 'What the hell is going on here?' she demands. Elizabeth gives the woman a stare. 'You gotta problem?' asks the woman.

'No problem. He was hitting on me, but I wasn't interested.' *Hitting on*, not *chatting up*. She is pleased with herself for using the American term.

'Oh, please,' says the woman. '*You* were hitting on *him*.'

'I was *not!*' cries Elizabeth. *Tough guy*, she whispers in her head. *Tough guy, tough guy.*

'So he isn't good enough for you?' The woman turns to leave. 'Fuck you, you snotty little bitch.' All the new words she has learned rush to Elizabeth's lips. *Fuck you* and *kiss my ass* and *kick the shit out of that cocksucking motherfucker.*

She grabs the woman's shoulders, then feels a jabbing kick on her shin. The red boots. At that, she begins to shake the woman violently. It is so easy to start a fight. And she will win. She is furious. Then two men take her by the arms and pluck her away, and the woman backs off, fear in her eyes.

As soon as the men put her down, Elizabeth wriggles away and rushes trembling to the men's bathroom, past a blur of faces. *Find Spencer and leave*, she thinks. *Just forget about it, tough guy, forget, forget, forget.*

Spencer and Mr Whip are standing with their backs to her by the urinal, talking. She feels immediately soothed by the white bathroom, and leans her hot cheek against the wall as she watches them. Maybe this is really why she needs Spencer, for his empty desert. The blank expanse. The cleansing of what has gone before.

Spencer and Mr Whip finish up, then Mr Whip raises

his hand as if to touch Spencer. She sees her spit fly across the room, as graceful as the coin falling through the water in the Dairy Queen. It lands on Mr Whip's neck.

'What the—' says Mr Whip. He touches the back of neck, looks up, then turns around.

'Elizabeth!' says Spencer. 'What are you doing in here? This is Dean, Four-Star Employee, remember?' She stares at Dean and recalls a gold-starred badge and a candy-striped uniform.

'But how come you're bow-legged?' she says. 'I thought that was from riding a horse.'

'She's sorry,' says Spencer.

'She made a mistake,' says Dean. 'Spirited gal. No harm meant.' He gives Spencer a small mock punch on the arm and leaves. Spencer puts his arm round her shoulder and says, 'What was all that about?' She doesn't know how to tell him, doesn't understand her anger. She weeps.

2

Love Hearts

THE MONKS OF ST Benedict's are praying for your soul. Gothic lettering, a gilt-edged card. There is no name, but Elizabeth knows who sent it. Her grandmother has always regretted not becoming a nun, and she tries to make up for it by her missionary efforts. Elizabeth's older brother Duncan told Granny he didn't believe in God long ago, ducking away from the holy water Granny tried to sprinkle on him and shouting, 'Get off, I'm an *atheist.*'

'Protestants do believe in God, you know,' Granny retorted. But finally Duncan made her understand. So there was only Elizabeth left.

She received a crucifix every birthday, a bigger one each year. It was as if Granny thought Elizabeth was growing indefinitely, needing bigger and bigger crosses as her face receded into the sky. Or perhaps Granny wanted the crosses to weigh Elizabeth down, so that she would stagger under them and remember Jesus's suffering. Eventually, Elizabeth fully expected her crucifix would be full-size, two planks at right angles, nailed fiercely together.

Elizabeth crumples up the card and feeds it to the Insinkerator. Americans are so efficient at disposal. At home the sweet scent of old chicken bones wafted from the rubbish bin, and sometimes the cat dragged something unrecognisable out and gnawed on it. But here everything is consumed by the Insinkerator, and washed away.

JESUS CHRIST LOVES *YOU*.

'Look how they italicise the "you",' says Spencer. 'As in "*even* you".' He laughs.

'Don't throw that away.' Elizabeth snatches the leaflet from Spencer's hands.

'I thought it was junk mail,' he says in surprise. As usual, the leaflet, printed on a background of billowing fire, urges her to repent and be saved. This can be done, she is informed, by reciting the following: 'Dear Heavenly Father, I respond to your invitation and come to you in the name of your son Jesus Christ.' A tear-off page with postage paid reads: *YES! I have been saved. Please send me more literature on the Christian life.* A note is also enclosed: *Dear Elizabeth: I hope you are well, Love Granny.* After that there is a line of kisses, meticulous as embroidery stitches.

Her parents told Granny Elizabeth was going to America to study, knowing better than to mention Spencer. 'I suppose they're all heathens out there, are they?' Granny asked, with a note of fascination in her voice. Elizabeth did not think it was worth the effort of informing her that many people in America were Catholics just like Granny. Granny had a fixed idea of foreigners: they were all heathens, and they all ate spaghetti.

'She's trying to get it in writing,' says Spencer. 'You should call her and explain that you're not a Catholic and never will be. Stop leading her on. And tell her you're here with me. She'll understand.' Spencer always advocates telling the truth. He does not understand that telling the truth is a different matter when it has been kept hidden for twenty years. In his experience, people speak their feelings, analyse them together in adult fashion, then apologise. Their hearts are swept as clean as Shaker houses.

'I was thinking about signing it just to keep her quiet,' Elizabeth replies. She picks up a pen, and sits down at the table. But she can't do it. Somehow the flimsy page seems portentous as a legal contract. She cannot lie and claim to be saved. It's not that she believes in God. But she can't rule out the possibility of His existence, however slim, and therefore of His vengeance.

*

Granny's house was full of portraits of God and Jesus and the saints. There was no picture of her dead husband; instead, in pride of place over the mantelpiece, there was a photo of Granny shaking hands with the Pope, a look of utter ecstasy on her face. Every surface was cluttered with religious statuettes, and at the top of the stairs stood a plaster St Francis who was fully three feet high. He had a tonsured head, a brown cowl and a miniature prayer book. Each yellowish plaster hand and foot had an incision neatly filled in with red paint.

When Elizabeth was ten, his stigmata began to fascinate her. They had been so painstakingly executed. Finally, one visit, she dared to touch him. She sat at his feet and rubbed one of the delicate grooves with her finger.

At dinner that night, she could not bring herself to swallow. It was always 'meat and two veg', then jam trifle and thick custard made from a powder. Granny did not like fancy food.

'Beddy-byes for you,' said Granny, as they cleared the plates.

'I'm not tired yet.'

'What's the matter?'

'I just don't want to go to bed.'

'You're a big girl now. Don't be such a little scaredy-cat.' Granny's baby talk enraged Elizabeth.

'I hate you,' she said. But nothing happened. She had

almost expected that Granny would burst, like a puffball fungus when kicked.

'God forgive you,' Granny said. She cast her eyes upwards, tilted her head to one side. Elizabeth was sure she had copied this expression from St Francis.

'I hate you so much I want to kill you.'

'But how would you get rid of my body?'

'I'd cut you up in tiny pieces and hide you in a bag at the back of the wardrobe.' Granny didn't respond, but she smirked a bit. Elizabeth realised that Granny was relishing the thought of her own torture and dismemberment.

'The joy of living is the joy of giving,' said Granny, handing the cake over in its hatbox. 'All that stirring wears my wrist out, but I know how you all love your fruit cake.'

'Can't wait to try it,' said Elizabeth's father bravely. Duncan had made himself scarce to avoid Granny's wet kisses, and her mother was upstairs in bed, which was where she spent Granny's visits. Elizabeth was fourteen and for the first time, a few months before Christmas, her mother had dared to phone Granny and asked her not to bother with a fruit cake that year. 'All that stirring tires you out,' she had said. But it was too late. Granny had already spent some of her slim pension on raisins, sherry, flour and eggs, and beaten the ingredients together in her tiny kitchen. The cake was already wrapped in brown paper in her linen closet, being 'fed' with brandy at intervals.

Her father carried Granny's bags upstairs and Elizabeth took the cake down to the kitchen. It was nubbled with coal-black raisins, burned and glittery. And it was as heavy as a meteor. It could have been a chunk broken from Granny's house, as if she stubbornly intended to bring it to London piece by piece. The greatest wish of her life was to move in with the family. But each year after her departure, as winter softened into spring, the cake sat in the garden, untouched even by the squirrels.

Granny installed herself in the sitting room and Elizabeth took her a cup of tea and a hacked black slice. Granny spent much of her visit sitting on the sofa with her embroidery and her book. She liked the lives of saints, but she also subscribed to *Reader's Digest*, enjoying the accounts of real-life disasters such as 'Thirty-Six Hours Down A Well' or 'Trapped In The Inferno.' Elizabeth or her father took turns sitting with her, but Duncan said if anyone made him do it he would write an article for *Reader's Digest* called 'Seventy-Two Hours With My Granny'.

So for hours Elizabeth listened while Granny talked about growing up on a farm and training as a nurse, and about scrimping and saving so that she could afford to send Elizabeth's mother to a convent school. Her husband had died at forty-five, after a lifetime of fried breakfasts. He could not read and signed his name with a cross, and he had loved to play jigs on his fiddle, the same one on which Elizabeth now practised obsessively. But that was all Granny had ever told Elizabeth about him.

They had Christmas dinner at four o'clock, when it was already dark outside. Elizabeth thought herself too old for Christmas. But Granny looked on with delight as Elizabeth's father bore in the Christmas pudding veiled in blue fire. Her father cut a large slice and her mother pressed Granny to try the lemon mousse as well. 'My word,' said Granny, holding out her plate. 'Very à la posh. I do love a sweet on occasion.' Granny was never without a tube of Love Hearts in her handbag, melting each one on her tongue with a solemn expression as if it was a holy wafer. 'When I was a child, I had nothing but a raw turnip for my lunch.'

'Oh, stop exaggerating,' sighed Elizabeth's mother. 'You had ham sandwiches.'

'Yes, I did,' said Granny. 'I had to pick it from the field on the ten-mile walk to school. What high living you have here.' Then she inverted the cream jug over her plate, smacking her lips and saying, 'Luscious, luscious.' She made the very word sound juicy as a grape.

'Pass me the pudding, Elizabeth,' said Duncan. She paused to put down her spoon and fork, and he barked: 'Today!' Granny looked on approvingly as he cut himself a second piece.

'I like to see empty dishes at the table,' she said. Duncan frowned. He got up and winked at Elizabeth, a party popper in his hand. There was a bang, then Granny's white hair was bedizened with thin coloured streamers.

'I think Granny's brains have exploded,' said her father, *sotto voce*. Granny was so deaf she had not heard the bang. Elizabeth's mother started to laugh.

'What is it?' said Granny. 'What is it? Have I got something on my face?' She dabbed at her mouth with a napkin, tried to run her tongue over her teeth surreptitiously. Even Duncan laughed. Watching Granny patting vainly at her hair was only funny in the way that watching a chicken running around without its head was funny. But they almost never laughed together. It was a relief to laugh, a relief to torment someone else.

After dinner, Elizabeth tried to watch television with Duncan, but Granny kept on talking. 'Even when I was on my feet from dawn to dusk, training to be a nurse, I still fasted for the full twenty-four hours before Mass. I can't get used to all this rich food.' The film was *Risky Business*. Tom Cruise played a teenager who decided to make money by using his house as a brothel when his parents went on holiday. He flashed his white teeth, shook back his hair. Granny gradually fell silent. Elizabeth did not dare take her eyes away from the screen. Finally it was over. 'Well, that was the devil's work,' Granny spat out, gathering up her embroidery. When she had gone, the two children looked at each other and their laughter showered like sparks from a live wire.

★

'What in hell is *that*?' asks Spencer. Elizabeth has hung the gold chain around her neck and the crucifix is cold on her bare chest. It is the biggest one yet, chunky and gilded, painted with a biblical scene. She looks down at her breasts, and flat, amazed faces look back at her.

'It's not even my birthday.' She did not sign the declaration of repentance. She has thrust the magazines, *The Modern Missionary* and *St Anthony the Messenger*, into the garbage. And she has not replied to Granny's letters. The crucifix is intended to woo her, as if gifts would work when words wouldn't.

'I must tell you that I am very devout,' she tells him, smiling. He advances towards her.

'In my view, sex is a religious experience,' he says. He pushes her down on to the scratchy blanket, sucks on her hard nipples, nudging the cross aside.

Elizabeth wonders whether anyone ever touches Granny, apart from the compulsory kiss or squeeze of the hand. Perhaps she doesn't mind. Probably she was pleased when her husband died. All Granny has ever really wanted is sugar, cream and heaven.

Watching a patch of light on the floor cast by the fading sun, Elizabeth forgets to breathe. She can sense each separate atom of herself, the electron clouds within. She is made of the same matter as everything else, and the same energy holds her together. This is what a revelation must feel like. More than a human being is made to know. So ecstatic it's almost terrible, almost enough to make her fly apart.

When the phone rings, the crucifix is warm. 'Granny's had an accident,' says her mother. Elizabeth goes cold. *It was*

26

my turn to write, she remembers, ashamed, then feels deeper shame at the trivial thought. 'But she's all right,' her mother goes on. 'She'll live. She fell down some steps on one of her pilgrimages.' Granny goes on a pilgrimage about once a year, usually to somewhere in England, but sometimes she ventures further afield, to the great Catholic shrines of Italy, France and Spain. An English priest leads her tour group, and they avoid eating the local food as much as possible.

'It was at Lourdes,' says her mother. Elizabeth has recovered enough to notice the care with which her mother pronounces the French word, its breathy 'r'. 'Granny slipped climbing the steps up to the cathedral. All the priests and monks nearby rushed up to help, and the paramedics bore her off on a stretcher. She liked all that. But she's terribly worked up. She keeps saying that it was a sign and now she's going to prepare for her end.'

'She isn't about to die, is she?' asks Elizabeth, her stomach contracting.

'I don't think so,' says her mother. 'She seems perfectly fine to me. She broke her wrist and she got a nasty bump on the head. But she's talked the ears off all the patients in her ward, and apparently some of them have made a particularly speedy recovery. She's still got the comatose ones. Actually,' says her mother, giving a nervous laugh, 'the knock on the head seems to have brought about a little renaissance.' She pauses. 'Dad let it slip about you and Spencer. And she's been telling all the other patients about her granddaughter's foreign beau.'

'Now I'll get even more hellfire pamphlets,' says Elizabeth. 'She'll try to save me from the jaws of sin.'

'No, darling, that's the thing,' says her mother. 'You won't believe it, but she's actually rather pleased about it. I told her you'd write her a letter and tell her all about him.'

Being with him is like looking at the world through a kaleido-

scope, junk glass and buttons turned into a perfect pattern. Even the red paper strawberries hanging overhead in the Dairy Queen seem like rubies. Attempting to describe her relationship in terms suitable for Granny's ears make it sound impossibly sentimental. But she has to try. She describes the bottle house, but not the Love Raft. She describes watching the sunset together from the side of the road, but not having sex against the side of the car.

Granny's reply is brief.

Dear Elizabeth,
   My wrist is still giving me trouble, especially when I write, but the doctors tell me they are impressed with my perseverance. I have had a chance to make some new friends here in the ward, so every cloud has a silver lining. I was thinking of learning to lip-read because you know my hearing is not up to much. But I do not think there is much point because I am now reaching the final chapter of my life. I hope you are well,
   Love Granny

In return, Elizabeth measures out a larger dose of romance. *Spencer cooked me dinner. He lit candles and threw a linen cloth over our table.* They sat on the floor and ate pasta with sauce from a jar, drank Mexican beer. *We shared a platter of succulent oysters, while outside the window the moon hung full and low in the sky.* Then almost three weeks pass without a reply, and Elizabeth wonders if she has provided too much detail, allowing Granny to intuit that Elizabeth is living with Spencer out of wedlock. Or perhaps she simply embellished beyond credibility this time.

'Granny's very busy with her shroud,' says her mother. 'That's probably why she hasn't written. She tried it on for us. It's a long white frock edged with Valenciennes lace. She kept hinting that she would like the bonnet and gloves

28

to match, but they cost too much. I think she'd like us to get them for her.'

'Poor old thing,' says Elizabeth.

'I know Catholics are morbid, but I think it's a bit much,' says her mother. 'She's very pleased because she got it half-price second-hand.'

'What?'

'Her friend bought it, but then she decided she liked another one better, and they wouldn't take it back. So she sold it to Granny.'

'Is she really going to die?' asks Elizabeth. Her mother pauses.

'She's been threatening to do so ever since I was a little girl.' There is a pause. 'But I think this might be it. She was fine last week, and her wrist was getting better. But as soon as she got her shroud, her angina got very bad. The doctors said she's got to carry an inhaler with her, and can't have any sudden shocks. It's peculiar. It's almost as if she's simply decided to let go.'

'Will you give her my love?' says Elizabeth. 'And I'll look into a plane ticket home. I want to say goodbye.'

'Actually, she gave me rather an odd message for you,' says her mother. 'The bump on her head really did something to her. She doesn't feel up to writing, but she wanted me to tell you that . . .' She pauses. 'Well, her exact words were: *All I ask is that I see her married before I die*. And then she said you were keeping romance alive in the modern world.'

Elizabeth sees Granny lying in her hospital bed, arms crossed over her frilled chest, her body strangely flat without her customary coat and cardigan and thermal vest. She always wore a lot of layers because she felt the cold. She was so soft and bulky that she seemed entirely made of cloth, as if the layers went all the way down and even her heart was wool and nylon. She seems incapable of such a passionate imperative. *She must be married before I die*.

29

Elizabeth has never really thought of Granny as having a body with breasts. She wonders if Granny was wearing special Catholic underwear, or if she was naked beneath the shroud.

Elizabeth has an inward tremor, the same she feels when she receives one of the cards letting her know that strangers are praying for her. Fingers laid on her soul, on some intimate place.

The women are wearing A-line frocks of flowery chintz. The frocks are so simply cut they look as if they were drawn by a child. Their faces are young too, pink-cheeked and empty. Elizabeth cannot stop staring at them. They must have sewn those frocks themselves. She takes up the laminated sundae menu and pretends to scan it, while watching the women surreptitiously. The women link hands to say grace, so that for a moment they look like a row of paper dolls. Then one of them gets a Bible out and reads aloud while the others eat their hamburgers.

In front of her, Spencer tucks into his Surf n' Turf. They have stopped for dinner at Denny's Diner on their way to the lake where they plan to camp. Spencer has three days off from the hospital, and he said Elizabeth needed a trip to take her mind off worrying about Granny.

Spencer catches her watching him, and gives her a big grin. Then he goes back to busily cutting up his steak. He eats neat and fast like a cat. She suspects he is just as happy here as he would be in an exquisite restaurant.

'Aren't you going to eat your dinner?' he says, eyeing her French fries.

'You can have them.' She tips them on to his plate.

The women have finished now, their plates completely clean, their milkshake glasses sucked empty. They hold hands again and bow their heads. Spencer puts down his knife and fork, reaches out to put his hand over hers.

'Are you going to eat that?' says one of the women,

marching up to their table. Elizabeth realises that she is not young after all. Her eyes have the empty look of a chick dazed from the shell, but she must be in her fifties or older. She points to Spencer's plate.

'Eat what?' says Spencer. 'That's a garnish.' A twisted orange slice lies on a frill of lettuce.

'Eat that,' says the woman. She points to a scrap of the steak that he has left, the outsize portion in the end too much for him. They stare at the woman for a moment, and Elizabeth realises she is giving a command.

'I don't want it,' says Spencer.

'But it will go to waste.' The woman's feet are planted firmly on the floor. She is wearing white ankle socks and Mary Janes. 'You must not refuse what the Lord has given to you.'

Her eyes take in their ringless, entwined hands. She stares, then pulls a pamphlet from a straw bag slung over her shoulder and turns to Elizabeth. 'We are the Daughters of Grace,' she says. 'And you are living in sin. But if you ask the Lord for forgiveness, you can reclaim your chastity.'

Elizabeth looks back to her table and sees that the other women are looking on eagerly. She shivers. Then she stabs a finger at the woman's shrouded body. 'Look at you,' she says. 'You might have been beautiful once. But you let it go to waste.' The woman takes a step back.

'Sweetheart,' says Spencer warningly. But Elizabeth stands up and advances on the other women, who have begun hastily counting out a tip in change, preparing to leave. 'Sex is a religious experience,' she announces to them. 'And you –' she waves her finger accusingly – 'you have squandered the Lord's gifts!' The women gasp, spilling their nickels and dimes, then as one they rush from Denny's Diner into the night.

Spencer is scuffling in the shallows of the lake, stabbing a stick into the water.

'What are you doing?' she says. The sun has risen, but it is a cloudy day. *The air was spiced with the scent of sage and the crickets were singing.* The sky is biblical, low, ominous clouds packed together in grey folds.

'Trying to get a crayfish,' he says. 'I thought I saw one. They're very small, but they taste like lobster. I was going to boil it up and surprise you.' She loves his lack of squeamishness, she has seen him crack lobster claws and gnaw on jerky with the bristles still on it. He is like an animal, living in the present, forgetful of past and future. To him, meat is just meat, not haunted by the creature that wore that flesh. Why must everything be so much more complicated to her? She crunches down the beach past rusty beer cans and shreds of dissolving tissues, and wades into the lake with him. *The sun was setting. In the west there were shining streaks, as if the blue was being scratched off to reveal the silver underneath.*

'Will you marry me?' she says.

His eyes are very green. A weak ray of sun catches his unshaved jaw and turns the ginger in it to flecks of gold. He wraps wet arms around her and holds her tight as a caught fish. Who else would put up with her unexpected rages, her recent torpor? Then the clouds close again, and she realises that in her head she is already shaping this into one of the letters that Granny waits for like injections of a life-giving drug. *He asked me to marry him and when I looked down he had slid a diamond ring on to my finger.*

3

Vinegar and Plum

HER MOTHER IS LATE picking her up from the airport. Elizabeth waits for more than half an hour with her suitcase and bag of gifts. Cactus candy, a bottle of hot sauce, tequila with a worm in it for Duncan. Then she remembers suddenly that of course he won't be there. When she left for America, he declared that he was leaving home too. He said he would get a bedsit and watch the football in peace. Two years older than her, he lived in his attic room until the day she left. He worked at Domino's Pizza and afterwards went drinking with his friends. She almost never saw him, except occasionally in the middle of the night, when she would find him in the kitchen making precarious stacks of buttered crackers, or cheese on toast. Sometimes she just found the plate, the cheese as smooth as cooled wax, like a candle left to gutter out after a party.

She twists the diamond ring on her finger. Spencer bought it as a surprise, although she was the one who proposed. She keeps touching it, in the same way fingers stray to a scab or a bite. It reminds her that Granny is dying and that her last wish is for Elizabeth to keep romance alive, as if it were a rare orchid demanding continuous attention.

Spencer will join her in two weeks, two days before the

wedding. It was all the time he could get off from the hospital. She will miss him, but at the same time she's glad. He must spend as little time at her family's house as possible. She dreads his meeting with them. But perhaps everything will be different this time.

It's Duncan who has come to collect her, not her mother after all. He shambles up, wearing dirty combat trousers and an ancient creaking leather jacket. Around one eye there is a bruise, dark and ripe. He shies away when she tries to hug him. 'I see you've become all American then,' he says, marching off. She runs after him pushing the trolley with her suitcases.

'What happened to your eye?'

'Ran into a door.' He keeps walking.

'You mean you ran into someone's fist at Kebab Delite.' He swings around on his heel and transfixes her with half an angry glare. But the black eye looks as sad as a clown's. She falls silent.

Kebab Delite is where Duncan and his friends go after the pubs close. Elizabeth has been herself in the past. In the window a brown cylinder of animal origin turns on a spit. The word 'Delite' on the sign is done in red, with stylised red and yellow flames lapping at it, indicating spicy heat. She knows the ritual. Duncan and his friends down seven pints, then order kebabs. The pukers bend over the gutter and groan, and the ones who don't puke crow with victory but wish they did. The pale youths just spilled out from the pubs are sometimes too drunk to count out the right change, too drunk not to lose their tempers if someone shoves them in the queue.

Duncan comes to a halt in front of a black two-seater speckled with rust. 'Look at that,' he says. 'Car only cost me a hundred pounds.' He puts her luggage in the boot, gets in, then reaches over to unlock her side.

'There's a hole in the floor,' Elizabeth says. She can see

34

the concrete between her ankles, and the carpet is damp with dew.

'Only thing wrong with her,' says Duncan.

'Is it safe?' she asks.

'If you don't put your feet down.' He slips in a tape and there's the thud of techno. The car revs furiously. He navigates out of the car park and they shoot down the motorway. She wants to thank him for coming to pick her up at the airport but doesn't dare, doesn't dare even mention the tequila.

He frowns ahead, and Elizabeth stares at the road rushing between her knees. She doesn't believe that he got the black eye at Kebab Delite. If that were true, he wouldn't have been able to resist boasting about the sorry state of his opponent. He didn't get the black eye from a drunken stranger, but from someone else, only she's not sure whom.

When they pull up, her mother emerges from the house in a grey tracksuit that hangs off her. She kisses Elizabeth, then bends down and plucks ineffectually at the handle of one of her suitcases, while Duncan screeches off, tingeing the air with exhaust.

Elizabeth's mother has always been too thin. She has worried eyes and long straight hair that she scrapes back in a chignon. It isn't like her to wear a tracksuit. She usually favours skirts and cashmere sweaters or silk blouses, knotting little scarves round her neck in order to look French. Her mother first went to France on a school trip, and at once fell in love with the golden bales of hay in the sun, the real mayonnaise filming her tongue. At dinner with her penfriend's family, she ate an entire tin of foie gras, not realising it was a delicacy. When she talks French, her voice changes, becoming dreamy and soft. Elizabeth sometimes wonders if perhaps she fell in love unhappily there, and that's why she's always so sad.

'I don't think I can lift this. What have you got in here?' says her mother.

'Where's Dad?'

'Oh, darling, I'm afraid he had to go on a business trip. It's just the two of us. Look, the cat's going to get out.' She shoos Elizabeth and the cat into the house. 'He caught a bird earlier,' she says. The cat is an old tabby that leaves a black snow of fur everywhere he goes. He has a mysterious hold over her mother, like Rasputin.

'Oodgy woodgy,' her mother coos. 'Who's a fat boy then?' The cat yowls as Elizabeth's suitcase swings dangerously in his direction.

'When will Dad be back?' she asks.

'I don't know,' says her mother. 'I don't like to be interrogated, darling. I'll go and put the kettle on, shall I?'

The framed pen and ink drawings of sailing boats, the davenport with the grain in its wood in the shape of a leering face, the rooms painted in slate and cream. The house is as refined as a pedigree greyhound, exactly as Elizabeth remembers it. Then she looks closer and sees that the davenport has been thrust closed on a mass of bills and circulars, and there is dust on the mirrors. She has never seen the place this way. Her mother always pored over *Ideal Home* and *House and Garden*, longing to be like the families in the pictures, raising champagne glasses around a grand piano, eating cornflakes from blue-and-white pottery bowls. She always kept the house punishingly neat, perhaps because, although she is a lapsed Catholic, she never lost the dream of heaven instilled in her by the nuns. Then there is a scream.

'Ugh, ugh, ugh!' When she goes down to the kitchen, her mother is waving her hands in the air as tiny moths flutter around her. 'I was just making the tea and they flew out from behind the sugar.' Elizabeth looks in the cupboard in search of their origin, and is amazed by its disorder. A jar glued to the shelf by the honey that has trickled down its side. Crumpled bags of flour, containers of ancient glacé cherries. At the back she can see the cod liver oil yellow of Granny's marmalade. Another moth flies out in her face. 'The house is in a state,' says her mother. 'I know.' She puts the teapot lid down and shakes her head as if trying to clear it. 'I've absolutely got to water the petunias.' Elizabeth follows her into the garden. Water drops from every bush and twig, the lawn is muddy underfoot. At the end a space has been cleared and filled with gravel.

'Are you planning to build a gazebo?' she asks, looking at the space. That has always been one of her mother's dreams. Her mother used to talk about things they would do: buy a villa in France, hike the Pyrenees, take a sketching trip in the Alps, and build a gazebo in the garden where they could read their books in the summer. Her mother was enraptured by each plan in turn, her excitement filling Elizabeth too. But they never did any of these things.

'Dad was planning to build a meditation garden,' says her mother. 'It was an idea he got from the Sunday supplement. They're very fashionable and they're meant to relieve stress.' She rakes her foot in the ground where a fountain has been choked by leaves, and it bubbles up feebly. 'Emptiness and the sound of water, that's what he wanted.'

'When's he going to finish it?' asks Elizabeth.

'He never finishes any of his projects.' She nudges the fountain with her foot.

'Mum?' says Elizabeth. Her mother frowns.

'Honestly, the least you could do is offer to take care of the petunias.' Scooping up the cat on her way, she marches back to the house with an aggrieved air.

Elizabeth unwinds the hose and douses the flowers. When she goes inside, two cups of tea are cooling on the kitchen worktop, but her mother has vanished, perhaps to do some errands, perhaps to play with the cat in some far corner of the house. When Elizabeth has unpacked her things in her old room, there is nothing to do.

She wanders about the house idly, opening one door after another. Her mother is not in her bedroom, and Elizabeth enters, raises the blind, plumps up the pillows. She opens the wardrobe and flips through the clothes until she finds her mother's old fake leopard fur. She buries her face in it for a moment. It smells of rain. It was a gift from her father to celebrate her mother's escape from the Catholic Women's Home.

Granny had refused to let her mother go to university unless she stayed at the Home. It smelled of the fish they ate on Friday nights and the doors were locked at nine o'clock. Elizabeth's mother hated it. But one day Elizabeth's father got her attention in the library, pretending to tickle the faces of Victorian scientists with a feather duster. Their college library had a marble dome and a circular balcony, and the busts were ranged at intervals on ledges. Down below students hunched in carrels and in one or two of them couples embraced. Elizabeth's father was in the habit of taking photos of them for a gossip sheet, the 'College Nudesletter'. There was nothing prurient about this; he just liked practical jokes.

Attempting to impress her mother, her father leaned out dangerously far over the balustrade with his duster, and she caught his feet. In return, he took her out for coffee and blackberry pie at a greasy spoon, then to a James Bond double bill. When they got to the Catholic Women's Home, the doors were locked. So he drove her to his place in his pink car. He planned to get a pink jacket to go with it. He was so gentle, not like other men, who would never have wanted a pink car or a matching jacket. It was the pale pink of sunset in early spring.

Elizabeth's mother moved out of the Home the next day, while the nuns flapped around her praying loudly. To celebrate her moving in with him, her father bought her mother elbow-length evening gloves and the fake fur. They went to parties every night and took black and white pills so they could dance all night long. That was more than twenty years ago. The fake fur is no longer worn, the satin gloves are balled in a drawer. Elizabeth's father never bought the pink jacket.

Elizabeth closes the wardrobe and goes upstairs, then climbs the ladder up to Duncan's attic. The door is locked. But when she rattles the handle angrily, it opens.

Inside, it looks as if he never left. The window is open and his papers flutter on the noticeboard. A postcard from a friend of a large brown breast with a mouse face inked on to it, the pink nipple for a nose. A list entitled 'Things To Do', which has only two items on it: 'Get Up', and 'Buy Cigarettes'. On the desk there is a chocolate cigar that she recognises as a stocking-filler from the year before last, perhaps a hint that he should stop smoking. No one would have dared to do more than hint. The flat roof outside his window is littered with cigarette butts, and the room smells of him. Stale smoke, mixed with earth and dead leaves.

Next to the cigar is a heap of small change. Duncan always won in slot-machine arcades. His favourite game was Coin Niagara. One step grated back and forth on another step, both loaded with coins. The top shelf nudged constantly at the coins on the bottom shelf, so that they seemed poised to fall at any moment. When Elizabeth dropped her coin, it fell harmlessly on top of the others. But Duncan always dropped his coin down the glass chute at exactly the right moment, so that coins were pushed over on to the bottom shelf, and money came flooding down. Constantly rubbed and abraded by his teasing, she grew up knowing what it felt like to be one of those coins.

*

Elizabeth was relieved when Duncan stopped accompanying them on family holidays. The spring she was fifteen, her parents took her to Italy. Duncan didn't want to go. He laughed and said Elizabeth could have the boring Roman ruins all to herself.

Their hotel had wallpaper with green stripes, red curtains held back by gold ropes. Her father discovered that if you ran down the corridor fast enough, the passing stripes would give you the impression that you were running through one doorway after another. It was like time travel in a bad B-movie. He called the place 'Hotel Infinity'. 'I've always imagined infinity as a sort of vast hotel,' he said. 'Each day a new guest arrives. No one ever leaves, but the hotel is never full. There is always one more room.' He gave a whoop and plunged down the striped corridor as fast as he could, shouting, 'Hotel Infinity!'

The hotel filled Elizabeth with desire. It offered the possibility of chance meetings with strangers. Already, she had heard several cries of '*Ciao, bella!*' as she trailed along the street behind her parents. But her mother sat on the edge of her double bed with its lavish gold headboard, and lamented. She had lost her contact lens. 'I wanted things to be perfect, but something always goes wrong. Why don't you two go off and enjoy yourselves?' Elizabeth and her father offered suggestions. Elizabeth could go and find an optician. Or her mother could make do with just one contact lens. Her father even offered her one of his. He thought seeing the world slightly wrong didn't matter. But her mother was intractable. 'You don't know enough Italian to make them understand what you want in the optician's,' she pointed out. 'Anyway, I didn't come on holiday to be left on my own.' Then suddenly she changed her mind. 'My day's been ruined by all this arguing,' she said. 'All I want is to lie down and have a rest.'

So in the end, Elizabeth and her father did leave her in the hotel, wandering together through overgrown gardens filled with cypresses and orange trees. They strolled comfortably along and finally stopped before a headless body in flowing stone drapes. 'This is the perfect opportunity for a Theme Photo!' cried her father. He loved Theme Photos. A head poking from behind a rock. Two feet disappearing into the water. With her mother as their reluctant photographer, they had once created a whole sequence. It had begun with Elizabeth peering into a gorge, her father's head visible, hands gripping the edge. In fact, he was standing on a ledge just below the lip. Then his hands reaching up, clutching the air while she clutched back. And in the last picture she had been alone, looking down in mock dismay.

Elizabeth let her father arrange her behind the statue, head dutifully balanced on its amputated neck, her body concealed behind it. And then he took the picture. 'See, Elizabeth!' he said triumphantly. 'We can still manage to enjoy ourselves. And now let's have a fine dining experience!' Her father revelled in peculiar euphemisms, seductive periphrases like those found on restaurant menus. Sometimes he slipped into this language himself, and Elizabeth joined him. He was an accountant, and she thought that spending so much time with numbers made him starved for language, the more elaborate the better.

'Let's commence our mastication,' she said, Boswell to his Dr Johnson.

The hotel restaurant had an outside terrace covered with vines, a view of the blue lake. 'A pastoral enclave,' said her father, throwing himself down at one of the white-clothed tables. They ordered a bottle of wine. Elizabeth had to help her father because he only spoke a few words of Italian. He believed the key to fluency in a foreign tongue was just a matter of assuming the right persona. Learning the cadences, the gestures. Then everything else would follow. His Italian persona was a lovelorn opera singer. '*Spaghetti alle vongole!*' he cried with great drama. But he got the pronunciation all wrong. He was tone-deaf. She had tested him by playing a note on her violin, then telling him to sing it. Two notes at angles to each other. Sometimes that was how she thought of her parents.

'You never have *spaghetti alle vongole*,' said Elizabeth. 'I thought you didn't like shellfish.'

'I didn't want to keep on ordering the same old thing,' said her father. 'Maybe if I revisit it, I will like it. Don't you think the secret of happiness lies in variation? The universe is essentially a monotonous continuum, but we can defeat that monotony through variation. Look at literature! Literature is merely a million variations on the dull continuum of language.'

They ate their spaghetti with messy gusto. Her father said that was how the Italians did it, dangling hanks of it into their mouths, not winding it up prissily on their forks. 'And now I must perambulate to the nearest public convenience,' he said.

'Shall I order you a demitasse of your favourite beverage?' she said. He loved to have an espresso in the afternoons – he had got into the habit of drinking them to get him through his work.

While he was gone, her mother came downstairs, looking around in a dazed way. Elizabeth waved to her, and she came over and sat down. 'Hello, beautiful,' she said. It was her word reserved for moments of great affection, unspoken apology. And yet the way she said it left an aftertaste of irony. Elizabeth was just learning to find some beauty in herself, in her long legs and clear pale skin. *You think you're beautiful,* that was what her mother meant.

Her mother sniffed Elizabeth's wine, swirled it around, then sipped it.

'Mum!' said Elizabeth, unable to restrain herself. 'Can't you get your own glass?' When her mother was angry, Elizabeth was capable and calm. Then as soon as she recovered, Elizabeth couldn't control her childish irritation. Their moods alternated predictably. There was never either apocalyptic rage or perfect forgiveness.

Her mother made a face. 'There's something wrong with it anyway,' she said. 'It's vinegary.' Her father came back and sat down. 'Darling, there's something wrong with this wine,' she said.

'Tasted fine to me,' replied her father. He sipped and savoured it theatrically. 'I taste notes of oak and plum. I would say this is a coquettish wine with a darker after-note—' Elizabeth couldn't help joining in.

'Redolent of peatbogs,' she finished off. Her mother sighed.

'You're so embarrassing. I can't believe you sat here and drank this.'

'Then why don't you complain?' asked her father.

'Because you're the man. You should have complained. That's how it's done on the Continent.' Her mother's good mood had faded. 'Why can't we be a jolly family?' she said.

'We are a jolly family,' insisted her father. He really believed it. Between the two of them, her parents could taste vinegar and plum in the same glass of wine.

Her mother didn't say anything. Her father took the bottle cork, stood it on an upturned water glass, and stabbed two forks into it so that they balanced. The cork rotated uneasily with its fork propeller, first one way, then the other. Then he looked out across the lake, and began to sing one of his sailing songs under his breath.

All I want is a tall ship, and a star to steer my way.
All I want is a tall ship, on the lonely midnight sea.

He liked to hum tuneless little songs, which he claimed were drawn from his favourite book, *Authentic Sea Shanties*. Elizabeth looked out over the lake too. 'The thrill of voyaging,' her father said. 'Wouldn't it be amazing to set out across the open sea and not even know where you were going?' He had a rapt, joyful expression, and she felt suddenly annoyed. It was she, not her father, who had the right to unexplored continents. He was supposed to be looking after her mother.

And he did so faithfully, until he bought his yacht, when Elizabeth was in her last year at college. It was called *The Black Pig* and he spent first days, then nights, then whole weekends on it. Her mother went sailing with him once, then did not accompany him again. Even Elizabeth didn't much like the swinging boom and heaving sea, the way the kettle rattled dangerously in its clamp on the stove. But her father was not worried about the weather. On her mother's sole voyage with him, he shouted, 'Don't worry, crew!' while the mainsail flapped madly and the boat lurched. He cut across the wake of a speedboat, narrowly avoided a larger yacht labelled *Princess*. He called, 'Ahoy there!' to the blazered crowd on deck holding glasses of champagne. When they looked in another direction, he took his boat in a neat circle around theirs, waving the whole time and promising to see them at 'the Club' later, while her mother hunched down into her life jacket in embarrassment. Her father thought people who rode in boats that big weren't real sailors. 'There's nothing like being alone with the wind in your face, battling against the elements,' he told Elizabeth. His blue-grey eyes held the distant look of a sailor used to having his gaze fixed on the horizon. As soon as the boat was moored, her mother climbed off it, saying, 'Thank God for dry land.' Then she tramped up the wooden dock towards the car park.

*

When she goes back downstairs, Elizabeth hears a cough in the cellar and realises that's where her mother must be, loading clothes into the dryer. She descends into the cellar but her mother is not there, although the dryer is open, a

44

pair of jeans dangling one leg in, one leg out. Something is different and she realises that the shelves at the far end are bare, the shelves that usually hold a tangle of ropes, galoshes and yellow oilskins. The box of canned provisions that her father keeps for long trips is gone too, and the telescoping aluminium brush he uses to get at the dirt in the corners of the deck. The only things of his remaining are his toolbox and his set of miniature drawers. They are carefully labelled: 'Large Screws', 'One-Inch Nails', and 'Wood Glue'. Towards the bottom, the labels become more perplexed: 'Things That Fasten Things', 'Things That Look As If They Belong To Something', and 'Things That Defy Categories'. Her father always liked the idea of order, but deep down he didn't believe in it. She realises suddenly that her father is not away on business. He has gone, and she doesn't know where, gone on some strange sea journey.

A click and she's in darkness; the door up to the house bangs shut and the bolt rattles. A pause. 'Who's there?' Elizabeth calls. The boiler clanks and sighs. She takes a few steps forward in the dark and walks into the embrace of ghostly shirts hanging from the hot-water pipes overhead. There's the rasp of a cigarette lighter.

Duncan hasn't left home at all. He's still here. These are his shirts, warm from the dryer. Even though they've just been washed they smell faintly of him. She goes up to the cellar door and listens. She hears him exhale and the scent of his cigarette drifts under the door. She knows him well enough to realise that there is nothing to do but wait.

4

The Red Shoes

DUNCAN IS IN THE sitting room watching TV, sprawled full-length on the sofa. Elizabeth sits on the floor and frowns at the screen. He doesn't seem to appreciate her unselfish silence. Her mother had gone out to get some groceries, and when she came home she heard Elizabeth calling and let her out. Elizabeth didn't say anything about Duncan. Instead, she told her mother that the wind had slammed the door, then the cat must have patted the bolt shut. Her mother accepted this, perhaps because she thought it inappropriate to question further, perhaps because she believed the cat was capable of anything.

'I told Mum I locked myself in the cellar by mistake,' Elizabeth reminds Duncan, giving him a sideways glance. He grunts, not taking his eyes away from the TV. Thick greasy hair flops over his eyes. A black-and-gold beer can in his hand like a royal orb. Elizabeth looks ahead and scowls. He hasn't apologised, and now he won't even look at her. When they were growing up he would have done anything, anything at all, to get her attention.

She stamps down to the kitchen and nearly stumbles over the cat, strutting about waiting for his dinner of milk-poached fish. The vet said their cat was the fattest he had ever seen. He said he was surprised the cat was still alive.

The cat is too fat to get through the cat flap her mother has installed, or at least he pretends to be. Elizabeth suspects that he likes the ceremony of having someone get up and open the door for him. He always pauses for a moment and seems to swell a little before swaggering across the threshold like Henry VIII.

Spencer would call that *a power trip*. The exercise of power for its own sake. He has a whole vocabulary for feelings dark and hidden, which before she met him she had never openly discussed. *Passive aggressiveness* is his phrase for unspoken anger, and *codependence* his word for constricting love. When she heard him using these words, it was like discovering these things were common diseases. It gave you the impression they could and should be cured.

'What shall we have for dinner?' her mother asks. She starts flipping through one of her cookbooks. 'Golden Root-Vegetable Couscous,' she muses. 'That sounds lovely, doesn't it?'

'Mm,' says Elizabeth. She's afraid to show too much enthusiasm for fear her mother will embark on some impossible feat on her behalf, and they'll end up having dinner at midnight. Her mother loves these recitations, these phantom banquets. But when she actually cooks, she tries too hard, worrying over the one spice in an ingredient list that's impossible to find, throwing out whole cakes, instead of scraping burned bits away. When her mother swims, she holds her head out of the water like a dog, panicked concentration on her face. She looks the same way when she cooks.

Her mother opens the frost-furred freezer and roots about. 'We need to start making a list for the wedding,' she says over her shoulder. 'Photographer. Cake. Flowers. I thought showers of baby's breath and roses would be nice. I don't like those tight bouquets. And we need to sort out your dress as soon as possible, in case it needs to be altered.

I've made an appointment at a bridal shop tomorrow. What do you think about ivory silk? I think you'd look so beautifully Pre-Raphaelite.'

'Don't you think Dad would like to help us choose the dress?' asks Elizabeth. Her mother frowns.

'What does Dad know about dresses?' Her mother was right. He wore socks that didn't match, and the sleeves and legs of his suits always seemed too short for his lanky frame.

'Where did you say he'd gone?' Elizabeth asks. 'Was it on a sailing trip?'

'I told you that already.'

'I thought you said a business trip.'

'No, he's off on the boat. I did tell you, darling.' Cold exhales from the open freezer. Spencer once told Elizabeth that the ice at the North Pole is so hard that when red-hot meteors fall in winter they just lie on its surface. Maybe her mother doesn't know where her father is, or perhaps she simply doesn't care.

'Don't you agree, darling?' says her mother.

'You're right.' Elizabeth pauses. 'Dad doesn't know anything about dresses.'

Elizabeth helps her mother cut vegetables for the couscous, and after dinner they sit together looking at dress catalogues and fabric swatches. Oyster, pearl, moonstone. The brides wilt over stone balustrades or against weeping willows, as if dragging so many yards of material about has exhausted them. 'These dresses aren't quite me,' says Elizabeth. 'I don't want to look like a melting dessert.'

'It's "pudding", not "dessert",' says her mother. '"Dessert" is what the Americans say.' Then a paw shoots out and scoops up the square of moonstone satin. 'Silly billy,' her mother murmurs. She rubs his shaggy chin and a wet rag falls out of his mouth. 'You don't have that many friends, do you?' says her mother. 'We'll be able to have a small wedding.'

'Yes, I do,' says Elizabeth, stung.

'No, you don't, darling. You're an introvert. Not like Duncan. He's an extrovert.' In her mother's eyes the two of them have always been opposites. It is as if her mother has room for only one child, so that each of them has to be cut to fit the space. Two opposite halves. 'He's not a worker like you. He likes to have fun.'

'Everyone likes to have fun. By definition.'

'I know, darling,' says her mother. 'But at heart, you're a quiet person. Like me. You like to stay at home.' Elizabeth sighs. That is why in the end, like the Red Queen, her mother can't be defeated by logic. She has a trick of pretending to agree, then simply making a variation of her original point.

Duncan comes bounding down the stairs, opens the fridge door, slams it. 'Why don't you ever buy anything nice to eat?' He opens a cupboard door and starts shifting its contents around with clumsy swipes. He looks over their shoulders at the glossy photographs, stabs his finger at them.

'Who's going to pay for that?'

'Stop stirring,' says her mother. It is her word for trying to start an argument. It makes Elizabeth think of unsettled sediment. It implies that bringing things to the surface is cruel.

'You can talk,' Elizabeth says to Duncan. 'You're still cadging off Mum and Dad. You don't pay rent. I bet you don't even contribute to the grocery bills.' Duncan moves so quickly she almost isn't aware of what he's done until the fabric scraps and scented magazines and thick catalogues are lying on the floor, and tea is slowly dripping off the edge of the table, and he's gone. The front door slams and the room shudders. Their house feels as fragile as a sitcom set.

'Now that wasn't necessary, was it?' says her mother. Elizabeth isn't sure whose actions she is referring to, or whether her mother is even capable of distinguishing between attack and defence, between words and blows.

Elizabeth has forgotten how cold it is at home. The wind blows through cracks in the windows and under ill-fitting doors until the house creaks like a ship in a high wind. But her mother has put a hot-water bottle between her sheets. Elizabeth gets undressed, switches out the light, slips into the warmed bed. Then she doesn't feel right sleeping naked alone. She drags a shirt belonging to Spencer from her suitcase and pulls it on in the orange light cast by the street lamp outside.

She can't sleep, can't keep her eyes closed. Instead, she stares ahead of her at the wardrobe. She looks at one spot for so long that it seems to move, as if the wardrobe door is slowly opening. When a man steps out, she's too frightened to scream.

'Excuse me,' says Duncan as she snaps on the light. 'I came in here to borrow a book, then I must have taken the wrong door. I've been wandering around in there for hours.' What amazes her is his supreme patience, the way he could stand among the old coats without moving or coughing for what must have been half an hour.

'Fuck off.'

'Don't be like that. It was a perfectly understandable mistake.' He grins, but his top lip curls up slightly in one corner, a genetic quirk. That slight snarl is natural to his mouth.

'What do you want?' says Duncan. He is genial, expansive. He insisted that Elizabeth have a drink with him to prove she wasn't angry about the wardrobe trick. She surveys their parents' liquor collection. Most of these bottles have been here ever since she can remember, the emerald Gordon's gin, the swan-necked grappa. Her parents prefer wine to spirits. 'Brandy, whisky?' he offers. 'G&T? You used to like it.'

'OK,' she says. He pours a liberal slug, opens the freezer for ice. When there isn't any, he chips some off the inside with a knife.

'Old-age pensioner's drink if you ask me.' She doesn't feel like a drink, and the tonic is flat, but she sips anyway. Duncan tosses back his head and takes a swig of his beer. Jasmine used to say he looked like Heathcliff.

'So what's new?' he says. Any moment she could say the wrong thing, or not say enough, or say too much.

'Just hanging out.' That useful phrase, the phrase that makes doing nothing sound like doing something. You could say you were hanging out when you had been sitting in your room all day.

Duncan lights a cigarette and unfastens the kitchen window so that he can blow the smoke outside. 'How's America?'

'All right.' He nods. The end of his cigarette glows, a tiny speck of warmth. 'You still working at Domino's?' she ventures. A shrug, then silence. Ash falls from his cigarette.

'Did Jasmine say anything to you about me?' He has spoken, his face nearly completely turned away from her. All she can see is his stubble-shadowed jaw, a hunched shoulder.

'Jasmine?' She has not spoken to Jasmine for years. 'Why?'

'No reason.' Jasmine has been going out with Duncan sporadically for nearly six years, although it seems to have been more often off than on. Jasmine has dyed blonde hair and pouting lips. Although Elizabeth stopped talking to Jasmine, and Duncan was as secretive as ever, other girls at school told her the stories of what they had done. Jasmine went without underwear so that they could have sex wherever they wanted. They did it in a shower stall in the men's bathrooms in Duncan's college dormitory, and they broke into Elizabeth's school gym and did it there, among the exercise mats and climbing ropes. They were rumoured to have done unspeakable things with a banana in Elizabeth's kitchen when everyone was asleep.

'I chucked her,' says Duncan. Even now, when it doesn't matter any more, she is filled with relief.

'What happened?'

'Nothing happened. Why did anything have to happen? I just got tired of her.'

'OK, OK,' she says. 'Relax.'

'It's you who aren't relaxed. You've never been fucking relaxed your whole life.' He flicks the butt into the garden. 'Nothing happened,' he says, knocking her shoulder as he pushes past her.

★

She was ten and the dining room was ice blue. Duncan passed his fingers back and forth through the candle flames. 'Bet you can't throw a higher number than I can,' he said. Elizabeth threw a one. He flicked the die. Six. He grinned, then rolled the die twice more. Two more sixes.

'How did you do that?' she asked.

'It's my secret power.' The die was an ordinary one from a lost game.

'It's just another one of his tricks, Elizabeth,' said her mother. 'Don't take any notice.'

The winter afternoon was already dulling into twilight. From outside, the lit room was framed by the elaborate red brocade curtains, which were never closed. She thought they must look like a puppet show, Punch with his stick, Judy with her smile.

'Elizabeth, look at me,' Duncan demanded. She kept her eyes on her plate, chewed. 'Elizabeth, I've got something to show you.'

'Leave her alone, Duncan,' said her father.

'Just ignore him, Ellie,' said her mother.

'Will someone pass the potatoes please?' said Elizabeth.

'Ellie, look at me,' Duncan commanded. She looked. She always did. He opened his lips to show her the chewed-up food. She stared into his mouth's dark cave. He could not stand impassivity.

'Smelly Ellie,' he said hopefully. She ate. 'Ellie smelly welly. Wellington boot. I'm going to call you Wellington from now on. All right, Wellington?' By concentrating she could make his voice go small and faraway. He started passing his fingers through the candle flames again, faster and faster.

'Duncan, you'll burn yourself,' said their mother. But he never did.

At seventeen, Duncan still acted as he had when he was twelve. 'I've got a lovely bogey here, Elizabeth,' he said. Even at twelve, he had not acted his age. She went on watching television, her homework spread out on the coffee table. 'It's a present, Wellington. Aren't you going to say thank you?' He was fascinated by his own secretions, and demanded that she must be too. Then he reached out and put it on her arm. Elizabeth shrank inwards, thinking, *My arm is not part of me. I'm not in my body. I'm in my head.* She thought of the stories Granny used to tell her about the temptation of saints, the crude offers of beautiful women and bags of gold. No wonder they were able to resist. Endless polite coaxing would have been harder. *He wants to cover me with his slime*, she thought, *but I will stand fast.* The old-fashioned phrase comforted her.

As soon as he went out, she crept up to his room. These secret visits were her only indulgence. If she did anything he would find out about, she would only incur a worse retaliation. And she was hungry for knowledge of his life. She did not know the names of his friends or much of what he did with them. The answer to 'Where are you going?' was always 'Out.'

In his room a Coke bottle was filled with a sour-smelling amber liquid, which she knew better than to taste. If he could, he would have preserved every precious drop of his bodily fluids. She picked up the Coffin Bank and rattled it. When you put a coin on a button and pressed it, a skeleton sat up, extended a hand, and drew the coin into its coffin. His collection of lighters was arranged on a shelf. She picked up her favourite, a pelican. Its yellow beak snapped open to reveal a tongue of flame. She snapped the beak open, closed, open, closed. And then it didn't work any more. There was the bonfire whiff of lighter fuel, but no flame. She shuddered. She was usually careful not to disturb anything, like a detective at the scene of a crime. He would notice this, she knew, and then he would exact punishment.

Elizabeth ran downstairs and phoned her best friend Jasmine. She would arrange to go out. Jasmine would take her to the second-hand market where she bought her Indian skirts and the silver powder that sparkled on her eyelids. Or just for a coffee, for a walk, anywhere. All Elizabeth knew was that she had to get out of the house before Duncan got back.

Jasmine flounced ahead, her mirrored skirts trailing along the ground. Elizabeth paused to sniff the incense in the air, the foreign spices, the rich smell of cooking meat. One stall offered bracelets and necklaces displayed on black velvet; another sold fringed shawls. They stopped before a thin man dressed in black, lounging behind a stack of skulls. 'Human skulls, girls, honest!' he called out as they passed. Jasmine laughed and blew a kiss at one of the bald heads. Then she stopped and dragged down a backless velvet top and a purple skirt from the garments hanging above the stall.

'Try them on,' she said. The skirt had two layers of tassels.

'They're not really me.' Elizabeth was wearing a sweater and jeans.

'Come on, Elizabeth. You look like Jane Eyre. You need to get a new image. You could be really sexy if you tried.' Elizabeth's hair fell down her back, long and straight and brown. She practised her violin and won prizes for her Latin translation, and she was bored of it. She marched into the man's makeshift changing room, a corner of his stall curtained off with a sheet.

He had not done a good job and she caught his eye while she was wriggling into the velvet top. He winked. She pretended not to notice. It might have been the dim light beneath the stall's awning, but in the mirror she looked different, older and mournful. 'There, you look brilliant.' Jasmine squeezed Elizabeth's bare shoulder. 'Now I'll be able to take you out with me.'

When the man counted out Elizabeth's change, she saw that he was wearing a silver ring in the shape of a tiny naked woman. 'Do you like having a woman wrapped round your finger?' she asked. He looked up and gave her a grin. She saw that he was not a man at all, he couldn't have been more than eighteen. He took her wrist and drew it towards him, then he wrote a number on the inside. 'Call me and find out,' he said.

'Creep,' said Jasmine, turning to look back. The boy watched them go with his heavy-lidded lizard's eyes.

Elizabeth was in the bathroom getting ready to go out when she heard Duncan come home. She swore under her breath. She had assumed he would be gone all evening. He entered the kitchen, and she followed, hoping to stop him from going up to his room and discovering his damaged treasure. When he saw her, he stuck his arm out before him, fist clenched, and put on a flat voice, like a robot. 'Guided Fist, Guided Fist,' he said.

'I've got to go out, Duncan,' she said. 'I haven't got time for this.' She was wearing the velvet top and the purple skirt, but he didn't comment on her new look. He walked towards her with his fist forward, and she stepped aside. His fist hit the wall, then he started towards her again, bleeping, 'Guided Fist, Guided Fist.' The game continued. He never hit her, since the rules were that he must walk slowly and could not change direction until he banged into something. Besides, at fifteen she was too old to hit. Their game was not a serious fight but a ritual, its moves elaborate as a minuet.

Jasmine opened her door and surveyed Elizabeth appraisingly. Then she made Elizabeth sit down in her bedroom while she dragged a kohl pencil under her eyes, over the fainter lines Elizabeth had drawn earlier. She brushed Elizabeth's face with a big white brush, then blew to get rid of the excess powder. She filled Elizabeth's lips in with the black kohl pencil. Jasmine stepped back to admire her work. 'There,' she said appreciatively. 'You look like a vampire.'

At the club that evening, the man at the door just grunted when Elizabeth passed him the entry fee. He didn't ask her age. His eyes followed Jasmine's lemon-blonde hair, made luminous by the strobes. They danced until they were so hot they asked for ice at the bar to drop down the fronts of their tops, and when they got back to Elizabeth's house her parents were asleep.

Elizabeth left Jasmine in the hall unlacing her leather boots, while she slipped up to the bathroom. Inside, the air was warm and prickly with the scent of Lynx Oriental, and there was a tub of pink wax open in front of the mirror, which Duncan used to slick back his hair. He was usually out in the evenings. But tonight he must have stayed here after he discovered the pelican, to wait.

When Elizabeth went back downstairs, the hall was empty and she could hear voices from the kitchen. Duncan was sitting at the kitchen table eating Frosties, and Jasmine was sitting opposite him with a glass of clear liquid in front of her. The Finnish vodka that had never been opened stood on the table.

'Want a drink, Elizabeth?' he asked. He was gruff, polite, transformed.

'I don't know.' She looked at Jasmine, who raised her glass in a mock toast.

'It's still early. I don't feel like going to bed yet. Let's *do* something,' Jasmine said.

'We might wake my parents up,' said Elizabeth.

'Don't be so boring.' Jasmine picked up the vodka bottle and poured Elizabeth an inch or two.

'Why don't we play a game?' said Duncan. They sat round the kitchen table and played blackjack, one round after another.

Jasmine's face was flushed and she swallowed her drink in deep gulps. The drink scalded Elizabeth's throat, set her insides on fire. Finally, they decided it was too hot inside, and outside they would be less likely to wake up 'the olds', as Jasmine called them. They sat in the grass at the bottom of the garden. No one had a coat, but they didn't feel cold, even though it was late autumn. The air smelled of burning. Elizabeth remembered the pelican and realised that Duncan hadn't mentioned it.

'This is so weird,' said Jasmine slowly. 'Who'd have thought that tonight I'd be lying in the garden with Elizabeth's brother?' She burst out laughing.

'This is a weird, weird night,' agreed Duncan, lying on his back. Elizabeth lay back too and looked up at the sky and laughed to herself, and when she sat up again, Jasmine was straddling Duncan and kissing him. She really was kissing him, and Elizabeth was being sick, over and over in the grass. She couldn't stop shivering even when they took her inside to the bathroom. Then they disappeared. Elizabeth would never forgive Jasmine for that night.

The next day Elizabeth refused to give Duncan Jasmine's

phone number, but he sneaked into her room and stole her address book. Then the whole thing was out of control. Now when Jasmine phoned their house, it was to speak to Duncan, not to Elizabeth. When she passed Elizabeth in the corridor at school, her lips puckered sulkily.

Elizabeth began to spend her time with Cleo instead, a studious girl with long red hair who shared her hatred of Jasmine. They called Jasmine's sulky pucker 'the Glout', because it was a cross between glowering and pouting. They called Jasmine 'the Cockroach'. They were jealous of her name, the name of a golden flower, but not limply feminine. Cleo had changed her name from Claire. Elizabeth could not think of what she would change her name to. How could she ever be a temptress if she was an Elizabeth? Her name was as unyielding as a stiff-backed brocade chair. She lay in bed and tried to think of alternatives, listening for the sound of Jasmine and Duncan creeping up the stairs. In the mornings she sometimes tripped over Jasmine's bright red high heels, placed carefully side by side in the hall.

One day Elizabeth was practising Bach on her violin in the ice-blue dining room. She liked to look out on the street while she played. Magnified by echoes in the huge room, the music filled the whole house. The violin had been lovingly cared for. Her grandfather had kept it wrapped in a silk cloth and Elizabeth had inherited it without a nick. Her mother always said that although he hadn't had much training, he made up for it in feeling. But Elizabeth's strong suit was technique, rapid position shifts and triple chords, her fingers fluttering at the instrument's goose-thin neck.

Then she saw Jasmine and Duncan coming up the front path. Jasmine was wearing a white jumper that showed the shape of her breasts. The fingers of Elizabeth's left hand pressed down on the strings so hard that when she stopped each tip was scored with a red groove. Holding the violin too tightly had given her a sore on her neck, like a love bite.

She could hear them going up the stairs, right up to the top of the house, his door closing. It was an old house, and seemed to vibrate at every touch. Walls thrummed, banisters shook. Rooms echoed and sound carried easily. She could not avoid hearing Jasmine's cries, tearing open the afternoon. They were so loud they seemed to be coming from Elizabeth's own mouth. Jasmine's voice was practised, theatrical. The sounds went on and on.

5

The Funeral Game

AN ASSISTANT SHOWS THEM past the racks of jewel-coloured ball gowns to the glass-walled bridal room at the back of *Dresses for Princesses*. A baby chandelier hangs overhead, and pale dresses throng the racks. Elizabeth didn't want to come to this particular shop. She knew it would be expensive. All her life, her parents have never refused her any money. And now she doesn't want to take any more. She touches one of the dresses, and its silk skirts rustle like banknotes.

But it's too late to go somewhere else. She and her mother balance themselves on a diminutive sofa, and the assistant shakes a sheet out over the floor to protect the costly fabrics. She holds up the first dress on its padded wooden hanger, and announces: 'Shirley Temple.' She dangles Ginger Rogers and dances Elizabeth Taylor in the air. But none of the dresses are right. They see Titania and Cleopatra, Lady Di and Jackie O, Lucrezia Borgia and Marie Antoinette. The embroidery of lace and pearls makes the gowns look like thick candles with layers and layers of drips. Elizabeth's heart sinks. They must cost thousands of pounds.

Finally she picks one to try on. A simple sheath, no seed pearls, no silver thread. Just plain white, sleeveless. She emerges from behind the cubicle's velvet curtain, does a doubtful pirouette.

'Beautiful,' says her mother. 'Perfectly beautiful.'

'But I don't look sexy,' Elizabeth says sadly.

'You're not supposed to look sexy,' her mother replies. 'It's a wedding dress. You're supposed to look appropriate.' Elizabeth sighs. 'It's your decision,' her mother goes on, 'but I think it looks beautiful.' Elizabeth decides to take it. This must be the cheapest one.

The assistant stands behind Elizabeth and gathers up a handful of loose material. She inspects the shoulder straps. 'It will need to be adjusted,' she says. 'That will cost extra. You could pick it up tomorrow.' Elizabeth twists around to look anxiously at her mother. But her mother is nodding, bending over to help undo the dress's double row of tiny buttons, red-knuckled maid to a spoiled girl in silk.

★

Elizabeth squirmed into one skimpy garment after another, shy, wanting praise. 'Will that be warm enough, darling?' said her mother. Elizabeth wriggled and tried to get a view of herself from all sides.

'It's not meant to be a coat,' she said. Her face was moon-shaped and serious, her hair a ragged mane, but she could at least make the most of her figure. Besides, she was sixteen, old enough to wear whatever she chose.

'Is that a top or a dress?' asked her mother.

'A dress,' said Elizabeth. She looked in the mirror. 'But do you like it?' It *was* short. Her mother disappeared for a minute, then came back with a lilac garment. Elizabeth thought it looked like an old woman's nightie.

'Here's a pretty frock,' her mother said.

Elizabeth took the dress reluctantly and went back into her cubicle. When she was still in her underwear, someone yanked the curtain open, said, 'Oh, sorry,' and pulled it closed again. Then opened it. It was Jasmine, a wisp of a silver vest in one hand, a half-eaten Mars bar in the other, a strand of caramel on her lip. Her breasts had swelled, and their outline was visible through her pale-blue school blouse. She had begun to wear her hair up and a narrow ribbon around her neck in place of the required school tie. Even in her uniform, Elizabeth thought, Jasmine managed to look like a Toulouse-Lautrec whore. There was a rumour going round at school that she was a nymphomaniac.

Jasmine surveyed Elizabeth's flat-chested frame. 'I thought that slinky little dress you just had on looked quite sexy,' she said. Elizabeth stared. She had expected an insult. Jasmine sucked copper-coloured goo from her fingers and Elizabeth understood that Jasmine was trying to arouse her. Not satisfied with Duncan, Jasmine wanted Elizabeth to want her too. It was an insult after all. But Jasmine caught her eye in the mirror and swept her gaze over Elizabeth's breasts and pouted. 'Piss off,' said Elizabeth.

She pulled back the curtain a crack and watched to make sure Jasmine left. Dangling the silver vest from one finger, Jasmine glided past Elizabeth's mother with her nose in the air, but was not rewarded with the slightest flicker of recognition. Jasmine had grown up too much. And when she came over these days, she arrived after Elizabeth's parents had gone to bed. Elizabeth turned back to the mirror. In the stiff linen dress she looked as thin and sexless as a knife in a napkin.

She wished she had told Jasmine that she and Cleo were having some fun of their own that night. Although the phone number of the man she had met in the market with Jasmine had faded from her arm, she hadn't forgotten him. His name was Dax. She recognised him when they saw him strumming the guitar with the heavy metal band in her and Cleo's favourite pub, the Slug & Lettuce, and now they had invited him to dinner. But not just any dinner. The card they had written together invited him *to an alfresco supper in the Egyptian Village.*

Elizabeth tried on the original dress again. Two thin straps criss-crossed on her back, marking her body like a target.

'I preferred the other one. But it's what you think that matters, darling,' said her mother. Elizabeth sighed, swept up her armful of garments. She thought of the picture of herself displayed on the mantelpiece at home, the one her father had taken in Italy last spring. Her grinning face stupidly balanced on top of a draped statue. Her mother loved that picture. Elizabeth preserved for ever with a chaste stone body. She didn't want to be like that any more.

She saw a long white list, spiralling on and on, a list of all the things her mother had ever done for her. School bills, shoes, presents, outings. Instead of having a career, she stayed at home to look after the two children and keep house. However much her mother complained, her generosity was unstinting. But if Elizabeth couldn't please her mother, she might as well displease her. What could she do with such a debt except enlarge it?

The assistant totted up the prices, while guilt swirled in Elizabeth's stomach and she hated herself. It was not too late, she could put the clothes back. Later they would be strewn all over her floor, deep as autumn leaves, while she searched for something to wear that evening. Her mother was getting out her credit card, but Elizabeth did not stop her.

At tea she forgot about Jasmine and Dax. Her mother sipped from her cup like a little girl on her best behaviour. She loved to have tea, a proper tea, the kind with a three-tiered silver stand holding crustless sandwiches and tiny pastries. There was soft rose-coloured carpeting and pistachio walls, little tables with lace cloths. A miniature fountain. Fat old ladies eating éclairs. And then a string quartet started up among the potted palms. 'Listen, isn't that lovely?' said her mother dreamily. 'I've always loved the idea of a *thé dansant*. Why don't they have those any more?' She had been brought up starved of elegance and luxury. 'Look at that,' she said. She pointed to a calligraphic flourish of chocolate on one of the little cakes. 'You spend all that money on the opera or traipsing round art galleries. But maybe the most beautiful things happen by accident.' Sometimes nothing could please her, but sometimes it took so little.

Elizabeth was all solicitude. She had made sure her mother had the most comfortable seat on the pink velvet banquette, and now she poured the tea and chattered about nothing. She felt as if she would have done anything at all for her mother. They talked about what they would do if they won the lottery. Her mother said she would lie in a hammock all day. Elizabeth thought she would build her mother the perfect house she longed for, furnished with antiques, set among rolling lawns. 'If I could resurrect Capability Brown,' she said, 'then I'd get him to landscape it.'

She paused for a moment and saw that her mother was already somewhere else, in that mysterious place where Elizabeth couldn't reach her. Her eyes had wandered away and she picked up the crumbs on her plate with a licked fingertip, abstractedly. She might as well have been lying in a darkened room.

What was it, what was she thinking about? Who had she loved and lost, who had died, who had hurt her? They tried to make her feel better. Her father bought her a foot spa to soothe her feet while she watched television, but she never used it. Elizabeth bought her things for her bath, anything that said 'Relaxing' or 'Uplifting' on it, bath bombs that hissed themselves to nothing, shhhshsh, soothing, leaving the bath fragrant, milky, full of petals. But nothing made her feel better. Elizabeth wasn't sure if she believed in her mother's suffering any more. In her flurry of affection she felt foolish suddenly, a pampered pet dog wagging its tail.

When they got home, her mother said: 'Darling, why don't you show Dad what you bought?'

'Yes, show me your fripperies,' said her father.

But Elizabeth mumbled, 'I've got to get ready for tonight.' She locked herself in the bathroom. The plumbing was old and after one person had had a bath it took a long time to produce more hot water. She ran the bath deep and lay back among all the cold soap hearts she had given her mother over the years.

When Elizabeth had soaked herself enough, she stood up and admired her pink body in the steamy mirror. Lined up on the counter there were expensive lotions with French names, promising to smooth and firm, designed to prevent ageing. *Crème Hydratante. Huile Relaxante.* Elizabeth got out of the bath, put her nose to the glass and scrunched up her face. She tried to imagine what she would look like old and wizened. Then she rubbed on a little cream to keep her skin soft. She also put a tiny dab of perfume on her wrists, not too much, or her mother would smell it. It came in a bottle of thick green glass with a gold stopper. When she was little she called it Green Water. When her parents went out and left them with the babysitter, the scent of Green Water hung in the air. It made her think of leaves after rain.

Her mother's make-up came in gold tubes and boxes. One by one Elizabeth examined each item, like an archaeologist in an Egyptian tomb. All the make-up Elizabeth had of her own was one kohl pencil. She had been in the habit of letting Jasmine paint her face. But now she carefully crayoned her mouth with lipstick, then opened a case of eyeshadow and dusted purple on her lids. They throbbed beneath her fingertips, powdery as butterfly wings.

'I'm off now,' she shouted as she walked down the hall. Her parents were watching television in the sitting room.

'Hang on a minute,' called her father. 'When will you be back?' She wanted to get out of the door before they saw her.

'I'm staying the night with Cleo, remember?' It was too late. Her mother came into the hall.

'Why doesn't Claire ever stay the night here?'

'Her name's Cleo,' said Elizabeth. It was because Cleo's father was never there and they could get back any time they liked. When her parents got divorced, Cleo chose to live with her father. He was a psychiatrist and had also written a book on why marijuana should be legalised. There was a copy of the Kama Sutra right out on the bookshelf. In the fridge there were always cartons of Chinese takeaway. He let Cleo order whatever she liked to eat. He didn't do any cooking himself.

'You're going to be cold, dressed like that,' said her mother, taking in Elizabeth's low-cut neckline. 'And what have you done to your eyes? They look as if you've been at them with a lump of coal.'

Elizabeth looked in the hall mirror and her eyes filled with tears.

'She looks very glamorous,' said her father bravely. *Glamorous.* A clumsy word, implying: *You've tried too hard.* Like an ancient film star trying to deny her age.

'You look too severe,' said Cleo. 'You need something more. I've got an idea.' She made Elizabeth sit still while she drew on her with face paints, looping tendrils and blue flowers all over her shoulders and chest.

'What about you?' said Elizabeth. Cleo's hair was naturally red, but she'd dyed it and now it was almost blonde. She had sandy eyelashes and her fair skin was thin, almost transparent, like a sheet of filo pastry. She could have been beautiful if she tried, but she often didn't.

'I've been busy taking care of the food. I went to a delicatessen. Vichyssoise. Brioche. Don't you love the word vichyssoise? It sounds like some unspeakable sexual practice.'

Cleo's flat was full of her father's books, and she had read most of them. She was an expert in many things: ancient sexual positions, modernist art, and the history of marijuana, even though she had never smoked any. They had begun to tell each other everything. When she was with Cleo, Elizabeth felt they communicated so perfectly it was almost as if she and Cleo were two halves of the same person. It was Soul Sex, said Cleo, and each lamented the fact that the other was not a man.

They intended just to have some fun with Dax. Cleo said he would assume that by 'alfresco supper' they meant sex, because that was what people were rumoured to do in the Village. 'He couldn't resist our invitation,' said Cleo. 'Vichyssoise, *ménage à trois*. We'll drive him crazy. Then we'll run away, possibly leaving him naked.' They had decided to save themselves for *la grande passion*. Not like Jasmine.

They squeezed between the gap in the iron railings, dragging the picnic basket after them. The cemetery had been filled two centuries ago, but now was open to the public at select hours because of the eminent Victorians who lay buried there, writers and thinkers, the owners of diamond mines and newspaper empires. Old lady volunteers led tour groups. But at night the cemetery had a different sort of visitor. Schoolkids with nowhere to go, sucking on forbidden cigarettes, and people from the Slug kissing in the bushes. There were beer cans and the occasional luminescent condom underfoot.

The old ladies had done their best to weed the paths and rake the ivy from the tombs, but the place was still completely overgrown, a riot of ferns and rhododendrons and huge ivy-strangled trees. Crosses and obelisks and pillars stuck up all along the path and filled the woods beyond.

The Village was built at the height of the Egyptian craze, and it was the place for serious trysts, deep in the cemetery's heart, away from the schoolchildren and casual kissers. A stone archway led to a street of locked wooden doors, the yellow tombs ornamented with fudged hieroglyphs and crumbling scarabs. Someone's idea of Egyptian, rather than the real thing, the place resembled a film set. It was hard to believe there were really any inhabitants lying inside.

At the top of the street there was a courtyard lined with black dead leaves, flanked by pocked yellow-grey columns that resembled gnawed corncobs. This was where they spread out their rug. Swags of wild flowers dangled festively over the tombs. With a shock, Elizabeth realised he was already there, leaning against one of the pillars, in a long black coat. 'Hello, girls,' he said, stamping his cigarette out under his boot. 'Want a drink?' He scraped aside the leaves until he uncovered a bottle of gin. 'I keep it here to be prepared,' he said.

They all sat down, and Dax leaned back against a tomb door and lit another cigarette. She and Cleo were nonplussed. Now it seemed as if he was the one who had set the scene and planned their parts. The gin, which was half empty, gave Elizabeth the feeling he had done this many times before.

Dax spooned up the vichyssoise and frowned. 'It's cold,' he said.

'It's meant to be,' Cleo told him. 'It's vichyssoise.'

'Huh,' he said. 'I knew that.' After the soup course, Elizabeth slipped off her cardigan. She and Cleo had planned that this was the moment when she would display herself to Dax, tattooed with Cleo's fanciful flowers. Anyway, the gin was making her hot. They had nothing to mix with it and were swigging it straight from the bottle.

'Cool,' said Dax. 'Is that real?' He reached out and rubbed Elizabeth's shoulder, sending little waves of sensation up and down her arm, leaving a bruise-blue smudge. 'Why don't you get a real one?'

'Because my mother would kill me,' Elizabeth said.

'She's just jealous of your developing sexuality,' said Dax. He blew a smoke ring. 'But it's essential for you . . .' He paused. He was two years older than her, so perhaps, she thought, his advice might be worth listening to. 'Not to stop yourself from exploring these things.' Elizabeth nodded. He didn't say much, so it seemed important to pay attention to what he did say.

Cleo had gone very quiet. She was lying on her side, looking like a plump courtesan in an eighteenth-century painting. After Dax's last remark, she glanced at Elizabeth and began giggling quietly to herself. She slid down lower and lower and finally she was lying on the ground. She pulled her jumper over her face and lay there, mummified.

'Are you all right?' said Elizabeth. She put her hand on Cleo's shoulder.

'Fine,' came her muffled voice.

'Maybe she just needs a little nap,' offered Dax. 'Sleep it off. We could go for a stroll.'

'I'm not leaving her by herself,' said Elizabeth.

'No, do leave me by herself,' urged Cleo's voice. 'I'll just have a sleep and then be fine. Need to sleep, that's all. Off.' Her shoulder shook in a final convulsion of laughter. So they went.

The maze of tombs and mausoleums made Elizabeth think of a many-roomed mansion, trashed after an all-night party. It was completely quiet, as if the party was at last over and strangers were asleep in all the bedrooms. 'You know what people used to do here, don't you?' said Dax.

'Drink beer and shag,' she answered, feeling rather streetwise.

'They were Satanists. They opened up some of the tombs and scattered human remains about. They kidnapped babies and drank their blood here.'

'Oh,' she said. 'But that must have been a long time ago.' The gin no longer warmed her and she was starting to find him melodramatic.

Then she gasped as he shoved her chest and pushed her into one of the tombs. It was a square one like a little house and its mouth had no door, only a bit of wooden slatting that easily fell away. Inside was utter blackness. He stood in the doorway blocking her way out, silhouetted against the sky. 'They had orgies in honour of the devil,' he said.

'Dax, this isn't funny.' To her embarrassment, there was a sob in her voice. She really was frightened now. She stepped towards him, wondering if he wanted to kiss her. Let him get it over with. He grabbed her and pressed his groin against hers. Then he yawned.

'We really should go back and get Cleo,' he said, stepping out of the doorway, offering her his arm in gentlemanly fashion.

'What?' She'd been expecting the kiss. Then she understood. 'I get it. You're a joker,' she said. He wanted to show her that he could play their games too. He grabbed her by the hair and then he did kiss her.

'You weren't meant to actually go and snog him,' said Cleo.

'Oh,' said Elizabeth. She was never sure with Cleo what was real and what was a game.

'Well, it's done now,' said Cleo. 'Fast or slow. Wet or dry?'

'Wet,' said Elizabeth. 'And slow.' She could still feel the cold tips of Cleo's face paints moving over her skin while Dax's long fingers pinched her nipples. But he made her feel grown up. He was almost a man. He had left school and had stubble. It was, she told herself delightedly, *a sordid liaison*. He put something in his hair so that her fingers tangled in it. Cleo sighed.

'Dax,' she said, 'is not your intellectual equal. He is your false animus. You are using him to prevent yourself embracing your true anima.' The book face down on her bedside table was *He: The Workings of Masculine Psychology*. She was into Jung at the moment.

'I'm not going to have sex with him,' said Elizabeth. It was all play-acting and sex would make it real. 'It's just for fun.' She was flattered that someone like him would be interested in a schoolgirl. And Dax gave her life drama, the appearance of rebellion. Together they projected mysterious suffering. He was playing a part and she knew that, but he was good at it. When they walked together down the street, people looked at them as if they were drug addicts.

Cleo shook her head. Her hair was growing very long, and the blonde dye was fading. She had begun to look like a saint in a medieval painting, the kind who would lacerate her own flesh and be martyred for her fixed ideas. She lay down on the bed and it fanned out around her.

'I'm going to die a virgin if I don't meet the right man,' she said dreamily.

'Welcome to the Purple Chamber.' Dax gave an elaborate bow. The walls and ceiling of his attic were deep purple. It was the first time Elizabeth had been to his house. When she came out of school that day, she had found him waiting for her.

'It's like being inside an enormous blueberry,' said Elizabeth. He looked momentarily annoyed. He didn't respond well to flippancy. Maybe he wanted to bat it back, as her father would have done, but he didn't know how. He put on *Boys Don't Cry* and pulled her on to the bed. Then there was a thumping sound. Someone banging on the ceiling below with a broom. Dax got up and turned the music down.

After an hour or so, he descended the ladder from his attic room to get them some instant coffee. Elizabeth heard unintelligible shouting down below. When she lifted the attic trap door and listened, she heard someone saying: 'Why can't you bring her down and be sociable, Daniel? I'm sure she doesn't want to be shut up in your room all evening.' It was his mother. When she heard Dax returning, she quickly shut the door and rearranged herself on the bed. After that, they didn't go to his house any more. She knew it was a bad idea to bring him back to her house, so they kissed in the cemetery instead.

She was not entirely satisfied with this arrangement. The air smelled mouldy. And when they kissed on top of tombs, somehow it was always she whose back was pressed against the hard damp stone. In the daytime she worried about being discovered by one of the old ladies who day after day told tales of deaths by pneumonia and prussic acid and expounded the symbolism of urns and upside-down horseshoes to the visitors. She worried about being discovered with Dax's hand inside her bra or up her skirt. Dax said not to worry. 'Don't you know why those old bags love this place so much? What would make someone keep coming back day after day? They don't earn anything.' He paused. 'They get turned on by all the dead guys. If they found us, they'd probably be pleased.' Then he bucked his hips and closed his eyes in mock ecstasy. 'They'd rub themselves against the crosses and straddle the pillars as they watched.'

Something about the crude gesture offended Elizabeth. Maybe it was because she felt sorry for the old ladies because she too would be old and dried-up one day. She was glad she was never going to have sex with Dax. She was not in love with him. She knew that love was much more complicated than what she felt for him. She liked his lizard eyes and loping walk. Love, Elizabeth thought, would be more like what she felt at home: meaningful silences, two-edged compliments, different feelings blurring together. People knowing each other so well they didn't know each other at all. It surprised Elizabeth that her mother should have been convinced by the charade with Dax.

Her mother expressed her disapproval in sudden, oblique attacks. 'I don't know why you're bothering with your homework,' she said. Elizabeth was lying on the sofa with a Latin grammar on her lap. Her face was white, her lips black. She wore her favourite skirt, streaked purple and black, and thick black wool stockings. Dax liked that. He said she looked beautiful and doomed. 'What's the point of you getting an education if you're just going to end up with someone like that Dax? It'll all be wasted. I don't see why Dad and I should pay for something you're just going to throw away. We might as well spend the money on Duncan.' Elizabeth knew this was a bluff. Besides, she wasn't getting educated to get herself a husband. She thought she would never get married. But what came out of her mouth was something entirely different.

'You don't even know Dax,' she said. 'You're judging him.'

'You won't let me know him. You never bring him back here. I work all day to keep the house nice and you never show the slightest bit of appreciation.' Her mother had a trick of shifting ground, so that Elizabeth was momentarily confused. In any battle of logic, Elizabeth would have been victorious. So her mother always resorted to complaint. In any argument, no matter how small, she reminded Elizabeth who gave birth to her, who

73

took care of her, who looked after the house. It followed, in her eyes, that Elizabeth was always wrong and she was always right. Her mother's mind was a sewing basket where needles had fallen out of their packets and got mixed up with ends of thread. Everything had become so tangled up that if she tried to take one thing out, everything else was dragged up too. 'Anyway,' said her mother, 'you're going to have to stay in more. I need you to help get the house ready for Christmas.'

'Fine,' said Elizabeth. Dax would be busy at the Slug the next few nights anyway, playing his guitar for the band.

Her mother took Christmas seriously. She made her own mince pies and polished the silver and gold balls for the tree until they shone like waxed apples. Meanwhile, Elizabeth and her father stuck a sprig of holly above every picture. The walls were bristling.

On Christmas Eve, Elizabeth's father was dispatched to get the champagne. He drove off declaring grandly that he would get a jeroboam. He loved the ceremony of opening champagne. And although Duncan usually held aloof from festivity, this was the one time when he could always be persuaded to join in. Egged on by their father, he had once made the mistake of shaking the bottle first, so that when uncorked a jet of foam powered it across the room.

Elizabeth hovered in the kitchen. But her mother wanted to do everything herself. Finally, when Dax called, Elizabeth was relieved to escape. He wanted to meet her that evening at the Slug, after the performance. She put on a dress of cobwebby black lace, and stood in the kitchen doorway until her mother looked up. 'What are you all dressed up like that for? You look like you're in mourning.'

'Dax invited me to the pub.'

'But it's Christmas Eve. Don't any of your friends have families of their own?'

'Mum, everyone goes out on Christmas Eve.' Elizabeth didn't bother saying that Duncan was out too. He was not subject to any rules. Her mother treated him as if he could take care of himself or, at least, as if she did not expect him to take care of her.

'You'll freeze, dressed like that. And what about your dinner?'

'I'll have something later. I'm not really hungry.' Her mother's face fell. Her mother had envisioned a jolly family around the dinner table, pulling crackers and cracking nuts, even though it wouldn't have been that way. Elizabeth felt a throb of regret. Then her mother said, 'You don't think about anyone except your stupid boyfriend. All you've done all day is sit in your room tarting yourself up.' Elizabeth wanted to say that she tried to help all day, but her mother wouldn't let her. She didn't ask to be born, she didn't ask for the sacrifice that her mother had bestowed on her, her whole life for the perfect happy family. Then what she really wanted to do was beg, beg for forgiveness, beg to stay and help. But that would have meant spending all evening in the overheated house, and she couldn't bear to do that. Her black lips wouldn't move. She had to leave. Only she wished her mother would let her go without bitterness. 'You ungrateful little bitch,' said her mother. Elizabeth was shocked and almost exhilarated, as if she had just been immersed in icy water. Everything was calm and clear. *I don't feel anything*, she thought, *nothing at all*.

But in the Slug with Dax her mother's words repeated themselves over and over in her head, so she had to bite her tongue not to say them. They marched round and round. What if they got stuck there only to fly out again in ten years' time when she had a daughter of her own? She watched Dax smoking, tapping his finger to the music with one arm around her. She thought how she despised him for smoking, then she thought how sexy it made him look.

Late that night Elizabeth made Dax take his boots off so they could tiptoe into the dining room. She trod on the edges of the stairs where they didn't creak and eased the door's bolt from its socket so gently that it made no sound. There was champagne left, and they finished it, drinking messily from the bottle. ''Twas the night before Christmas,' Dax declaimed loudly. She hushed him, then turned the key of the sitting-room door so slowly that its click was almost inaudible. The scent of pine needles reminded her of Green Water. Dax pulled her down to the sofa, then they rolled on to the floor. He fumbled with her dress, and she wished she'd worn something with buttons. Buttons would have slowed things down, and at each button she would have had a new chance to change her mind. He pushed her skirt up and tried in one motion to scoop her dress over her head. 'No,' she said, trying to hold on to it.

Dax gave up trying to remove Elizabeth's dress. Instead, he slid off her knickers and edged himself between her legs. Then he was inside her, much more easily than she had expected. She had imagined what sex would be like for so long. But it wasn't very different from what had gone before. She had already had Dax's fingers in her, after all. She lay back with his body on top of hers, wondering what her contribution was supposed to be. She breathed heavily and writhed a little. She considered moaning.

Elizabeth had expected unimagined new pleasures, but she didn't feel anything, except a faint boredom. She was more excited about telling Cleo than about the act itself. She wanted to be able to recount every detail, but she drifted into a reverie. She began to play the Funeral Game. Each player had to design his or her own funeral. Duncan said he didn't see the point of playing a game without a prize. And her mother refused to join in too. So when she was little, at night Elizabeth fell asleep by imagining it for her. The details were always the same: a car accident, a telephone call. She would say 'thank you' politely, then hang up. She saw again the same scene she used to see: herself looking down into the grave, in black with a black veil. Underneath the veil, she was pale and drawn, but did not cry. They were in the cemetery. Elizabeth had chosen something magnificent: the biggest mausoleum. The other mourners looked on at her tragic figure. *So young, yet so brave,* they whispered. At that point each time, she would fall asleep, weeping deliciously into her pillow, her body pulsing with guilt.

When she woke up, pine needles were prickling her back. The sky was getting light and the red bird in the stained-glass window was emerging from the blackness. She let Dax out and then tramped upstairs and fell into a deep sleep. When she came back down into the sitting room, blinking and dazed, it was late, almost midday. Her mother was sitting on the sofa, waiting for her. Elizabeth panicked. She hadn't plumped the cushions before going to bed. Could her mother tell that two bodies had made those indentations? And pine needles still nestled in her hair.

But her mother didn't seem to notice anything. 'We decided to wait to open the presents until you got up,' said her mother. 'Happy Christmas. You're not too old to hug yet, are you?' She embraced Elizabeth and Elizabeth remembered the argument of the night before. She understood that they would neither mention it nor apologise.

Beneath the tree her mother had piled up many perfectly wrapped presents. There was even a bunch of bright balloons, exuberantly festive. But because of too much static, they rose outwards, fastidiously not touching, yet unable quite to fly apart.

Elizabeth felt hot and humiliated. She wondered if something about her body told her mother, maybe some smell. Then she realised that if her mother did know she would never mention it, and that Elizabeth herself could never ask her mother if she knew.

Elizabeth was not used to embracing her mother. She had an involuntary memory of Dax. She almost caressed the back of her mother's neck, as she would have done with him, pressed her breasts against her mother's chest. She tried to shrink away, but her mother held her close.

6

Jazz

A BLACK AND WHITE tiled hall with doors leading off it. Watercolours of boats on nacreous seas, a couple of armchairs upholstered in pastel. There is no sign of anything medical or administrative. Elizabeth is surprised not to see the usual religious knick-knacks, the portraits and statuettes. Granny is out of the hospital, but was transferred here to this Catholic nursing home because the doctors said at this stage there is nothing they can do. Elizabeth's mother, generous with money as always, has paid well. This place might almost be someone's home, except for its sweet stench.

The nurse who opened the door says, 'She needs another minute. Would you mind waiting and I'll call you when she's ready?' Elizabeth nods, and sits down to wait. The nurse is dressed in an ugly black dress, with a wooden crucifix dangling from an ostentatiously long chain, and Elizabeth suspects that either she is a nun, or would like to be. The nurse makes up for the tendency to worldliness in the decor. Granny must feel at home.

After a few minutes, one of the hall doors opens a crack. Then it opens all the way and an old woman in a nightdress emerges. She shuffles to one of the armchairs with clockwork steps. Then she says, 'Can I ask you a question?'

'All right,' says Elizabeth. The smell is carbolic soap and urine. She breathes through her mouth.

'Why do gorillas have such big nostrils?'

'I don't know.'

'Because they have such big fingers!' The woman cackles heartily, and Elizabeth manages a smile.

'What's the difference between bogeys and broccoli?' the woman continues.

'I don't know.'

'Children don't eat broccoli!' Her face cracks open in illicit mirth.

'Ugh,' says Elizabeth, smiling.

'Yuck!' cries the old woman. 'Yuck, yuck, yuck, yuck, yuck!'

'That's enough,' says the nurse, as she comes back down the stairs. 'No need to get overexcited.' The old woman looks down at her lap and pleats her nightgown nervously.

Upstairs, the corridors are lushly carpeted in green, and polished side tables hold Chinese vases filled with silk flowers. The nurse puts her hand to a doorknob, then pauses. 'She might be a little different than you remember her,' she says.

But Granny looks surprisingly well, rouge brushed on to her cheeks, her white hair softly curled. She is fully dressed in a startling fuchsia suit with lipstick to match. A large cameo brooch is pinned to her chest, St Francis with a shepherd's crook, lambs at his feet. The only sign of her accident is the bandage on her wrist. Elizabeth kisses her.

'Granny, you look glowing!' she exclaims.

'And look at you! You've put on quite a few pounds! Marriage must agree with you!' She leans forward and peers at Elizabeth's engagement ring. 'A solitaire diamond,' she says. 'Quite understated, isn't it?' Elizabeth cringes a little. She had forgotten Granny's talent for barbed compliments. 'When did you get back?' Granny asks.

'The day before yesterday. But yesterday I had to go and

get my dress. I came to see you as soon as I could. If I'd come earlier, I wouldn't have had my dress to show you.' She raises the square silver box she has been carrying. Her wedding dress nested in tissue paper. She has just picked it up from the shop, fitted now and newly snug. Granny has requested a preliminary viewing, but Elizabeth is not quite sure what she will make of the sleeveless sheath, the absence of a veil.

'I'll get you two girls a cup of tea then,' says the nurse.

'Sorry about the smell,' says Granny in an undertone. 'It's not me, I assure you.' There is a bed with a cover sprigged with rosebuds, a dressing table with a chintz valance and a row of silver-backed brushes. A young girl's pretty bedroom. But vials of pills are ranged on the table and a foam sling hangs over the back of Granny's chair.

In the en suite bathroom, Oil of Ulay and Pears Facial Cleanser are ranged by the sink. There is a dainty little cosmetics bag too, pink silk edged with lace, its mouth half open to reveal a tube of lipstick, a palette of eyeshadow. Elizabeth does not recall Granny ever having worn make-up. Why is she doing so now? Is it some resurgence of long-lost vanity, or just an attempt to conceal the final marks of age?

Elizabeth opens the box and pulls out the dress, steps into it. By contorting herself she manages to do up most of the buttons. And when she emerges, Granny gives a rapturous sigh. She doesn't comment on Elizabeth's bare shoulders, the sheath tight as a bud. Elizabeth takes the hook at the end of the train and slips her finger through it. 'That's so you don't trip over it when you're dancing,' she says. She unhooks her finger and strides across the room, turns so that the train does a graceful flip, and comes back. 'And the train just follows you wherever you go.'

'Like the perfect groom,' says Granny. 'You look beautiful, perfectly beautiful. Your dad will be proud.' Elizabeth smiles. Unease about him throbs in her temples.

Coming in with the tea, the nurse looks at Elizabeth in her tight dress and sniffs. When she disappears, she leaves the door open.

'They always do that,' Granny whispers to Elizabeth, her mood suddenly changing. 'So that they can keep an eye on you and make sure you haven't died.'

'Oh dear.'

'They wouldn't want to miss it. They need to get the priest in. But don't worry, I'm all prepared. Look.' She leans behind her and opens the wardrobe. A white zipped bag dangles to and fro. 'My shroud,' she whispers. 'I don't want to get it out now though. I want to keep it nice. You'll see it soon enough.' She shuts her shroud up and turns back to Elizabeth in her ivory gown. 'Isn't that lovely?' she says. 'These silks and satins feel like cool water on your skin.'

After packing the dress carefully away, Elizabeth stands before the mirror in Granny's tiny bathroom and stares at herself in her underwear. She sees her body rubbed out and redrawn a great many times, until it blurs into age. She imagines what it must be like to be Granny, lonely and unravished.

When the phone rings late that night, Elizabeth immediately thinks of her father. She bursts out of her room, snatches it up.

'Could I please speak to Jazz?' says a gruff male voice.

'There's no Jazz here,' says Elizabeth crisply. She hears her mother whimper in her sleep. She should have realised it wouldn't be her father. Elizabeth used to have such long conversations with Cleo that in the end her parents installed a second phone line upstairs for her and Duncan to share. Her father would have called downstairs.

'I've rung her here before,' says the man. When she and Duncan were together, Jasmine adopted the irritating habit of giving out the upstairs number to her friends. 'Tell her it's Ally.' He pronounces it to rhyme with 'scaly'.

'Jasmine doesn't live here. She never did. Anyway, do you realise what time it is?'

'I just got off work. Come on,' he pleads. 'She didn't show up tonight. I'm worried about her. If she isn't there, at least tell me where she is.'

'My brother might know,' she says.

'I don't want to talk to him,' says Ally. 'Look, just forget about it, all right?' Something in his voice makes her suspicious.

'Why don't you want to talk to him? Who are you anyway?'

'Don't get your knickers in a twist,' says Ally. He pauses. 'It's just that he's all fucked up, yeah?' *Fucked up* is a dry pellet that drops into her mind and unfurls its suggestions. It could mean very drunk. It could mean your parents had given you a bad childhood. Or it could mean beaten up. *I fucked him up.* So it is Ally who had the fight with Duncan. But why?

At once Elizabeth knows what it is. Jasmine has been up to her old tricks again, unable to rest until she's Circe with her wand, all men beasts at her feet. Either she has been having an affair with Ally, or she has made Duncan think she has.

'Anyway, he deserved it,' adds Ally. Elizabeth feels a surge of anger on Duncan's behalf.

'That's a bit rich,' she says. Surely, if anyone is at fault, it's Jasmine. And Ally. 'I'd say you and she deserve each other.' However much she dislikes Duncan, protecting a family member is a reflex, irresistible biology, a goose hissing to defend its young.

★

Jasmine sucked in her cheeks to put on blusher, making a supremely haughty expression. Then she extracted a handful of shoplifted Fudge Sticks from under her sweater and began passing them out to her friends, a group of girls who all rolled their skirts up at the waist to make them shorter. But Jasmine wore the navy tracksuit they were supposed to use for hockey, a pair of narrow white stripes piped along the arms and legs. It was too small for her now and showed her curves. Some quirk of fashion had made it cool.

Elizabeth and Cleo sat together on the other side of the common room, huddled by the ancient radiator. They called Jasmine's haughty expression her Mirror Face, and imitated her behind their sandwiches. They were in their last year of school and couldn't wait to be rid of her. They had both got places at Oxford. Jasmine was going to the same university as Duncan, to study fashion. After she began seeing him, she had stopped doing any work to speak of. She bunked off lessons and went shopping. Her chemistry teacher had even said she didn't have to attend class any more, because all Jasmine ever did was melt biros in Bunsen burners and laugh at the resulting flaccid shapes.

'Boy on the Square!' someone shouted. The school faced a public green with stone-flagged paths and mean little rose bushes. Jasmine rushed over to the window of the common room and wrenched it open. She stuck her head out.

'Hey!' she cried. 'Are you wearing Y-fronts or boxer shorts?' She drew her head in and dragged out her leg from under a chair. It was a mannequin's leg she had extracted from a tip. She thrust the dirty, shapely limb out the window and joggled it about. 'Hey!' she yelled again. Elizabeth could not resist craning her neck to look. Jasmine had had her long hair cropped short and sleek, and what was left was dyed white blonde and slicked with gel. Elizabeth thought she looked like a Bond heroine who had just stepped out of the waves.

'Don't you want any then?' shouted Jasmine and poked the leg towards the boy invitingly. He put up his arm to shield his head, and quickened his pace. The girls surrounding Jasmine cheered. Cleo and Elizabeth frowned.

'If people were chocolates,' Cleo said under her breath, 'Jasmine would be a Fudge Stick. Everyone likes them, but no one loves them. You and me would be violet creams. Not everyone appreciates them, but the ones who do like them, adore them.' Elizabeth was silent. When boys passed along the street below or, worse still, were foolish enough to linger there, Jasmine laughed at them like a tourist among the Amish. Even though they came to her, squinting up at the tall Georgian windows, cigarettes burning between their fingers, their school shirts rakishly hanging out, they ended up looking prudish and stupid. Even though she hated him, Elizabeth didn't want her brother to be treated that way.

'How do I know that anything exists?' asked Cleo. It was after school and they were lying on their backs on the grass, on a hill in the park by Cleo's flat. It was never really dark in the city. At dusk the air simply seemed to thicken, like water in which a dark paintbrush was repeatedly rinsed. 'It could all be a dream,' Cleo said. 'My dream. I could be dreaming *you*.'

'Or it could be someone else's dream,' said Elizabeth.

'A malevolent demon,' Cleo murmured dreamily.

'Maybe I'm the demon,' said Elizabeth.

'Are you?' Cleo propped herself up on her elbow and looked down at Elizabeth. Elizabeth widened her eyes so that the whites appeared all the way round. She had practised this on herself in the bathroom mirror. If you stared into them long enough, your eyes seemed to revolve, two blazing Catherine wheels.

'Stop it.' Cleo lay down, rolling over to face away. 'I'll tell you what's really frightening. What if when we stand up there's nothing there? What if London's gone and there's nothing left but us?' Elizabeth tried to imagine this. An abyss opened at her feet.

'I'm going to read all the philosophy I can, and if I haven't discovered the meaning of life by the time I'm twenty-five, I'm going to kill myself,' said Cleo. She sat up. Elizabeth didn't say anything. Was it true that everyone else led lives made tolerable simply by wilful ignorance? She was afraid. She was eighteen and it was not the first time she had come across these ideas. But they had never seemed to matter before. Now they were real. Cleo had given her a new and terrible way of seeing. She felt Cleo's fear and it magnified her own. Fear was a voluptuous falling, a long dark corridor opening inside her. They were like two mirrors that multiplied for ever when placed face to face.

'Do you love Dax?' asked Cleo suddenly. Elizabeth had told Cleo about losing her virginity to him. 'What about *la grande passion*?' Cleo asked.

'Of course I don't love him. I'm waiting, just like you,' Elizabeth said. In theory she and Dax were still going out, but he was hardly ever in London any more, so it didn't seem worth the effort of breaking up with him. He had joined the army and was doing his training at various mysterious locations scattered around England. Even if she decided to tell him she wanted to break up, she didn't have his address.

'The ideal man,' said Cleo, 'will have four essential qualities. Strength. Sincerity. Soul . . .' She paused.

'And Sexiness,' added Elizabeth.

'But no more men until we meet the Ones,' said Cleo. It was not as if they were giving up much. Like Jasmine, they saw men – at least the ones they knew – as helpless and slightly stupid. They were fun to torment, but you couldn't fall in love with them. It was women who were fascinating and difficult.

'What's the matter with you?' said Duncan. It was late that night and Elizabeth was in bed trying to read. Draped around her neck and shoulders was the blanket she had had since she was born, unravelling and grey with age. Elizabeth had pared down her life to the bare essentials: eating, sleeping, reading, talking to Cleo. Now that she spent most of her time in her room, Duncan had actually taken to paying her the occasional visit.

'I wasn't expecting visitors.' She turned back to her book. It was Frazer's *The Golden Bough,* a gift from Cleo. Its tissue-thin pages were dense with tiny print. Elizabeth spent her days shut in her room, studying ancient texts, memorising irregular verbs. She read philosophy and literary theory, and she had begun to teach herself German. Cleo was learning about genetics and anthropology, and her German was already better than Elizabeth's. They told each other it was so that they could fit in at Oxford, where they expected that everyone would know much more than they did. But also, although neither of them mentioned Cleo's promise that night in the park, it was because they were looking for a reason to live.

'You look Emily bloody Brontë,' Duncan tried. Cleo had decided that Elizabeth should get rid of most of her clothes, the purple dresses with their tasselled fringes, the ragged velvet opera cloak that came down to the floor. She said that they were affected. Besides, they would not have time for such distractions. Instead, they would wear a uniform as plain as that of a religious order: black trousers or skirts, and black jumpers. They had stopped wearing make-up too. Cleo looked different now. With her pale lashes and brows, her features lacked definition. She was soft and white, as if she had never been exposed to light, as if she had not been born yet. Her skin looked as thin as the membrane inside an eggshell.

Duncan twiddled at the knob on Elizabeth's wardrobe until it came off in his hand. He inspected it, then began tossing it from one palm to another. He hooked his feet under her desk and swung back in her chair.

'Where's Jasmine, anyway?' Elizabeth offered finally, when the chair was about to tip.

'At work.'

'What does she do?'

'Stuff at the Silk.' He and Jasmine travelled all over London to disused docks and ruined warehouses. Elizabeth had overheard them speak of their favourite places: the Needle Factory, the Slaughterhouse. She had never heard of the Silk.

'What stuff?'

'She helps with the ambience. Dances. This and that.'

'Where did she learn to dance?'

'It's *club* dancing. There aren't any rules. You don't have to learn it.'

'Yes, I know people don't do the foxtrot any more,' she said. Duncan threw her wardrobe doorknob across the floor and slammed the chair back to the ground.

'You just don't understand anything that doesn't involve swotting with a book,' he said. 'Mum and Dad are really worried about you.' He got up to go. Elizabeth was outraged, all the more so because in fact she did feel ugly and strange. She had begun to blush when she went into shops to ask for things. But her teachers wrote on her report that she was a natural scholar and musician. Surely anyone would have said that Elizabeth, with her string of As, was the ideal daughter. Duncan must be twisting their parents' words.

'It's you they should be worried about!' Elizabeth shouted after him as he left, then regretted it immediately. Duncan would only take this as a compliment, an allusion to his mystery friends, his seedy haunts. He was as secretive as a film star hounded by fans.

Elizabeth flung her book down. Had they all been talking about her behind her back, the same way they talked about whether Granny should be put in a home? 'A few sandwiches short of a picnic,' she heard her mother saying, while everyone nodded solemnly. But no, she couldn't imagine them holding a meeting, sitting comfortably together at the kitchen table. People in this family relayed their thoughts only indirectly. The house was full of rumours, like a Renaissance court, and only some of them were true.

Elizabeth waited until she heard Duncan go out. He stamped down the stairs and slammed the front door. He always made as much racket as possible, wanted his arrivals and departures to be known. But her parents never chided him, perhaps because they knew their word had no power over him at all. They must have seen Jasmine's shoes in the hall, the two mugs of coffee Duncan made in the mornings, the bottles of Diet Coke in the fridge that fuelled their late nights. But they pretended not to.

Elizabeth went to their shared upstairs bathroom to see if she really did look like Emily Brontë. The bathroom was blue and white, and the tiles had a border of fat little yellow ducks. When they were very young, she and Duncan used to have baths together there. Their bubbles came in a bottle with a sailor's face on it and the top was a sailor's cap. They thought the bubbles looked like clustered frogs' eggs, each one holding a reflected child.

Jasmine's things now lay scattered across the counter. A stick of roll-on Body Glitter. Instant Beauty Gel, Five-Minute Revitalising Cream, Get Up And Go-Go Two-in-One Shampoo. Jasmine led a life that seemed twice as fast as Elizabeth's. She liked things you could cook in the microwave and have ready in minutes. Elizabeth had seen the French Bread Pizza boxes in the bin, the Boil-in-the-Bag Cod in Butter Sauce bag brazenly left by the sink. Jasmine always shunned the kind of laborious preparation that Elizabeth was good at. She lived her life in a rush, as if her flight number had just been called for some exotic place.

Jasmine's work at the Silk occupied her nights, and she drowsed through the mornings at Elizabeth's house, rarely bothering now with school at all. Her parents didn't care. Her father was a theatre critic who went to plays most evenings. He wrote his reviews in the small hours and slept all day, and her mother lived in France. Jasmine could do whatever she wanted.

Elizabeth heard the front door click shut. She leaned over the banisters and Jasmine appeared below, creeping stealthily upstairs. She must have forgotten something and come back for it. Elizabeth dodged back into the bathroom and flushed the toilet. When she came out again, she passed Jasmine on the stairs. They pretended not to see each other.

'She's practically living in your house!' said Cleo, outraged. 'Why don't your parents do something about it? Don't they care?'

'She usually comes in at dawn,' said Elizabeth, 'before they get up. She sleeps in the day. And she's gone by dinner time.'

'But you must mind,' said Cleo. Once Elizabeth and her father had thought of a way of making London less crowded. They would divide the population in two: Day People and Night People. Day People would go to work in the day and sleep at night, but Night People would do the reverse. The waiting time for restaurant tables would be shorter, the Tube less packed. A single house could accommodate several people leading entirely separate lives. Elizabeth's life barely brushed the edge of Jasmine's. That was how she managed.

'You should do something to get her back,' said Cleo. 'Post a dead wasp to her in an envelope. Go to her house and stick gum in the keyhole. Throw up on her.'

Elizabeth laughed. When they were eleven, Jasmine was known to have a phobia about vomit. It was rumoured that once, seeing another girl throw up, Jasmine had become hysterical. She claimed that she had never thrown up in her life. But Elizabeth could not imagine Jasmine hysterical now. Despite her hectic life, she always seemed as calm as a racecar driver.

'She's probably grown out of it,' Elizabeth said. 'And then we'd just look stupid.' She thought of Jasmine's fashionable blonde crop, and of Go-Go Two-in-One. 'We could put depilatory cream in her shampoo bottle,' she offered. 'If you're serious.'

'Of course I'm serious,' said Cleo. 'I think there's something profound in the very nature of a prank. One response to the great Question is to seek the Answer. But if there's no Answer, then you should just embrace the absurdity, take advantage of meaninglessness. I mean, if nothing really exists, then we can do whatever we like, right?' She picked up the phone and dialled, then passed it to Elizabeth. 'I dialled randomly,' she said. 'Whoever it is, I want you to ask them. Ask the Question.' Elizabeth tried to give the phone back, but then a man answered. 'Yes?' he said.

'I'm on the verge of suicide,' said Elizabeth. She thought of putting a sob in her voice. 'Give me a reason to live.' She looked at Cleo, her red hair fanning over her milky shoulders. Cleo's skin was paler than ever because she so rarely went out now. Sometimes Elizabeth wished they could just be normal.

'I would, love,' said the man, 'but the football's just starting on the telly.' His voice was kind, with a slight edge of irritation.

'For a moment I thought he answered *I would love*,' said Elizabeth after she had hung up. 'I mean, I thought that was his answer. That was his advice.'

'How ridiculous,' said Cleo. 'Who is there to love? Probably when we get to university the men there will be exactly the same as the ones we know now. I'm never

going to meet anyone that I get on with as well as you.'
Elizabeth's heart sank. For a long time it had been their
one hope, the thing they waited for. Love. And apparently
they didn't even believe in that any more. The universe
was a great blank, an empty skating rink in which she and
Cleo twirled and pirouetted. It was only two o'clock and
the afternoon stretched out ahead of them. 'Let's have a
drink,' Elizabeth said.

'OK,' said Cleo. 'But I want to do this properly. I want
cocktails.'

Cleo's father was away, at a psychology conference in
Tuscany. He had a well-stocked drinks cabinet, and they
drank sour-apple Martinis, sitting on the leather sofa with
their feet up on the coffee table. Then Elizabeth began
pouring things into the shaker indifferently, hoping to
discover a new drink. She added vodka, then cassis. The
cocktails evoked a vanished gentility, ladies and gentlemen
aboard the *Titanic*.

'This will be very dark and powerful,' she said. 'We'll
call it—' She stopped to think.

'The Winged Demon! The one whose dream we are,'
cried Cleo. 'In his honour.' They drank and tasted fruits
they could not name. Cleo wiped her mouth with the
back of her hand. And then they kissed. It was the softest
and gentlest of all kisses, and it was impossible to say who
kissed who. Cleo smelled of clean clothes and vanilla.
Elizabeth couldn't feel Cleo's teeth, only her gums and
tongue. Elizabeth wanted to scrunch her up, like something wrongly made. Cleo was too white and soft-not *real*
enough. Elizabeth suddenly felt that a man's hard, rough
body would refute Cleo's theories like the stone that Dr
Johnson kicked.

On the way home, walking through the park at dusk,
she still felt dizzy from the Winged Demon. She looked
down on the black city dashed with gold, and it seemed to
swirl about her like a cape. The man on the phone could

tell that she was not serious. Something in her voice. And to her surprise, she realised that she was not. She clung to life. There was food and sex and pain, music and dancing and people. Whether these things really existed or not. They had allowed themselves too much time to think. Their angst, she thought, was the luxury of spoiled girls.

A key in the lock woke Elizabeth late that night, a quiet grating like crepitus in a joint. She was dry-mouthed and starving. She read or talked to Cleo until she forgot what time it was, and she had been forgetting to eat. They had been living the sequestered life of scientists working to prevent a comet hitting the earth, surviving on occasional meals.

Elizabeth stuck her head cautiously outside her bedroom door. Through the landing window the night sky was already turning from black to blue. The smell of toasting cheese drew her down to the kitchen. Duncan was sitting at the table, slumped in his chair with his legs spread wide, his eyes a little glazed. Jasmine was microwaving a pizza. She was going through a phase of wearing metallic fabrics, and she looked like a visitor from the future. Pushed back on top of her blonde hair was a pair of goggles sprayed silver. She was shod in moon boots covered in blue fur and her puffy silver jacket was slung over a chair. Elizabeth intended to snatch something from the fridge and carry it up to her room, but Jasmine spoke.

'All right,' she said.

'Jasmine.' Elizabeth nodded.

'It's Jazz, by the way. As in "jazz it up" or "all that jazz".' Elizabeth thought that Jasmine suited her new name, a single hard syllable. It was still a name you could give a perfume, but *Jazz* would be citrusy and unisex, a fragrance of the new century.

The microwave pinged and Elizabeth started. Duncan laughed. 'Don't worry, it's not dangerous,' he said. 'It doesn't emit harmful radiation.' He always sensed when she was afraid and then tried to make it worse. When she used the microwave, she secretly expected it to blow up. For Elizabeth, whether machines would work or not depended not on wires and switches but on their mysterious whims. They had personalities of their own and they did not like her.

When she and Duncan were young, their father had offered to show them how to grow salt crystals on a string, how to make tiny drops of solder. Elizabeth had always preferred to read her book. Duncan began a salt garden then got bored with it before its ghostly ferns could grow. But he liked playing with the solder gun or hammering in nails, and when they got a video, he was the only one who learned how it worked. He pushed Elizabeth away when she tried to use it, and later when they were old enough to drive he monopolised the family car so that she could not practise. Now the whole world seemed a machine governed by energies and connections that Elizabeth did not understand.

Jasmine picked up the entire pizza in both hands and took a bite out of it. She looked at Elizabeth looking at the pizza. Then she said unexpectedly, 'Do you want a bit? We can share.' Elizabeth nodded.

'You can pick the sausage off,' said Duncan. Elizabeth did not like meat. 'I'll even clear an area for you,' he added. He got up, meticulously staked out a third of the pizza, and plucked the pinkish-grey lumps off. Elizabeth took the piece he offered her, feeling a little treacherous towards Cleo.

'I've been thinking,' said Jasmine. 'You could be quite striking if you tried.' Elizabeth flushed a little, pleased despite herself. 'Duncan thinks so too,' Jasmine added. 'Don't you, Duncan?'

'No,' said Duncan.

Elizabeth put the pizza down. While she herself had a

cautious diet of live yoghurt and vitamin pills, Jasmine and Duncan lived on junk. Their blood was coursing with toxins, with sugar, caffeine, and radioactive particles. No wonder Jasmine had so much energy.

'Diet Coke is bad for you,' Elizabeth said.

'So what?' said Jasmine.

'It's full of aspartame. Aspartame causes brain tumours.'

'That hasn't been scientifically proven,' said Jasmine uncertainly. It was obvious that Jasmine was going to fail her A levels, except art. She hadn't even bothered taking the mock exams. She had stopped by the school hall where the exams took place just long enough to wave at her friends through the window. When Elizabeth came out, her fingers blue with ink and her head swimming, the sign outside that read QUIET PLEASE EXAMS IN PROGRESS now said QUIET PLEASE SEX IN PROGRESS.

'Anyway,' Jasmine added, 'I don't care if my life is short, as long as it's exciting.'

'You're like Achilles,' said Elizabeth. 'That's what he said when the gods asked him if he wanted a short, glorious life or a long, quiet one.'

'It's obvious which one you'd choose,' said Jasmine. 'The quiet one.' Elizabeth realised that she had played right into Jasmine's hands. She felt tricked. She should have stayed upstairs.

'Not necessarily.'

'Come on,' said Jasmine. 'You hardly leave the house.'

'I go running,' protested Elizabeth. At dusk, sometimes, in her old black tracksuit.

'There's no risk in running, no adrenalin, no challenge,' said Jasmine scornfully.

Although she had cleaned her teeth before she went to bed, Elizabeth decided to brush them again after the pizza. In the bathroom she pushed Jasmine's scatter of cosmetics roughly to one side. She looked at the green bottle of Go-

Go shampoo and felt irritated enough to use the depilatory cream. But it was too obvious, too childish. And the very act of revenge flattered its object.

She would simply leave a book in there. That would annoy them both, a seemingly unintentional reminder that if Duncan was the handsome one, Elizabeth was the clever one. And if he had Night, then Day was all hers, knowledge and ambition and success. She chose *The Golden Bough*, for its impressive size and copious footnotes. She placed it face down on the edge of the tub, as if she had been reading it while she soaked, brooding on the grove where the king is killed each year by a stranger who succeeds him.

Elizabeth got back into bed, but couldn't sleep. She still felt angry. And the morning's scrubbed light stopped her eyes from closing. Perhaps she should simply get up. She went up to the bathroom to put her contact lenses in. But the door was locked and the taps were running. She heard a giggle, breathing. Then a sudden vigorous splash like wings beating a lake, wild geese taking flight too quickly to be stopped.

7

Night People

ELIZABETH SCRUBS THE DIRT from the curlicues of picture frames with an old toothbrush. She waxes the banisters and rubs them with a soft cloth, removes minute flecks of black from the silver with creamy viscous polish. Since she and her mother have so little time to plan the wedding, they have had trouble booking a venue. Elizabeth suggested that after the official ceremony at the registry office, they should simply throw a party at home. She relished this solution, thinking it would be easy and cheap. After all, they are only inviting a handful of guests. But her mother has begun to talk of filling the cellar with champagne, installing a string quartet in the sitting room, and hiring caterers to serve fillet of Dover sole and pyramids of profiteroles.

Elizabeth wishes her mother would not spend so much. Instead, she dreams of a wedding to match her love, simple and pure. Back in the west, on the shore of a lake, with a wedding breakfast of fresh water and marshmallows charred from the campfire. She might have dared to do that if it hadn't been for Granny. But now the caterers are booked and the champagne ordered. And the house must be cleaned from top to bottom.

The surfaces of the house are silted, the shelves and

tables, the worktops and mantelpieces. It's as if her mother has several times begun to clear up, then lost her resolve. Hoarded foreign coins, layered receipts. Screws and tiny coils of wire, pieces that belong to lost objects. And toppling stacks of magazines, like pillars in a ruin.

Elizabeth sweeps pennies into her palm from the coffee table, wonders where to deposit them. Her father was always careless about money. Coins rained through the torn linings of his pockets and poured from his trousers when he sat down, but he never noticed that he had left a glittering trail.

Elizabeth is worried about him. This is the third day that she's been home and as far as she knows, he hasn't phoned. Why would he leave when he knew she was on her way back? Elizabeth's mother refuses to furnish more than her terse statement: 'He's off on a sailing trip, I told you, darling.' Elizabeth considers bullying. *Where is he and why?* But then she might discover that her mother really doesn't know.

'I had to go outside for a minute to get my head together,' says Spencer. He is telling her about his day. He had to clip out a cancerous stretch of a man's intestines, then sew the shortened tube closed. 'The poor guy had already had so many cancer operations that his intestines didn't even look like regular intestines any more. They'd been trimmed and patched-up so many times, and it seemed like the other doctors had put things back any old how. After I cut the bad part out, I suddenly realised I had no idea where anything went. I looked at the other guy and he looked at me, and he said, "Let's go get a cup of coffee."'

'You sorted him out in the end, though.'

'Yeah. But I was panicking for a moment.' Elizabeth tries to imagine Spencer panicking, and can't. She wants to tell him that she doesn't know where her father is or when he'll be back. It should be easy to tell him things. Spencer has the doctor's manner, the implicit reassurance that nothing she can confess will upset or disgust him, that things will, almost always, turn out all right.

But she finds herself talking about the wedding instead. 'Have you been measured for your suit?' she asks.

'One of the other doctors recommended a suit place to me and I'm going to check it out this weekend. Don't worry, I'm on top of it.' Elizabeth tries to imagine Spencer in a suit. After only a few days apart, for some reason she is unable to summon up his face. She can only recall parts of it, a shadowed jaw, a green eye. She has been worrying that her father will miss the wedding, but now she finds it difficult to imagine Spencer's presence either. Perhaps because her mother is determined to pretend he doesn't exist, the wedding all seems to centre around Elizabeth. Not even around her, she realises, but around her body. How it will be draped and bedecked and photographed, as if this were a funeral. It is difficult to believe in a life afterwards. What went before it now seems so important, as if it might help her understand why her father is gone.

As soon as she hangs up, Elizabeth feels guilty for not paying more attention to Spencer. Since he sleeps at the hospital every fourth night and often works round the clock, it's been hard for them to talk and she doesn't want to waste their precious minutes. She's about to call him back, when the phone rings and it's him.

'I was just about to call you,' she says.

'Guilt call,' he says.

'What?'

'Oh, it's just something me and my dad used to do. Especially when I lived in England for that year and there was the time difference. It's hard to really talk on the phone anyway, and sometimes you misunderstand each other, or you're too busy to really listen. A guilt call is when you call back. Just for a couple of minutes. To say you feel bad.' Elizabeth envies Spencer and his father for being able to dissolve guilt so easily.

That night she dreams of people being opened and stitched shut. When Spencer operates on a man's heart, the chest cavity is filled with crushed ice to keep it from spoiling in the air. Duncan and Jasmine are leaning over her, peering at her chest. Cold floods her and she wakes in a shock.

★

The phone rang at three in the morning. 'Do you know what time it is?' Elizabeth snapped. The only person who would call at this hour was one of Jasmine's friends. There was always music in the background, shouting voices.

'It's not that late,' said a voice, then paused. He was looking at his watch. 'Oh. I'm sorry. Were you sleeping?' The voice had a touch of an accent, like cinnamon, cloves, unknown spices.

'Actually, no,' she said, relenting a little. 'I was up reading. But my parents are sleeping. Who is this anyway?'

'This is Valentino here. Valentino Silk.' Could that be his real name, shaken out with a flourish, like a red handkerchief from a breast pocket? 'If you're wondering, my mother is Brazilian,' said Valentino. 'I'm calling for Jazz.'

'She's not here.'

'Damn. I need to find out whether she can work an extra night tomorrow.'

'Sorry.'

'What were you reading?'

'Excuse me?'

'You said you were reading.'

'Oh. It's the *Metamorphoses*.'

'Ah, Ovid!' Valentino sounded triumphant. 'One of my favourite books. I must have read it a thousand times.'

'How do you have time? You run the Silk, don't you?'

'I own it, yes. But at heart I am a lover of the arts. I have many strings to my guitar.' *To your bow*, she thought. 'May I ask you a question?' he said.

'Yes.'

'What are your favourite lines of poetry?'

'*Then let us tear our pleasures with rough strife/ Through the iron gates of life.*' They were the first that came to mind.

'Bravo,' he said. 'Now, what shall I do about my little problem?'

Elizabeth thought. He got his clichés wrong. But he had read Ovid, which was quite impressive considering that he claimed to be Brazilian. Besides, it was time to stop Jasmine taking all the adventures.

'Jazz has gone away for a couple of days,' she said. 'But I can dance.'

'Oh?' He hesitated. 'But do you know what kind of dancing our girls do?'

'I can do any kind.' She used to go to clubs with Jasmine all the time. She knew how to dance, she told herself sternly. It was easy. Especially if you had a drink first.

'Excellent,' he said. He paused. 'Tomorrow at six?'

'Six is a bit early,' she said. 'I've got a violin lesson after school, and I'd have to come straight to the Silk from there. In my school uniform.' Then she bit her lip for revealing that she was still at school.

'Do that,' said Valentino. 'Ciao.' She hung up, disappointed. If he didn't mind her turning up in her uniform, then presumably the work wasn't so glamorous after all. Maybe Jasmine didn't dance. Maybe she rinsed glasses or swept the floor or something. But now she would have to go.

'Please come,' said Elizabeth. 'Come on. I'll need protection.'

'I don't want to,' said Cleo, her jaw set like Joan of Arc.

'And I don't think you should go either. You don't even know this Mr Silk.'

'That's part of the fun,' said Elizabeth. Cleo shook her head. She was hunched in her father's leather armchair with a blanket over her knees. She had begun to gain weight. It was because she lived on takeaways. Sometimes, when Elizabeth stayed over, Cleo got hungry in the middle of the night and ordered Indian food. Cleo's beauty depended on a kind of radiance, it came from her translucent skin and her long red hair and her eyes that were sometimes green and sometimes grey. It came from the animation she had when she was expounding one of her ideas or devising a new scheme. But now she slept a lot and her skin was dull. It was as if the moon had stopped strewing light and you saw it was nothing but craggy stone. Elizabeth was not sure if this was something to do with her or whether Cleo was like this with everyone now. 'I'll go alone, then,' she said.

Elizabeth did not tell Jasmine about the phone call. Instead, she sneaked into her brother's room, where she had seen flyers for the Silk Academy. She wrote down the address. The next day, after her violin lesson, she stowed the violin in her locker, then did her best with the school uniform. It consisted of a white blouse and a navy skirt, a tie with the school colours, and a navy blazer with a blood-red oak tree on the pocket. There was a hat, but she left that with the violin. In theory, you were supposed to wear navy knickers too, to preserve your modesty in mischievous breezes. But Elizabeth was not wearing them. She was wearing Jasmine's silver vest, the one with the overlapping sequins like chain mail. She had filched it from Duncan's room where it lay tangled with his jeans on the floor. She knew no one could see it, but it made her feel glamorous and invulnerable. She brushed her hair with her head hanging down so that it rose up with static, put on red lipstick and rolled up the skirt as far she dared.

When Elizabeth saw the Silk, she almost wished she hadn't bothered. It looked like a hotel whose grandeur had faded. There was a scalloped blue awning, and underneath there was a varnished wooden door with a photograph stuck up next to it. It was a picture of a hotel lounge with pale yellow walls, a red carpet and shabby plush chairs, a bar with a row of glittering bottles, and artificial palms in brass pots. She was disappointed. She didn't know quite what she had expected, but it had been something darker and more dangerous.

The door was locked. When she rang the bell, no one answered. She rang again, and after a great rattling of bolts, a man appeared. He was wearing a suit. His hair, though grey, was sleek and thick. He was tanned as if he had recently returned from some tropical clime. He pointed at her like a hypnotist selecting a volunteer from the audience.

'You,' he said. 'Elizabeth.' He kissed her on both cheeks. She smelled aftershave. Musk, leather, cigars. She liked it. 'That's how we do it in Brazil,' he said.

'Sorry about my uniform.' She looked down ruefully. 'I thought maybe you'd have something I could change into.'

'No, it's perfect, perfect. I wouldn't change a thing.' He kissed his fingers and blew a kiss, not to Elizabeth, but to underscore his point. She couldn't place his accent. 'First,' he said, 'I want you to come to my office. I'll explain a bit more about the work, and you can have some coffee and refresh yourself. You've got a long night ahead of you.' She didn't like the sound of that. She thought of wiping beer-ringed tables, picking up sodden napkins from the floor.

'Let me show you to my headquarters,' Valentino said. He stepped outside, closing the main door behind him. He led her into a side alley, down some basement steps, then through another door. Elizabeth knew that what she was doing might be considered foolish, but that was why she was doing it. She wanted to let herself go, to throw herself, to be a pinball ricocheting here and there, not knowing where she would end up. But the office disappointed her. Walls of unpainted brick, a tiny window set at street level, through which you could see the alleyway. A battered filing cabinet, a desk with a stack of black ledgers. 'Coffee?' said Valentino.

'That would be lovely.' He vanished into another room, and a few moments later returned bearing two espresso cups on a tray. The drink was aromatic and thick, almost gritty. She sipped. 'Turkish coffee,' he said. 'My speciality. What is that proverb?' He held up one finger, commanding her silence while he thought. 'Yes. *Black as hell, strong as death, and sweet as love.*' He smiled at her. 'You'll fly high.' She drained her cup. 'And now let's get to work,' he said. 'And listen! I want plenty of theatre.'

'OK,' she said. She felt docile and light-headed. Maybe it was because she hadn't had anything to eat since lunch.

The throbbing began in the passageway. For a moment she thought it was her head. Then she realised it was the music. He opened a door and they were in the Silk Academy. It was recognisably the hotel lounge depicted in the photograph by the front doors, but someone had made an attempt to magnify its grandeur. The moth-eaten plush chairs had been replaced by red velvet seats and elegant little three-legged tables. The walls were covered with huge mirrors with baroque golden frames, and there were booths installed around the walls, framed by red velvet curtains with little gold tassels. Some of the booths had their curtains drawn. She looked around and saw that the customers were all men in suits. But no one turned round when they entered.

Some of them were chatting and drinking as calmly as if

they were sipping mineral water at a conference. But many of them were looking at the stage. It jutted out into the main seating area, and it was obviously a later addition to the room, although its creator had made an attempt to fit in with the hotel decor, installing mock–Grecian pillars of white plaster. On the stage there were dancing girls. Some of them had plaits and some of them had pigtails, and some of them wore thick white knee socks. Some of them, she realised as Valentino drew her closer, had freckles pencilled on to their faces. They were in varying stages of undress, but it was clear that they had all been in school uniform at some point.

'Up, up, up, up,' said Valentino, and he fluttered his hands like an exacting dance teacher demanding a difficult position. Then Elizabeth realised what he meant. Up on the stage. Of course. Why not? If Jasmine could do it, so could she. She felt completely relaxed. She climbed up on to the stage and began to dance, letting her body ripple to the music. She twirled her tie round her finger and pouted at some men sitting at a table near the front. Gathering courage, she pulled it off and threw it towards them. It landed around one man's neck, and he at once pulled it between his teeth and bit it like the stalk of a rose, flashing his eyes at her. She slipped off her blazer and began to unbutton her shirt.

Usually when she danced without drinking, she was a cartoon character before it had been animated, moving jerkily from one position to the next. But tonight something had dissolved all awkwardness into fluid motion. There was no harm in it, she thought. No harm in just dancing. She found a pillar and began to wrap herself round it, to slide up and down it, to make love to it, as the other girls were doing. She forgot about them, she forgot about Valentino. She even forgot about Jasmine. It was just her and her dance. Then a hand gripped her ankle.

'You're a natural,' said Valentino. She smiled, trying to

dance away. 'Come here,' he was saying. She bent down and he touched her cheek. Bending down made her dizzy and she swooped lower. Then his fingers brushed her nostrils, and she felt something go inside. 'Mr Silk,' she said. 'I wasn't expecting—' He gave her a smile of infinite benevolence.

'Don't worry,' he said. Something fluttered in her nose and she realised how stupid it was to worry about anything. She shook off her old fearful self, but who was she? She was a white explosion, she was the universe slowly expanding and filled with points of light.

Elizabeth was sitting in a taxi with Valentino. 'It's amazing,' she said. 'It's still light.' There was no time inside the Silk Academy. In natural light, his tan looked suspiciously artificial.

'It's tomorrow morning,' he said. She looked out the window and saw that the streets were quiet and empty. He was right. Then what had happened to the night? She couldn't remember anything after inhaling that unknown powder.

'What did you give me?' she asked. 'First, you poisoned my coffee, then you stuck something up my nose.'

'Something to make you relax, and something to make you lose your inhibitions,' said Valentino. 'It was nothing. Come back to my place and I'll make you a soft-boiled egg and some milky coffee. I don't want to let you starve. Then I can drop you off at school.'

'I'm not a child,' she said. She looked down and saw that she was still wearing her school uniform. Her bag was sitting at her feet, and she was all ready to go to school. But she had lost the night. And her tie, she realised.

'Don't worry, I put your tie in your blazer pocket,' said Valentino. 'Why so sulky? I thought you knew what you were letting yourself in for. Why do you think it is called the Silk Academy? It's not named after me. It's because of schoolgirls with their training bras and their cotton panties and their wet, silky clefts.'

Elizabeth surveyed her body, searching for some sign, but there was nothing, no cuts or bruises. Jasmine's silver vest was still on under her shirt.

'I want to go home,' she said. 'I don't even want to know what happened. I just want to go home.'

'Relax,' said Valentino. 'No one touched you. It was all look, don't touch. I had a soft spot for you and anyway, it was your first night.'

He drew the tie from her pocket and put it round her neck, then tied it expertly in a perfect knot. Something about the brisk way he did it made her realise. She was just a good business prospect to him, a competent employee. He probably hadn't laid a finger on her after all. He picked a thread from her shoulder. 'There's no need to be so scared. Smile.' She didn't smile. 'You're a pretty girl, especially when you smile.' He offered her the compliment like a toy from a Christmas cracker, something cheap and small.

'Was I as good as Jasmine?' she asked.

'Jazz? Well, she did other things as well.' There was a mischievous look in his eye. Elizabeth wanted to know what things Jasmine did, but she did not want to give him the satisfaction of asking. She was silent the rest of the way home, not even opening her lips when Valentino leaned across and tucked some notes into her blazer pocket. 'Pocket money,' he said, giving the pocket a little pat. The pat was as brisk as if she was a dog, as if it had not been on her breast. She had planned to get out the taxi without a word, but then she remembered something and tapped on the window. He wound it down and she said, 'Don't tell Jazz that I filled in for her tonight, OK?'

'Why not?'

'She loves her job. She'd hate to think she'd missed even a night of it.' He nodded and she walked towards her house. As the cab drove off, he called: 'Let's get together and talk poetry some time!' She didn't turn around.

★

Elizabeth is scrubbing the hall tiles when the post drops on to the mat. The *Yachtsman's Monthly*. And a postcard showing a glossy red plant shaped like a lobster claw, its top hanging back to reveal a wet pink throat. She is about to read it when the phone rings.

'I just wanted to check about my suit,' says Spencer. 'You don't wear tuxedos to weddings in England, do you? It should just be a regular suit, right?'

'A nice suit,' she says. 'Dark grey or something. And a smart tie.'

'I think I'll look respectable,' says Spencer. He starts to tell her about how one of the other doctors dropped a contact lens into a patient's open chest, but she's not listening. On the back of the postcard, a printed note reads: *The Rajah's Pitcher Plant is one of nature's most spectacular treasures.* The card is addressed to Duncan and filled with tiny handwriting. *This plant tempts insects inside to drink its sticky goo, then eats them instead. It is well hard, not like the kind we have in England. The clubs here are better too. In Pussy Hits Bull's Eye, the woman puts a dart inside herself, then fires it across the room. In Pussy Blows Out Candle, she puts out a candle without using her mouth. And I've been studying massage. The things I've learned in Bangkok would blow your mind.* A sweeping J precedes a postscript: *Don't think I've forgiven you.*

'We thought we'd have to leave it, but then we found it stuck on the edge of the sterilised sheet,' says Spencer. He pauses. 'Sweetheart? Are you still there?'

'You'll look sexy,' she says vaguely before she remembers that they are no longer talking about the suit. In her mind Jasmine is dressed in crotchless fishnets with a hibiscus flower in her hair. She scales a pole, hooks her feet through the spokes of a horizontal wheel and whirls herself round and round as banknotes snow the stage. Whatever she herself does, Elizabeth thinks, Jasmine always manages to make it seem too safe.

8

Kebab Delite

'AND TAKE THE GIBLETS out,' her mother adds. She has been trawling department stores for lengths of silk ribbon and lace to decorate the house, and she has stopped at Fortnum & Mason's to order the wedding cake. Elizabeth wonders what Spencer will think when he tastes the heavy fruit cake made heavier with its burden of royal icing. American wedding cakes are fluffy and white, frosted with daffodil-tinted cream. This will be more symbol than cake, she will warn him, designed to last like the marriage itself. Like English soil, she thinks, clayey and dense with centuries of crumbled weapons.

The wedding is in twelve days now and there is still a lot to do. Her mother's errands are taking longer than she expected and she wants Elizabeth to put the chicken for dinner on to roast. Although she doesn't eat very much, and Elizabeth doesn't eat meat at all, her mother likes to cook it for Duncan.

'How do I do that?' When she was living in the bottle house, Elizabeth got into the habit of cooking dinner for Spencer, but she didn't usually cook meat. When she did, it was never a whole roast, just an individual breast for Spencer.

'Just stick your hand up its bottom,' says her mother briskly.

The chicken's skin is soft and loose. Like an old woman's skin, massaged for years with cold creams. Elizabeth cuts the string binding the legs to the body, and lifts it up. It's a big chicken. With her hands full, Elizabeth realises that she's forgotten to open the oven door. The cold bird grows heavier and then when she turns back to the worktop, its legs flop down, an awkward baby. It's just for a moment that it seems stubbornly alive, but it's enough to make her scream and drop it.

Duncan comes bounding into the kitchen. 'What the hell's the matter?' He has a greasy bag in one hand, wafting the aroma of cooked meat.

'Nothing. I just dropped the chicken.'

'What did you go and do that for? I'm trying to watch *The World's Greatest Police Chases*. Only good bloody thing to come out of America.'

'I didn't like the way it felt.'

'Poor Ellie,' says Duncan, 'poor little Ellie. Scared of a chicken.' She is halfway out of the kitchen when he says, 'Hang on a minute. What are you going to do about dinner?'

'I'll do it in a minute. Anyway, I don't see why you're so worried about it. You've got your kebab.'

'Don't you think about anyone but yourself? What about Mum?' His solicitude is unusual. Then she realises it is just another form of attack. But just as she is about to respond, Duncan gives a martyred sigh and puts down his kebab. He holds the chicken up to the light and examines it, then dumps it in the sink and gives it a cursory sponge bath. He plunges his hand into its purplish cavity, gropes around, and brings out a plastic bag full of fleshy lumps. He peers at them curiously.

'The giblets,' says Elizabeth.

'There you are then,' says Duncan. The bag thwacks coldly against her chest. 'Snack on that.' She can't stop herself from giving a little gasp. But it is important not to show fear. After all, he never touches her. When he whips the towel turban away from her just-washed hair, he doesn't brush a strand of it. He still has his old habit of throwing flick knives at her too. These weapons are illegal in England, but he smuggles them back from Calais on trips with his mates. The blades stick quivering at her heels, and he has not so much as nicked her skin. There is always decorum in their violence. As if they are two gentleman fencers, making a point of honour out of not leaving a scratch on each other.

'Chicken,' says Duncan. 'Chicken, chicken, chicken.' A tender chant. Through the oven door, the chicken looks as white as her own legs after a winter of wearing tights. He does not stop. 'Chicken, chicken, chicken.' He is right, she thinks. Once back with Duncan, she is soft and awkward and helpless.

'You're so irritating,' she says. 'No wonder Ally had to punch you.' His grin vanishes.

'Fuck off!' he shouts.

★

'Is that a violin or a machine gun?' She swung around. She had just finished her violin lesson, and was leaving school. There was a shaven-headed man leaning against the side of the building, in blue jeans and a fisherman's sweater. A man with watchful lizard eyes.

'Dax?' she said.

He stood to attention and gave her a mock salute. 'Queen Elizabeth Her Royal Highness's Paratroopers.'

'But what about your guitar?' she asked.

'No time. I've got my career to think about now. I'm going to become an officer.'

'Congratulations.'

'Hold your horses. I haven't found out if I've got it yet.' He frowned. 'Do you want to go for a walk or something?'

'OK.' Elizabeth was curious. She remembered his thin shoulder blades. His body would be different now. Without his shaggy dark locks, his cheekbones and jaw were more prominent, and his bare head looked blunt.

They strolled to the park where a couple of months earlier Elizabeth had lain in the grass and talked to Cleo, but instead of climbing the hill, Dax veered off into the wood. Usually there were people walking their dogs there, but today it was empty. Winter was coming, and the trees were dead and brown. On the path under foot there were pale blooms of flattened gum, dropped by generations of schoolgirls. 'So what's it like?' she asked. Dax shrugged.

'It's top secret.' He looked down at her and grinned, as if she were a child begging to try an adult liqueur.

'I bet I could wheedle it out of you.' She had hardly given him a thought for six months, but somehow she was becoming coquettish. 'If I were an enemy spy, I'd seduce your secrets from you, then kill you as you slept.'

'They prepare you for that sort of thing,' said Dax.

'What would you do?'

'This.' He grabbed her arm, and wrenched it behind her back, bending her forward. She dropped the violin.

'You're hurting me!'

'No, I'm not,' he said. He worked her arm up further, so that tears came to her eyes. '*Now* I'm hurting you. I know what you did. I know you fucked some sleazy night-club owner. While we were still going out, technically.'

'I didn't!' she protested, shocked by his injustice. 'I didn't do anything!' To her shame, her tears spilled over, but they seemed to mollify him.

'Say you're sorry.'

'This is ridiculous. Ow! I'm sorry.'

'Say you won't do it again.'

'I won't do it again.'

'OK.' He let her go, and she massaged her arm.

'How did you know?' she said, as he handed her the

violin. She decided not to bother explaining exactly what had happened, since Dax seemed to feel his honour satisfied.

'Your friend Cleo. She phoned the army base and said it was an emergency.' She was the only person Elizabeth had told. But she couldn't imagine why Cleo would have passed the story on to Dax.

'I don't believe you.'

'Then we'll go and ask her.' He hooked his arm through hers and marched her off. The ill-tended garden of Cleo's flat backed on to the wood. Rather than going round to the front door Dax insisted on climbing the fence. Leaving Elizabeth to detach herself from the brambles, Dax tramped up the lawn, and banged on the French windows. No one appeared. He peered inside, and banged some more, but there was no response. As they retreated, Elizabeth looked back and saw Cleo peeping from behind a curtain, her white face expressionless. She did not answer the front door either.

'Well, it was her who told me,' said Dax. 'Soldier's honour.' Elizabeth knew why Cleo had hidden from them, why she had told Dax in the first place. It was because Elizabeth had broken the rules, she had betrayed their monkish ideal. It was a mistake to have told Cleo the story of the Silk Academy. But they had always told each other everything.

Dax took a silver hip flask out of his pocket. 'Prepared at all times,' he said. 'Look at that.' He held the flask out for her to examine. It was old, tarnished silver, engraved with two crossed swords and a motto *Non sine praeda*. 'Family motto,' he said.

'Not without plunder.'

'You always were a brainy girl.' There was a note of irony in his tone. The word *brainy* made her think of a pale, bulbous forehead, of intellect as deformity. She frowned, and he leaned against a wall and took a gulp.

'Help yourself.' She took the flask from him and drank. It was whisky and she coughed.

'Is this really your family motto? I didn't know you had an aristocratic lineage.' Somehow it seemed unlikely. She suspected he had got the flask at some second-hand market. He shrugged.

'Well, it's my motto now.'

Walking home, she weaved slightly, and the violin banged against her legs. Dax put his arm through hers and told her about his training. His platoon was lined up in order of height and divided into pairs. Then each pair had two minutes in the ring. The goal, he said, was to do as much damage to each other as possible. It was to teach the men aggression.

'What if one man killed the other?'

'That wouldn't happen. These men are too evenly matched. But if it was you and me, say.' He looked at her appraisingly. So close to winter, it was already getting dark. 'I could kill you in two minutes.' She looked back at him. She had had sex with him before. She could easily do it again. It even had a certain logic to it, the same logic by which if you drank two inches of whisky you might as well finish off the bottle.

Elizabeth turned her key in the front door as quietly as possible. She needed to sneak Dax up the stairs before Granny had a chance to meet him. Granny had sprained her ankle descending from the coach on a church trip to the seaside, and now she was staying with them while she recuperated. Just as they got to the top of the stairs, her mother called out from her bedroom: 'Is that you, Elizabeth? Will you get me a cup of tea?' They froze, then she shoved Dax into her room, and called out, 'Coming!'

Elizabeth delivered the cup of tea, and went back to her room. But it was empty. She checked thoroughly, thinking he might be hiding, then she went downstairs. She could hear Granny telling one of her stories from nursing school. 'Once, we found three dead mice in the waiting room. We had to take in dinner to the young doctor on duty, and I laid them out on a plate. I got some of the labels we tied on corpses' toes, and I wrote out one for each of them: name, date of birth, and what they died of.' Elizabeth saw Granny lifting a silver cover and the mice with their labels in her careful copperplate: *Squeak, born 12 October 1932, Choked on Large Piece of Cheese*. 'I put a parsley garnish on it,' said Granny, and Elizabeth heard a man's laughter.

'Elizabeth!' Granny cried when she walked in. 'We've been having a lovely chat.' Dax was sitting on the sofa next to Granny, and he appeared to be listening to her intently. But when he looked at Elizabeth, she saw he had a twinkle in his eye.

'Your grandmother was just telling me about her special mixture,' he said.

'It's one part cider vinegar, one part honey and two parts whiskey,' Granny said. 'I took some on the coach trip and everyone was asking me for the recipe. Would you like a little taste?' She took the cup off the top of her plastic thermos flask and began unscrewing the lid.

'I couldn't,' said Dax.

'It perks you up,' said Granny. She poured some out, and thrust it towards him. He put the cup to his mouth and drank with gusto, his stubbled throat moving as he swallowed.

'Delicious,' he said. Granny beamed at him.

'Are you a Catholic?' she breathed.

'Dax, we've got to go and do that *thing*, remember?' said Elizabeth. He had had his little game and she had had enough.

'*Thing*?' repeated Dax.

'Now, now,' said Granny. 'Patience is a virtue, have it if you can. Always in a woman, never in a man.'

But Elizabeth was not patient, back in her bedroom.

'Pretend I'm a spy again,' she said, 'and you've just found out that I've been leaking military secrets. How would you punish me?' When she was a child, she used to fantasise about being a slave girl, sold in a market to a brutal master who made her serve him dinner naked. She thought of that now, and struggled as hard as she could so that Dax would be forced to dig his fingers into her arms, to turn her over on to her front and rest his weight on her wrists. He smelled of sweet aftershave and soap. Turning her head to where his hands gripped her arms, she saw that his nails were neatly trimmed. He paid a new, military attention to his toilet. She began to wriggle again, his erection pressed against her back. She wasn't sure what made her want to goad him. It was the same impulse she got sometimes when making toast. She would become obsessed by the idea of sticking the knife in the toaster, watching everything sizzle and explode.

It was over quickly and Dax immediately fell asleep. He had trained himself to snatch his sleep whenever he could, as would be necessary in war. When Elizabeth woke him up half an hour later, he insisted on leaving out the window. It wasn't necessary, she could have sneaked him downstairs. But he climbed down the trellis instead, to the sound of leaves rustling and branches cracking, then strode off into the winter darkness without looking back.

Her mother had risen from her nap too, and was ironing in the kitchen. Once a week, her mother did what she called 'a Big Shop', and 'a Big Wash'. These activities consumed nearly two days. She sorted the laundry into lights and darks, delicates and woollens, and as she sorted, the laundry seemed to multiply, like loaves and fishes, in a kind of inverse miracle. Then she insisted on ironing every item down to handkerchiefs and underpants. In her twenties she had even ironed her hair. She had wrapped it in a towel, laid it on the board and ironed it until she eliminated every kink. But tonight her hair stuck up in odd places from being in bed all afternoon. She smiled when she saw Elizabeth, and Elizabeth saw that Granny hadn't mentioned meeting Dax.

'Poor old Mum,' said Elizabeth, 'all that ironing to do.' She had realised long ago that it was useless to battle with her mother's moods. If she suggested doing the ironing herself, she would be refused. The only thing she could offer was sympathy. 'Poor old Mum,' she said again. But her mother didn't reply. When Granny was around, her mother retreated deep into herself.

'I'll take those sheets and put them in the linen cupboard,' said Elizabeth. She patted her mother's shoulder, but her mother shrugged, whether to shake off her daughter's hand or whether by coincidence, it wasn't clear. Elizabeth did everything she could to make her mother happy, but she had stopped *liking* her mother, she thought, last Christmas Eve, the night they had fought, and she had slept with Dax. After that, Elizabeth's love had hardened into a cold solicitude. As unfeeling as if she was a spiked wooden roller to massage her mother's feet, or a cluster of cedar balls to pummel the knots in her back. Elizabeth wondered if her mother knew this, and that was why she shrugged.

In the night her mother screamed. A scream of pure terror, she was being beaten, murdered. Elizabeth leaped up, but then she heard her father's voice, shushing her mother. 'A dark figure,' her mother was crying. 'Someone standing by the side of the bed.' Then her father murmuring again. It was only her recurring dream.

On *Strange, But True* Elizabeth had once seen the story of a man who murdered women wearing a suit with nail-studded shoulders. When he was caught, they found a secret room in his house containing an inverted crucifix and a Bible fouled with human excrement. After that, for night after night, Elizabeth had heard his step on the stair. She had discovered an antique letter opener, slender and sharp, in the davenport downstairs, and she kept it in her dressing-gown pocket. For two hours at a time or more, she had kept vigil at the top of the stairs in her pyjamas, guarding the house against the nail-studded man. But that was when she was a child. Her mother had never grown up, Elizabeth thought. And because her fear was so nebulous, there was nothing anyone could do to help her. The house eddied and swirled with fear, filling every room like carbon monoxide.

'What shall we do?' said Dax. It was midnight, and they were sitting at Elizabeth's kitchen table. When the pub had closed, and when they were not in bed, there was nothing to do. She was doing her best, but he was not a skilled conversationalist. Of course, she had never wanted him for his conversation. She needed him because he was stronger than her, simply that. It was because Dax, even if he didn't use it, had the power to break her bones. She never knew what he would do. When she was with him, she was not the one in control.

'Got any scoff?' said Dax. He had a big appetite, due to his ten-mile runs with sixty-pound backpacks, his bouts in the aggression ring. Tonight his face was pale, his eyes a little bloodshot. He had come to see her straight from a sleep-deprivation exercise. Seventy-two hours without sleep, digging ditches. At the end, the men had to polish their buttons before falling into bed, but instead Dax had taken leave and come to see her. He hadn't slept yet. He was testing himself further.

There was roast beef from dinner, rare and bloody. She got him the platter and let him carve off ragged pieces with a knife. He ate them with his fingers. When he had finished, they sat in silence and he played with the knife. It was a good knife, a french Sabatier. There was a set, which her father sharpened every week, drawing each one slowly over the sharpener, with a sound like a sword being unsheathed. It brought the cat running every time, because he associated it with the carving of joints.

Dax put the knife against her arm, then took it away. It had drawn blood.

'Sorry,' he said. 'Didn't realise how sharp it was.'

'It's all right,' she said. 'Didn't hurt.' Dax leaned over her arm and looked at it. Then he touched it again with the point of the knife, and when she didn't move, he dragged it over her skin. The blood ran to meet it. Now there were two lines.

'It's like Etch-a-Sketch,' he said.

'That's enough.' She rubbed her sleeve on her arm, and when she had wiped away the blood, she was disappointed to see how shallow the grazes were. But they stung.

Now when Dax was on leave she began to spend all her time with him. She didn't see Cleo any more. Their friendship had faded away without drama. She presumed that was how Cleo wanted it, because she hadn't answered the door that day, hadn't called since. At school, they were polite and distant. Elizabeth hated their restrained anger, their tepid etiquette. She wanted passion and pain. When Dax cut her, it felt real. Blood was irrefutable. And there was something else about it. It made her feel virtuous, as if the sacrifice she made was a useful one.

Before that, Elizabeth had always been worried. When she wasn't studying or reading or practising her violin, she felt that she should be cooking dinner or vacuuming the house. When she started on one thing, she worried that she should be doing something else. The feeling was all the worse for being vague, and pain cut through it like caffeine through exhaustion.

Dax cut her arms, avoiding parallel lines, because these would look man-made. Instead, he made random scratches, so that afterwards her flesh looked like something vigorously crossed out. It was better than sex. She drank with Dax and sat around in the kitchen late at night and it didn't matter whether she passed her A levels or not. She had got a place at college with no requirements attached. She didn't see why she should strive for awards and teachers' praise when it won her no more approval than Duncan. Besides, Dax didn't like her studying. Once, when she had tried to get up and read one night, he had thrown the book out of the window. She had retrieved it from the flower bed the next morning.

Granny was still staying with them. The doctor had taken the bandage off her ankle, but she insisted it was impossible to walk on it. She pottered about the kitchen and baked sponge cakes that were so dry they crumbled at a touch. Every Sunday Elizabeth's father drove her to church. It was a long drive, because she complained that the church up the road was 'too avant-garde'. Elizabeth's mother said it was because the congregation held hands while they prayed, and at Christmas Mass, everyone hugged their neighbours in the pew.

Elizabeth's mother had become thinner than ever. She made elaborate meals from her French cookbooks that were supposed to replicate simple country fare, but then she did not touch them. She couldn't eat, because Granny's presence put her off her food. As if Granny, in her layers of coats and cardigans, was a kind of resurrected mummy and if you unwrapped her you would find something hideous beneath. But the more time Elizabeth spent with Granny, the harder she found it to believe this. Whatever her faults, Granny wasn't evil.

Elizabeth sat on the sofa and listened to Granny talk. 'It says here that St Anthony is statistically the world's favourite saint,' Granny said. She was looking at the inside cover of *St Anthony the Messenger*. Whom had they asked? Elizabeth thought. She was only half listening, light-headed after too little sleep. Dax had visited the night before, and now she had a row of berry-coloured bruises on her arm, where his fingers had gripped her. She felt like a house after a wild party, wax melted into the carpet, cigarette burns on the furniture.

'One of my friends died just before I strained my ankle,' Granny confided. 'I helped the nun clear out her belongings. Guess what I found in the back of the wardrobe?' Elizabeth roused herself.

'What?'

'Three bottles of whiskey!' Granny sang out. 'The nun took one, and I took one, and we couldn't decide who should have the third, so we raffled it at the church bazaar.' She paused for a moment. 'It's interesting because the lady who died, her *son*, he had a lucky escape. He had a wild youth, then he started a window-cleaning business and reformed. Finally, he converted. And the very next day' – she paused for dramatic impact – 'he fell off a ladder and died. Wasn't that lucky, I always said.' Granny took a religious satisfaction in suffering and death.

When Granny ran out of stories to tell about people she knew, she retold stories from the Bible in the same tone, as if in fact she did know the saints and the apostles, at least distantly. In her house, their portraits far outnumbered those of the family. 'He was beaten with thorns and mocked and spat on,' said Granny emphatically. It was her version of the Stations of the Cross. 'They scourged his bare flesh with a cat o' nine tails.' She was embellishing. 'But he was meek,' she went on. 'He was meek and mild. He suffered for the world.' Elizabeth saw the Jesus who hung in Granny's hall, by the front door. He was thin and pale, and the sheet he was wearing had slipped down, exposing his hairless chest. He didn't look thirty, he looked like a foolish young addict, relishing his own destruction.

Late at night stones rattled against her window. Dax was

hauling himself up the trellis, and she let him in. He thrust a letter into her hand. It was a rejection from officer training school. They said it was because his academic qualifications were not 'up to par'. 'What the fuck does that mean?' Dax said, flicking at the paper with his fingers. He smelled of whisky. He was wearing a sleeveless khaki jacket with pockets. It looked as if it had been worn to conquer natives in the days of the Empire. These days he liked to dress like a lion–hunting aristocrat.

'What does it mean?' he repeated.

'You did leave school at sixteen,' she said.

'You think you're so fucking clever, don't you?' She was shocked. She was cleverer and more well read than Dax, but she'd always thought that she concealed that knowledge rather well, avoiding obscure words, not mentioning Oxford. Anyway, her intelligence was not something she valued or wanted. It had become a duty, the tedious route to approval.

'I hate being clever,' she said.

'You're a liar.' He gestured at the shelves where her books were. There were so many of them that she had had to stack them horizontally. For a moment she saw them the way he did, mysterious ziggurats. Then she said, 'You're drunk.' At that he lunged towards her books as it to topple them, and she grabbed hold of his jacket, tearing one of the pockets. He gave her face a hard slap, then another, so that she staggered. She put her arms up to protect her head, and he paused, then punched her in the stomach. It knocked the breath out of her, doubled her up to cradle the pain. Somehow, she had never believed that Dax had the courage to really hurt her. Then he left.

When she went downstairs to bolt the door after Dax, she heard the sound of the television. Duncan was in the sitting room, watching a late film. She sat down, trembling and wanting company. Her stomach hurt. Duncan didn't say anything. Then he turned and looked at her. Her eyes were full of tears, her arms were torn where she had been peeling the scabs. They came off in little strips.

'You all right?' he asked.

'Yeah.' She fixed her eyes on the TV. It was *L'Ami de Mon Amie*. She was surprised to see Duncan watching it. It concerned a love triangle but somehow, in their French way, the characters seemed nonchalant about their tangled affections.

Dax had always cut her flesh with ceremony, and she had offered it up, an Aztec maiden baring her breast. But there was nothing of the erotic ritual about a punch. Or maybe the problem was that he had simply gone too far. The knife had hurt, but not that much. It was just enough to wake her up and set her adrenalin flowing, but deep down, she knew it was all theatre. With the knife, she could say stop. Not with this.

'We had a bit of a chat on his way out,' said Duncan. 'I thought it was best.'

'What do you mean?' Elizabeth asked. Duncan smiled to himself.

'I told him the situation.'

'What situation?'

'I said you were going to break up with him when you went to Oxford.' He said it in a patient voice.

'What?'

'Well, you are, aren't you.' It wasn't a question. 'Come on, Elizabeth. I was trying to do you a favour.' It was true, she supposed. Although she had given up Cleo's dream of meeting the One, she intended to do better than Dax. Besides, her mother hated him. She called him Elizabeth's 'bit of rough', which made Elizabeth think of a cat scratching itself against a fence post, inflamed with shameful desire.

'What did he say when you told him?' she asked. Duncan paused, looked at the TV screen.

'He said he was going to kill you.' A thrill of fear went

through her, and she tried to concentrate on the lovers in Paris.

But Duncan couldn't seem to settle down. He wriggled about on the sofa trying to get comfortable. 'This is boring,' he said. When she didn't respond, he began to croon in a high falsetto.

'Shut up,' she said.

'What?' He pretended outrage. 'I'm doing my voice exercises.' He sang, and she stared straight ahead. If she ignored him, he would stop. His voice swam among the high notes. He didn't care what sound he made. He did whatever he liked when he was with her.

When he paused for a moment, she heard her mother scream, very faint and thin. It was the scream Elizabeth had heard over and over. She gave a start, but Duncan didn't seem to hear it. Why was she the only one who did? As if the scream was a whistle too high for human ears, and she was a dog who came running at its sound. The scream stopped. Elizabeth told herself to relax. She would stay where she was. There was nothing she could do for her mother.

Duncan had begun singing again. But somehow the sound soothed her. The underwater song of a dolphin. She fell asleep to his lullaby.

'Shish or doner?' Dax put his arm through hers and started walking. Elizabeth tried to pull away, wishing she had noticed him in time to slip down a side street. She had stayed late at the library revising for her final exams, in a halfhearted attempt to make up for the time lost with Dax. 'Keep walking,' he said. 'Smile.' He had abandoned the khaki waistcoat. Instead, he had on his battered leather jacket. His scalp was covered with a mole's fuzz. He was letting it grow back. She decided not to struggle. They were only going to the kebab shop.

Kebab Delite had a floor with speckled plastic tiles, and

a counter on one side set with salt and pepper shakers and squeeze bottles of Heinz ketchup and HP sauce. Someone had carefully trained plastic vines along the counter, and there was a sign on the wall reading *Approved by the British Heart Association*, with a large red heart underneath. She thought this was unlikely. Behind the counter, a man in a white apron and stained T-shirt was chipping the scabby burned bits off a griddle. He had a melancholy look on his face.

'I don't want anything,' said Elizabeth.

'Come on,' Dax urged her. 'My treat.' She shook her head.

'Suit yourself.' He bought a lamb kebab and told the man to keep the change. The man smiled for a moment, then went back to scraping at the griddle. The place wasn't busy yet because it was early and the pubs were still open.

'Try a bit,' said Dax.

'I told you, I'm not hungry.' They were in the street, and she tried to squirm away from him. People walked by them without looking at her.

'Not good enough for you, is it?' She clamped her lips shut, but he held her nose until she opened her mouth, then he tried to force in a lump of meat. 'You don't understand,' he said. 'I insist.' She felt something boiling up in her. Then she bit his hand as hard as she could. Dax threw her off.

'Fucking wild animal,' he exclaimed, examining his hand. She had tasted the minerals in his blood. When she turned round, there were four youths behind her. One of them was her brother. He stepped forward. He was holding a kebab, but he threw it to one side.

'What are you doing with my little sister?' he said. The others stood behind him silently. She had seen them before, in the pub with Duncan. They sat together and drank beer and didn't say anything. Or they played darts.

Then they went to Kebab Delite.

'Nothing,' said Dax.

'Yeah, well,' said Duncan. He looked at his mates, then back at Dax. 'Fuck off out of here.' Dax regarded them appraisingly. He was taller than any of them and he was taut, muscular. He was trained, Elizabeth suddenly remembered, to be aggressive, to attack without hesitation, to kill a comrade if necessary. He stepped forward. Then there was the rasp of a blade. Duncan had his flick knife open.

Dax turned around and began to walk, moving faster as he got further away. He turned the first corner, and was gone. 'Thanks,' Elizabeth said.

'Get in the car,' said Duncan. They got in and he sat there for a moment. 'Lost my fucking kebab.' He got out and retrieved it from the pavement where it had fallen. Then he turned on his music and started the car. He drove with one hand and ate his kebab with the other. Sometimes it was too messy to eat with just one hand, and then he drove without any hands.

'I can't finish it,' he said after a while. 'Want a bit?' Elizabeth hesitated.

'OK.' She took the bag and reached in, touching the lukewarm meat. She put it in her mouth and chewed. It wasn't that bad. Duncan stopped the car outside their house.

'Go on then. Haven't got all night.'

'Aren't you coming in?'

'Going to pick up Jasmine.'

'Oh.' Elizabeth got out and watched him drive away. She thought she could still taste blood through the pungent spices of the kebab. Dax had flapped his hand as if trying to shake away the pain. She must have really hurt him, she reflected with satisfaction. She was surprised by what she had done, but by now, she thought, she ought not to be. This was how she was. She swung between Day

127

and Night, between work and violence, between duty and embarrassment. Black, white, black, white.

Elizabeth went inside. She would take a bath, she decided, to calm down. She lay in the cooling water for a long time. When she heard Jasmine and Duncan creep past the bathroom door, she didn't want them to know she was still awake, or to suspect that she had waited up for them. She held her body still in its glass coffin.

9

Nude

JASPER USED TO HOLD himself as stiffly as a toy soldier. But he has relaxed since he fell in love. He greets Elizabeth with a wine glass in one hand. Her best friend from college, he has always been untidy. His shirt is only half tucked in to his grubby jeans, and he is barefoot, his dark hair rumpled. He kisses her on both cheeks then disappears back to the kitchen. He has promised to cook a special dinner to congratulate her on her engagement. The scent of rosemary and garlic fills the little flat.

Elizabeth wanders around, picking things up and putting them down again. The two rooms have high ceilings, but the walls are a clear red, and the place feels warm. There is a black marble fireplace, and set in the grate, pressed tight together, there are pots containing monkey orchids and wilting tulips. A strange white object on top of a bookshelf catches her attention. It is smooth on one side, nubbled on the other. 'What on earth is this?' she asks, as Jasper emerges with a saucer of olives.

'Actually it's a piece of bread. I forgot about it, and it got really hard.' She looks closer. It is white, with grainy flecks. It seems half quartz, half marble. 'Isn't it beautiful?' he asks her. She thinks of her ex-boyfriend Quentin, always so obsessed with beauty, only able to see it in silent galleries and chilly museums. As if his thoughts have followed the same course, Jasper says, 'Have you spoken to Quentin since you've been back?' She shakes her head. She has not told Jasper what she did to Quentin. She and Quentin will never speak again.

'Well, did you break his jar in the end?' he asks. When he read *The Rape of the Lock* at college, Jasper insisted that the breaking of the 'frail china jar' was a symbolic allusion to the loss of virginity.

'I'm not telling you,' she says, smiling mysteriously.

*

Dax had been a mistake, and after she broke up with him, she decided to seek his opposite. She explained it to herself with crude philosophy: if Dax had been Body, now she must seek Mind. She would dedicate herself to the intellectual life again, and to a man who could inhabit it with her. When she went to Oxford, she studied determinedly in her overheated room, with its fuggy gas heater, its bed and desk and single threadbare armchair. But it was hard to concentrate. The building she lived in was just by the bell tower, and when she opened her windows to let in the cold air, she heard the bells chiming four times every hour, always a few minutes late. And Jasper was always clattering up the stairs and knocking on her door, giving her the latest gossip, inviting her to the pub, to a party. To get away from her room and her books, she ran, down the muddy paths by the river, through the sodden woods.

He was sitting on a rock across the water and masturbating. It was a minute before Elizabeth realised what she was seeing. He was fat, his naked body a puffy white toadstool in the lush grass. His eyes met hers and he smiled.

She had been running along the path circling the college deer park, over the bright red leaves. A tributary of the river surrounded the park, and he was sitting on the opposite bank. Elizabeth faltered for a few steps, then continued, picking up speed. She was already halfway around, so it was just as quick to go on as to go back. She liked to finish things she had started, and besides, she had seen naked men outdoors before. At school they had sometimes emerged from the undergrowth by the tennis courts. Elizabeth and her friends had stopped practising their serves, and while one girl slipped back to school to alert a teacher, the others had shouted, waved their racquets round their heads, and charged for the man en masse.

She ran through the rococo wrought-iron gates, into the cloisters, and straight into another student. He was tall, with red hair and a long face. 'Whoops,' he said. 'Completely my fault. I'm so sorry. I was deep in thought.' Then he looked more closely at her. 'Are you all right?' he said. When she told him, he began apologising. 'I'm so sorry. How awful for you!'

'It's not your fault,' she said. It had not occurred to her until now that it was awful. But the young man said she must report the crime immediately. He ushered her towards the porter's lodge at the main college entrance, his hand discreetly supporting her elbow.

'He was naked and masturbating,' Elizabeth told the porter. To her surprise, she stumbled over the word. Masturbating. It stuck to her tongue like a hair. The young man, who had introduced himself as Quentin, was politely pretending not to listen. The porter perked up. He got a notebook from under his desk, and clicked his ballpoint out.

'And did he have any distinguishing features?'

At school the young policewoman who had warned them about flashers had said, 'Always take a good look.' After the laughter subsided, she had mumbled, pink-cheeked, 'At his *face*.' Elizabeth could not remember this man's face, only his body. She shook her head. 'Masturbating,' the porter wrote, slowly. 'No other special features.' He clicked his pen shut and put it back in his pocket. 'He'll be long gone by now,' he said briskly.

She would recognise the man's voluptuous rolls of flesh if she saw them again, but bodies in Oxford were so thoroughly concealed. The university officials paraded in their ermine-trimmed robes and students went to dinner in flapping academic gowns.

'You need to sit down and have a cup of tea,' Quentin told her. 'You've had a nasty shock to your nerves.' Quentin's room was in the old part of the college, up a spiral staircase. Three arched slits faced out on to a stone quadrangle. There were pencil sketches of nudes tacked to the walls. The bed was perfectly made, the sheets pulled taut, the college-issue grey woollen blanket tucked in under the mattress. There was a bowl of shrivelled oranges on the mantelpiece and a saxophone lying in pieces on the desk. Next to the saxophone stood an artist's figure, the kind with jointed wooden limbs and a blank oval for a head.

'I seem to have lured you up here on false pretences,' said Quentin, after rummaging in a cupboard. 'I don't have any tea. Is coffee all right?' He made her instant, with dried milk, and Elizabeth perched on the edge of the bed. She was enjoying being looked after, and she concentrated on trying to look wan. Quentin sat in the only chair, his long graceful legs crossed. 'At least he didn't attack you,' he said. He leaned forward and gave her knee a little pat. Then he seemed embarrassed. His spoon clattered in the cup while he stirred his coffee. The dried milk took a long time to dissolve. He smiled. 'Although, according to quantum universe theory, he *did* attack you. The theory is probably all hogwash, but it's hard to stop thinking about. The idea is that a new quantum universe buds out for every possible event. Our lives are played out in an infinite number of universes, some of which are almost the same as this one. But then there are some that are radically different. I've sometimes wondered,' he said, looking shyly into his mug, 'whether the universes are all equal. Maybe there's the Proper Quantum Universe, and there are all the other ones, all Improper, to varying degrees. Like a river, and all the other ones are merely streams leading off. And if you're being rushed along in the great roaring river of the Proper Quantum Universe, you know it. Do you ever get that feeling?' He looked at Elizabeth and turned a delicate pink, like the inside of a shell.

'Flame-Brain saved you from the flasher!' Jasper burst out laughing. 'I bet you're the first girl who's ever been inside his room. He's meant to be a genius. He'll probably end up as the youngest ever physics professor at Oxford.'

'He thinks he might want to be an artist or have his own jazz quartet,' she protested. 'Anyway, why do you call him that behind his back? What do you call *me* behind my back?'

'I talk about everyone. I've got a healthy interest in human nature. There's nothing wrong with that.' He was sitting cross-legged on his bed, and he leaned towards his tiny window and blew cigarette smoke outside with a dismissive air. Elizabeth was sitting on the chair, her feet in a pile of washing, which she had swept from the chair in order to sit in it. She would have preferred not to have her feet in Jasper's dirty clothes, but there was no other space for them on the floor. Every inch was covered with a litter of papers, books, magazines. On the mantelpiece, there was a jar of preserved baby peaches in brandy, which he was waiting for a special occasion to open. Postcards jostled with half-empty wine bottles and tubes of hair gel. There was a jar of mayonnaise too. 'That should be refrigerated,' she pointed out. Jasper snorted. He was eating a mango when she came in, and now he offered her the last piece. She shook her head. She had noticed what looked like a crust lying among the clothes at her feet. Jasper looked at her with bright squirrel's eyes.

'Maybe you should take him on as a project,' he mused. 'Strip him of his innocence.' He stubbed his cigarette out in the mango peelings, emphatically. A vision flashed before her: Quentin naked, a thin white candle, his red hair a dying flame.

Jasper liked to befriend those who sat in the dining hall alone, nervously mashing their steamed pudding into their custard. Girls in long skirts with their hair hanging over their faces, boys with pitted skin who walked hunched forward like question marks. Jasper referred to them as his 'projects'. By patient coaching, he hoped to transform them into paragons of beauty and wit. Elizabeth had been helping him. So far, they had not had much success. But Jasper said their present project had a lot of potential. Patrick was a surly youth studying engineering. He had a handsome Roman profile and thick dark hair, but his hair was slicked back with too much grease, and he became belligerent when drunk. He caught people's eyes and said, 'Yeah? Yeah? Yeah? What's your problem?' His hand had to be stitched up in several places when he had punched through a window. Another time, he forced Elizabeth into a drinking competition, kissed her in the college garden, then threw up on the lawn and went to his room to watch the football.

'I think Quentin's sweet,' she said.

'The insistent verticals are amazing, aren't they?' Quentin murmured over her shoulder. Elizabeth was standing in front of *The Holy Family on the Steps*. All three had the round rosy cheeks of choirboys. The family posed on a flight of steps, with large, waxen apples and pears lying at their feet. At the top there was a narrow view of the sky. The picture had no effect on her. It just looked very clean, with the scrubbed cheeks and artificial fruit, the spotless white marble. 'Yet you can see how there's an asymmetry in the picture,' Quentin went on. 'For Poussin, no matter how beautiful the earthly world is, it's always imperfect.' She turned round to look at him. He was wearing a silk shirt halfway between purple and blue, like the plumage on some rare bird. His eyes were fixed raptly on the Holy Family. He had invited her to see this exhibition at the Royal Academy because Poussin was his favourite painter. As they walked on through the airy rooms with their polished floors, he wondered whether beauty was universal. 'If you took a pygmy out of the rain forest and showed him a Poussin, would he recognise its beauty?' he said. Elizabeth's feet were aching, but she didn't care. The desire for self-improvement flooded through her, like detergent thrown over a dirty floor. She wanted not only to understand the paintings but to be moved by them. She wanted to see what Quentin saw.

They had lunch in the gallery café. It was in a conservatory and on every table a vase held a single lily. 'The ancients altered the human form to get rid of its flaws,' Quentin told her. 'They elongated the body. And they'd take one woman's nose, another's eyes, and so on, until they had an ideal woman.'

Elizabeth thought of the stubble in her armpits, the yellow undersides of her feet. She felt herself growing into a hairy pygmy, unable to understand Ideal Beauty. Quentin made it seem a delicacy that could only be appreciated by civilised adults, like caviar. Elizabeth gazed at him intently as he talked, taking little sips from her glass of white wine. While she and Jasper had been wasting their time at parties, Quentin had been roaming through museums and hushed galleries. So far nothing he had said had struck her as brilliant, exactly, but she had the impression of great reserves of knowledge, and more, a hunger for beauty and truth. She wanted to learn from him, or at least to share his passion. The only thing she could give him in return was her body.

'Don't you think that physical perfection can be in the eye of the beholder?' she asked him. 'If you love someone, it doesn't matter if she's asymmetrical.'

'Of course,' said Quentin. 'Of course when you love someone they seem beautiful. If we couldn't appreciate the human form as it is, we'd never procreate.'

Quentin had nearly finished his lunch, wielding his knife and fork neatly with his long musician's fingers. Elizabeth had time only to take a few mouthfuls of her salad before he was finished. His meal was accompanied by a little glass dish of gherkins, and he speared them one by one, then drank the liquid remaining, delicately as if it had been a cup of China tea.

Elizabeth assumed that once she made her interest obvious, things would proceed swiftly. But for a couple of weeks, she and Quentin continued their chaste visits to cafés and exhibitions, and she wasn't sure whether he really wanted her. In the end it was she who kissed him, standing on tiptoe to reach his face when he stopped outside her college gate to say goodbye one evening. When she opened her eyes, she could see his white lashes fluttering. His hands had stayed by his sides for a moment, then they settled on her waist, as if they were about to waltz. Afterwards, she walked not up the stone staircase to her room but across the quad towards the bar.

'Where are you going?' Quentin called.

'Just for a quick drink,' she called back, startled that he had not left.

'I'll take you,' he said, loping across the quad to join her. He was too polite to let her go alone.

The bar was in a vault with a pillared ceiling and a bare stone floor. On weeknights at this hour it usually contained only a handful of long-haired engineering students, playing disconsolate games of darts. But for some reason, tonight it was packed. Elizabeth elbowed her way through the crowd with Quentin following, then caught sight of Jasper and Patrick, and stopped. Patrick had somehow taped his chest together so that he had a cleavage. He was almost bursting out of a floor-length red evening gown that Elizabeth thought she recognised from the window of Cinderella's, a ball-dress rental shop. Jasper was wearing a sequinned white gown and a large number of silver bangles. He was slim-hipped, and fitted into his dress rather well, unlike Patrick. 'Patrick,' said Elizabeth. 'How you've blossomed!' Patrick lowered his blue eyelids and pouted his ruby lips.

'It's a cross-dressing party,' he explained.

'You look like a pair of ladies of the night,' said Quentin.

'That's exactly what we thought,' said Jasper in delight. He warmed to Quentin, taking his remark for a compliment. 'Can I get you two a beer?'

'Nothing for me,' said Quentin. He paused, as if considering something, then said: 'It's interesting, the question of pairs. If two things are identical, then are they perhaps only one thing? If I put two identical eggs on the table, same colour, size and shape, then are they really two separate eggs? Maybe there's only one egg on the table.' Patrick raised his eyebrows.

'Does it matter?' There was a long pause, during which Patrick fixed his gaze on Quentin. Even with the lipstick, Patrick had Heathcliff's dark stare. Quentin cracked.

'My mouth's dry,' he said, edging away. 'I need a glass of water.'

When he was gone, Patrick said, 'I know Jasper suggested him as a project, but he didn't mean you to take him so seriously.'

'He told you about our projects?' she said, looking at

Jasper in disbelief. *Patrick* was a project. Quentin was working his way back through the crowd, politely tapping on every shoulder and saying, 'Excuse me please, excuse me please.'

'Being with him must be like one everlasting tutorial,' hissed Patrick. Elizabeth ducked through the crowd to meet Quentin.

'Take me outside. I need to get some air,' she said. As they left, she slipped her arm tightly round his waist.

Quentin's bed was a narrow cot that sagged in the middle, and she couldn't quite get comfortable. She settled for lying on her back, arms crossed over her breasts. Jasper said college beds were purposely narrow so two people could not fit into them. He also said that in the morning the cleaners barged in without knocking on purpose, in order to surprise any overnight guests. Quentin was sitting in the chair. He was stripping away the pith from an orange. He looked down at the plate, concentrating on getting every bit of pith off, though the fading afternoon light was making it difficult to see. 'You didn't enjoy it, did you?' he asked.

'I did,' she protested. 'It's just that it was so fast. Maybe I'd like it better slow.'

He was trying to teach her to appreciate jazz. She closed her eyes, listened to a piece, then described her reaction. 'Jittery,' she said. 'Nervous. Like a moth.' Quentin sighed.

'Maybe it sounds completely different to you,' he said. 'How do we know that an orange tastes the same to you as it does to me?' He had taken to asking her these questions, then pausing and staring at her expectantly. 'What is the difference between a mouse and a picture of a mouse?'

Jasper fished out the last baby peach and dropped it into his mouth. His room was messier than ever. There was a saucer of assorted vitamin pills on the floor, a candle stuck in a wine bottle, a cigarette butt stubbed out in a bottle cap. Elizabeth didn't see much of him any more. He spent all his time with Patrick, drinking in the bar and playing fierce games of table football. She used to have breakfast and dinner with him in the college dining hall every day, but now he went with Patrick to have breakfast in the buttery of another college. And in the evening he and Patrick bought sausages and pheasant and different kinds of olives from the Covered Market and made their own meals in the tiny student kitchen at the foot of Jasper's staircase. Elizabeth spent most of her time with Quentin now.

'Here's a paradox for you,' said Jasper. 'You've seen a flasher naked, but not Quentin, and Quentin has seen a model naked, but not you.' She had tried. She had swept the books from his desk, seated herself, and pulled Quentin towards her, wrapping her legs around him, licking his cold ears. His pointed face and small prim mouth made her think of one of the stone saints in the cloisters.

She was not attracted to Quentin. She worshipped his mind, or at least, she wanted to. What she felt for him was a jealousy so pure it almost felt like love. But she had no desire for his body, white as a root. He had told her about an experiment in which a psychologist uncorked a bottle and said to a group of subjects, 'Raise your hands when you can smell the lovely smell coming from this bottle.' One by one, hands went up. But the bottle was empty. So you could convince yourself you felt something when you didn't, and how could you question the validity of the feeling, if, finally, you really felt it? She would make herself desire Quentin by sheer force of will.

The winter air was cold, and Quentin offered her his camel coat, which was the colour of English mustard. He held the coat up so that she could slip her arms into it. He treated her so gently, as if she were a porcelain shepherdess. Resolutely, Elizabeth turned to kiss him, but he took a step back. 'I think we should take it slowly,' he said.

'We *are*,' she protested. Then Quentin told her how his parents, who met at Oxford, advanced gradually, stage by stage. He got out his wallet and showed her a picture of them: their three-quarter profiles gazed into the distance, black-and-white and melancholy. She saw his parents taking autumn walks along the river, then toasting crumpets before the fire. His father sat in a leather armchair, with Quentin's mother at his feet. And then his father kissed her on the forehead and walked her home.

'The ultimate act was more beautiful because they waited,' said Quentin. She shrank. She'd thought she was the one holding back. Now she imagined herself through Quentin's eyes, and saw herself slobbering over him, a pig rooting for truffles.

The following afternoon, she was in the porter's lodge checking her pigeonhole for letters, when she heard a gruff raised voice. 'We've had incidents reported, you know,' the porter said. There was an urgent, murmured reply. 'Well, put yourself in my position,' the porter answered. 'How do I know that's true? I'm answerable for the safety of these young ladies and gentlemen.' When she stepped outside the mailroom, her father was there. He was wearing his old beige raincoat, and the belt was dangling from one loop only, as if someone had seized him by it. His trousers, as always, were slightly too short, and between cuff and shoe, his socks bloomed brightly. He waggled one ankle at her.

'Look, Elizabeth,' he said. 'Thought they'd be a splash of colour in my office.'

'This is my father,' she said.

'Are you sure?' asked the porter. 'I found him loitering in the gardens.'

'I was not loitering!' exclaimed her father. 'I was taking a stroll while waiting for my daughter to get back.' He turned to Elizabeth. He looked tired, old, the first grey in his hair. 'I knocked on your door but you weren't there.'

'You were in the undergrowth,' said the porter.

'I was admiring your flower bed,' her father replied grumpily.

'Anyway,' said Elizabeth. 'This man is not a flasher. Mystery solved.' She patted her father's sleeve. 'Come up to my room, and I'll make you a cup of tea.'

'I'll have to ask you to sign the visitors' book first,' said the porter, interposing himself between them.

'Oh, I'm just going to pop in and out,' said her father. 'I'm on my way back home from a business trip.' The porter gave her father a dark look.

'I need your name, sir,' he retorted. 'If there's a fire and you're burned beyond recognition, you'll have to be identified.' Her father gave a sigh, then signed the heavy book with a dramatic flourish, taking up several lines. As they started up the stone stairs, the porter shouted after them: 'You'll thank me for this when they start bringing out all the charred bodies!'

Her father flopped down in her shabby green armchair, and she plugged her electric kettle in. 'He thought I was a pervert,' he said. 'But I was just admiring his oriental hellebores. They're very difficult to grow, you know.' Elizabeth leaned past him to retrieve her milk, which was keeping cold on the window sill. The trouble was, in his flasher's raincoat and clown's socks, her father did have a vaguely suspicious air. He had simply managed to be in the wrong place at the wrong time. Elizabeth wished she had something more to offer him. She thought of YumYums, the sugary doughnuts he liked that came in a plastic package from the supermarket.

But when he had his mug of tea, he seemed to cheer up a bit. 'At least this will make a good anecdote,' he said.

'You can never have too many anecdotes. They are plums in the stodgy pudding of history. With enough anecdotes, you know you will never be lacking for dinner invitations.

'Anyway,' he went on, 'how are things? Everything trundling along nicely?' She considered telling him about Quentin, but thought better of it. She never told her parents about her boyfriends and she felt an ignoble twinge of embarrassment when she thought about introducing them to Quentin. An awkward intellectual in his father's old sports jacket. There were even leather patches on the elbows. It was obvious Quentin would never keep her out too late or offer her heroin or impregnate her. Maybe that was why she didn't want to introduce him.

'Same as always,' she answered. 'How are you, Dad?' she said. 'How was your business trip?'

'Oh, not bad as these things go,' he said. He stopped for a minute, as if waiting for something, then he pulled his handkerchief from his pocket and clapped it to his nose. 'Do you mind if I lie down for a minute?' he said. He laid his length on her bed and looked up at the ceiling. 'Bloody hell,' he said. He was prone to nosebleeds. Her mother said that was the trouble with having such a distinguished nose. Elizabeth felt worried about him. He seemed always on the verge of catastrophe, like a clown.

The second time she saw the man, a few days after her father's visit, he was standing up. He was further down the river than he had been last time, and he was masturbating again. More vigorously. 'Get yer tits out!' he yelled as she ran past. She had thought of him as harmless. Now she raced on as fast as she could, and she felt him coming after her. The two of them rushed round the circular path, about to converge any minute, like two hands on a clock. But when she got to the gate, there was no one behind her. She ran through the cloisters, up the stone staircase, straight into Quentin's room. Quentin was sitting at his desk cleaning his saxophone with what looked like a miniature feather duster. When he saw her, his face filled with concern and he got up and enfolded her in his long sinewy arms.

'He was masturbating again,' she said.

'Try to forget about it,' said Quentin.

'He had his clothes on this time, but he was masturbating. Hard.'

'It's better not to dwell on all the gory details. Just accept it and forget about it. Men have dark urges, women don't. That's all there is to it.' She drew back and stared up at him.

'Quentin, does that mean you have secret desires you don't tell me about?'

He cleared his throat.

'Not me personally. I'm just making a general point. Men have different needs from women, needs women just can't understand.'

Elizabeth imagined what it would be like to marry Quentin and grow old with him, in a house crammed with objets d'art and gold-framed paintings. She knew she wouldn't. Maybe that was part of his attraction: loveless scientific detachment, the possibility of a hypothesis proven or disproved, but not of pity or pain. And then she thought of the flasher again, shouting, 'Get yer tits out!' and saw herself tearing off her T-shirt and bra and plunging through the ice-cold water towards him.

10

The Whore of Babylon

'YOU NEVER TOLD ME how you met Spencer,' says Jasper.
The two of them are meeting for tea in the Empire Tea
Rooms, a place that she and Cleo used to like. Patrick was
going to come, but he had to stay late at work. He is an
assistant to an interior decorator, who lets him take home
wilting flowers and spare swathes of expensive silks to
decorate the flat he shares with Jasper.

The Empire Tea Rooms are not as grand as they sound.
A single room up a creaking staircase and cramped above
a hat shop. Shelves containing old boarding-school stories,
a record player playing waltzes from the twenties, and blue
mugs full of daffodils. The proprietor brews the tea and
butters the scones in a tiny kitchen in one corner of the
room. Elizabeth and Cleo had spent a lot of time at the
Empire because it was cheap, and private, and the
proprietor did not mind how long they stayed.

'I'm afraid it makes a very brief anecdote,' Elizabeth
begins. Then another couple enters and she stops.

They seat themselves opposite Elizabeth and Jasper
without looking at them. A red-headed girl and a tall man.
They make a fuss about having their table wiped, then
when they sit down the man orders Queen Mother Cake,
which is the proprietor's speciality, and the girl orders a pot

of tea. Elizabeth shrinks into her seat. It is Cleo and Quentin. She didn't even know they knew each other.

'Go and say hello,' says Jasper.

'No.'

'What? Go on. I want to find out what they're doing now. I'm curious.' He gets up and says in a tone both ironic and genial, 'Quentin! My dear old fellow!' She has no choice but to follow.

Quentin is better dressed than she has ever seen him. He used to wear his father's hand-me-downs, tweed jackets, shirts whose collars were slightly too pointy. Now he is in a suit, the jacket slung over the back of his chair. He has filled out too, and it suits him.

'What an unexpected pleasure!' says Quentin, getting up to peck Elizabeth on the cheek. He seems to have forgotten about their final meeting, but she knows he hasn't. It is simply that ignoring it is the gracious thing to do, as if it were light drizzle at a picnic.

'Elizabeth,' says Cleo. 'You don't mind if I don't get up.' Cleo has gained weight and her hair is shorter. She is wearing a polka-dotted navy dress and earrings that look as if they should belong to a much older woman, crimson onyxes rimmed with gold. They look like tiny shields. There is a large diamond engagement ring on her finger.

Quentin, Elizabeth suddenly notices, has diamonds sparkling in his cuffs too. And Cleo looks right for him, like a banker's wife.

'Lovely to see you, Cleo,' says Elizabeth.

'She's Claire now,' says Quentin.

'When did you change your name?' Elizabeth asks with a pang. Cleo always hated Claire, she said it was too ordinary. Cleo shrugs.

'This,' says Quentin proudly, 'is the most intelligent woman I've ever met.'

'Where did you two meet?' asks Elizabeth.

'At a reading party, at the college chalet.' Quentin looks

at Cleo and pats her hand. Cleo looks back at him and her green eyes light up like splashed beach glass.

But except when she looks at him, she has shaken off her beauty. She reaches out and twiddles Quentin's sparkling cufflink, a gesture that is partly nervous, partly proprietary. Will she and Quentin live in a house like the one he grew up in, expensive and safe? Maybe that was all Cleo really wanted, thinks Elizabeth, a man's protection. Cleo will become like Quentin's mother, gardening and going to the opera and reading in her spare time, a dilettante housewife.

'Elizabeth is getting married too,' says Jasper. 'To an American.'

'Oh. How did you two meet?' Quentin is expansive. His salary has given him a new air of authority.

'There's not much to tell really,' says Elizabeth.

★

There was a pubic hair stuck to the side of the tub, like a lavish signature. Elizabeth removed it and rinsed the tub out carefully. She had been taking a lot of baths recently. Feet were clattering up and down the stairs, and she heard the thump of fists on people's doors. There was always a party going on somewhere. In the morning when she walked through the college garden on the way to break-fast, empty bottles strewed the dew-wet grass. But these days, she did not have the energy for parties and late nights. She had put herself on a diet. She would never attain Ideal Beauty, but it might help, she thought, if she was thinner. For lunch and dinner, she had Slim-a-Soups, little sachets of powder. When you added water, bits bobbed up that were supposed to be vegetables.

Elizabeth lay back in the bath and admired her new, flatter body. The two bathrooms at the foot of her staircase shared a window because they were originally one. A wall

146

divided the room in two, but could not go all the way across because the window had a deep embrasure. There was a gap there. Through the gap, she could hear a lot of vigorous splashing in the tub next door. Then a voice began a scale.

'Doh, ray, me, fah—' There was a pause and he cleared his throat. 'You don't mind if I sing?'

'Not at all.'

She thought it must be one of the choral scholars. He would choose an ancient hymn, or perhaps a snatch of opera.

> *All my exes live in Texas,*
> *And Texas is a place I'd dearly love to be.*
> *But all my exes live in Texas,*
> *And that's why I hang my hat in Tennessee.*

Elizabeth smiled. Despite the plaintive lyrics, the voice was cheerful.

'You've got a very powerful voice,' she said.

There was a splash and the song suddenly got louder. It quavered for a moment. Now it was coming from above and behind her and his face must be at the gap by the window, the gap that was just large enough for a determined person to see through. He must be standing on the ledge of his bath, his feet braced next to the taps. She remained absolutely still, her whole body warmed by his gaze. The voice flooded forth.

Elizabeth checked her door was locked, dropped her towel, and lay down on her bed. She tensed herself in readiness. It was as if she was being squeezed tighter and tighter, all her molecules pressing closer together. Quentin had told her about dead stars, stars that absorbed light instead of giving it out. They sucked energy into themselves to hold their molecules together. She felt like this now, every muscle clenched. The blood pounded in her ears when she came.

Quentin's parents lived in a large, white Georgian town house. A heavy black door with a fanlight opened on to a cool, tiled hall. 'Tintin, is that you?' called a voice.

'Mummy!' cried Quentin. A woman came out of a door at the back of the hall. Elizabeth had imagined her to be elegant and slender, in a pastel two-piece suit with a string of pearls, but she was not. She was wearing muddy wellington boots and moss green cord trousers. She smothered Quentin in her embrace.

'I've been working in the garden,' she said. 'That's why I'm a bit of a mess. But let's have a look at you.' Elizabeth was wearing a red wool dress. Now she realised that she should have worn something less smart. 'Aren't you cold in that low-cut thing?'

'I'm fine, thank you very much,' said Elizabeth politely.

'Nonsense, nonsense,' his mother replied. 'I can dig something out for you to fling over the top.' She rummaged among a rack of coats further down the hall and found a brown cardigan. Elizabeth draped it gingerly over her shoulders. It smelled of earth. 'Why don't you go and wait for us in the sitting room, Elizabeth? Quentin can help me bring in the tea things.' Elizabeth began to open the first hall door, but Quentin darted in front of her.

'That's my father's study,' he said.

'Yes, Daddy's hard at work in there, darling,' his mother said. 'He's not going to join us for tea. Busy, busy, busy.' She opened the next door down for Elizabeth, and walked off along the hall, slipping her arm through Quentin's. As they disappeared, she heard his mother saying, 'Now, Tintin, tell me all about *you*.'

The sitting room had beige walls and a cream carpet, and large white sofas. There were French windows, but massed rhododendrons in the garden dimmed the light.

Something about the room struck her as odd, then she realised what it was: there were no books.

Then Quentin's mother returned with a tray, and served tea in tiny, thin gold-rimmed cups, and iced lemon slices. Quentin began telling his mother how he won the college prize for his essay on the friendship between Galileo and Milton. 'It is not widely known, but they did actually meet,' he said. 'Milton made a special trip to the Continent. Two visionaries face to face. Can you imagine?'

'And what does your husband do?' Elizabeth broke in politely. She had always assumed he was some kind of professor. She wondered why he was not present. Perhaps the invitation had really only come from Quentin's mother.

'He's a management consultant, darling,' said Quentin's mother briskly. 'And Quentin's going to follow in his footsteps. He wants to be able to afford his box at the opera and the finer things in life.' Quentin sipped his tea and didn't meet Elizabeth's eyes. So he was not going to be a penniless artist or a saxophonist playing in smoky candle-lit clubs. He was not even going to be a philosopher or a scientist. She saw herself dashing her lemon slice on the floor and grinding it beneath her heel, then flinging the little polished table aside. She wanted to smash things, or, worse still, to dash Quentin off the sofa and tear open her dress. She excused herself, intending to splash some cold water on her face. As she left the room, she heard his mother saying, 'No, I didn't mean I don't like her. It's just that she's awfully thin, darling.' When she came back, Quentin was lying full-length on the floor, laughing and holding on to his mother's foot, while she tried to shake him off.

'I won't let you, I won't let you!' he was shouting joyfully.

'Tintin, don't be such a silly,' his mother admonished him. She looked at Elizabeth with a little glint in her eyes.

'I said he should sit and chat with you, while I wash up the tea things. But he insists on doing it himself.' Elizabeth had always thought of Quentin as being older than her, even though they were the same age. Their relationship had seemed both decorous and perverted, as if she were having an affair with her aged professor. But now he looked young and thin, his face hairless. He got up and dusted himself off. Elizabeth stared at his flushed cheeks and had an idea.

She prepared carefully, putting on her best black lace underwear and spraying on Trésor. She had wanted to offer Quentin sex as a gift, a sacrifice even. Now it was something else. A way to make him cast aside his pretensions and admit what he was.

On the way to Quentin's room, she thought of all the people sitting inside having conversations, the tutorials and discussions and lectures taking place at that very minute. 'Are two identical eggs one egg or two?' 'Is there such a thing as universal beauty?' She almost heard a dull buzz from the old yellow buildings, as from a hive. 'What is the difference between a mouse and a picture of a mouse?'

Elizabeth sat down on Quentin's bed and waited while he made coffee. When the kettle boiled, she said, 'I've decided to let you draw me.'

'I couldn't.' He stirred in the powdered milk briskly, like medicine. His lips were tight.

Elizabeth used his trick, the unanswerable question.

'Why is it better to look at a stranger's body than at mine?' she asked. 'You do it in your life class. What's the point of calling it a Life class if you can't draw real life?' At first Quentin protested, but she wore him down. He wasn't used to such determination from her, and eventually he shrugged and tossed over his scratchy brown dressing gown.

'You can get changed in the bathroom,' he said. When

she came back, he was rummaging in a drawer for his pencils, and he didn't turn round at once, even though he must have heard the dressing gown fall to the floor. The artist's model on the desk had her head cocked, quizzically.

She arranged herself carefully on the bed, on her side, cheek propped on her hand. A breeze from the open window was cool on her bare skin, and the first scratch of Quentin's pencil grated loudly in the silence. His eyes flicked over her body, then back to his work. He didn't meet her gaze. His pencil scratched and scratched, like a mouse in the skirting board. Then he began to make smoother, more confident strokes. His eyes met hers, and a little smile played about his lips. Finally, he leaned back, and said, 'That's it. Ye-es, that's it,' with a sigh of satisfaction.

Elizabeth walked over to look at the picture. On the paper there was a ghostly outline, without hands, or feet, or breasts. 'Don't you like it?' Quentin said. She stared at the wraith he had drawn. He had not even looked at her. He refused to acknowledge her body existed.

'Quentin,' she said, 'what's the difference between naked and nude?'

'What are you talking about?' he asked uneasily.

'I'll show you,' she said. She reached out and placed his hand on her bare breast. He gave a violent start. 'What's the matter, Tintin?'

'Don't call me that!' he said, getting up and overturning his easel. She advanced, menacingly. She thought of the Bacchae ripping a man to pieces as a fertility sacrifice.

'Go away, go away!' he screamed.

Elizabeth did not understand the impulse that made her tear up her pencilled headless body and rip the other sketches from the walls. She considered breaking the artist's model over her knee, too, but in the end she spared her. Instead, she gave Quentin one last kiss, and his eyelashes fluttered, the head of a guillotined aristocrat, blinking in surprise.

After she got dressed, she walked into the deer park. She could walk for miles. She was aware of every rustle and shadow. She remembered the naked man standing on the bank, surrounded by the first small white crocuses. It was like stumbling on a gash in the universe, through which she caught a glimpse of something else. It was as if suddenly she'd seen a great tongue sticking out through the clouds. At the end of the deer park, there was a bridge that led to the Fellows' Garden, and at the end of the garden, there was a padlocked gate. There were so many rules, so many locked gardens and forbidden lawns. She squeezed through the hedge, and struck out along the river, through the wet, open meadows.

11

The Red Man

The wedding is in eight days. The dress is bought, the ceremony is booked, the cake ordered. Elizabeth sets a cup of tea down in front of her mother. 'Where did you say Dad went?' she says gently.

'Sailing, I told you.'

'Yes, but where? I've been home for a week. How long has he been gone? Why hasn't he phoned?' And why did he choose this particular time to disappear, the fortnight before his daughter's wedding? Elizabeth pauses. 'Did he leave unexpectedly?'

'I don't like your tone,' her mother says huffily. 'You obviously learned this routine in America.' The cat is lying on the sitting-room floor, playing dead, on his back with all four legs stuck out akimbo. 'Who's a pretty boy then?' her mother says, in her cat voice. It is slurred like the speech of the deaf. She leans over and palpates his stomach, knots her fingers in his fur. Elizabeth knows that deep down her mother is terrified. But she won't admit it.

'What routine?'

'You know what I mean. This good-cop bad-cop routine. This aggressive tone.' A counter-attack, thinks Elizabeth, a smokescreen. There is no suitable *tone*, no way of asking that does not sound accusing. *Where is my father?*

Elizabeth decides to take matters into her own hands. One by one, she phones his friends, the ones who sometimes crew for him on his sailing trips. One by one, his friends say: 'Sorry, love, can't help you. Haven't seen your dad for a while.'

The next step, then, is to go to his office and question his handful of employees. At the very least, they will be able to tell her the day he left.

No one answers the buzzer when she presses it, but she's able to slip in behind a workman carrying a pot of paint. She gets in the lift with him, and they both step out on the same floor. He marches straight into her father's office, and she follows him.

There's nothing there. The main room, the conference room, the offices – they are all empty. The porridge-coloured carpet has been torn up from the floor, leaving bare boards. The grey walls are dashed with yellow streaks, and another workman is standing over a splattered folding wooden table, working a roller up and down in an aluminium paint tray. 'Can I help you, love?' says the first man.

'Where's the place that was here before?' she asks.

'Dunno.'

'They went down,' says the second man. 'Yeah. Folded. There's a new lot moving in now.'

'Was that the bloke who run off without paying his debts?' says the first man. The second one scratches his head.

'Think that was him.' He pauses, looking at Elizabeth. He is a grizzled middle-aged man, his skin minutely flecked with paint. He has a kind expression. 'You all right, love? Want a cup of tea or something?'

'No,' she says. 'Thanks. I'd better get going.' She takes the stairs down, instead of the lift. That was what she and her father always did when she met him at his office. They ran downstairs as fast as they could, pretending they were James Bond and his beautiful accomplice and there was a bomb just about to explode.

★

Elizabeth was stuffing envelopes in her father's conference room. It was the summer she was twenty-one, and she was helping out, part-time. College was over and soon she would be following Spencer to America. He had already left.

The envelopes contained information about her father's company, quotes from satisfied customers. He was looking for more business. She did not like the work, but she was too old to take money from her father any more, except as wages. The problem was that the kind of work he gave her made her wages seem like a gift. She would rather have been scrubbing dishes or stocking shelves, real work, sweaty and back-breaking. The work her father gave her was too easy. Answering the phone, data entry and envelope stuffing.

An unaccustomed sun burned through the windows and the office smelled of toxic markers and photocopy ink. Her father's employees were a handful of pale young men. They tapped away at their computers and nervously swivelled in their upholstered swivel chairs. They were gangly like her father, but they didn't share his appetite for conversation. At the office Christmas party, they only drank one beer apiece. Behind their backs, Elizabeth and her father called them 'the Young Christian Soldiers'. She could see them now through the glass wall of the conference room, hunched over their keyboards, one leg wrapped around the other, tying themselves into knots like balloon creatures.

Her father stuck his head round the door. 'Would you

mind making some coffee?' he asked. 'And I'm going to have to chuck you out, I'm afraid. I've called an emergency meeting. You can do your work in my office if you want.' She got up heavily. 'The stronger the better,' her father added.

In the kitchen, all the cups were huddled dirty on the draining board, and there was no milk in the fridge. It was empty except for a saucer containing a half-eaten cream horn. The coffee would have to be black. She plonked the tray down on the conference table so that the cups shook, and the young men bobbed their heads shyly. When she left, the blinds of the conference room dropped down one by one. She wondered what was going on.

Elizabeth did not feel like doing any more stuffing. She strolled into her father's office and opened one of the financial statements splayed on his desk. Column after column of numbers. If she stared at them for more than a second they seemed to march.

Her father did not really like being an accountant. But he was a maths whizz and he made money at it. He survived by drinking coffee and playing with his desk toys. Two Chinese silver globes that you were supposed to roll around in your hand, relieving typing cramps. A row of metal balls dangling from a frame. When you lifted one and let it drop back, the one at the other end would rise and drop back, and the motion would continue for a while, before slowly coming to a stop. *Tap, tap, tap.* But her favourite was a mound of silver diamonds clinging to a magnetic base. They could be sculpted into different shapes, and they felt as cool and slippery as little scales.

She shaped the diamonds into a rearing wave, then she put her feet on the desk. She called Jasper. After more than an hour, she went back into the main office. Silence. Nothing but the hum of computers. They had reverted to sleep mode and on their screens spirals rotated and patterns budded. But behind them was blackness, pathways into space, leading away, as if her father had just that minute decided to step through one of those dark doorways and was gone.

'Ready to go then?' he said. He was sitting in the corner with his raincoat already on. 'I sent the Young Christian Soldiers home for the afternoon. Useless bunch anyway.' It was only four o'clock. He sighed. 'Let's get a couple of KitKats, shall we? I'm feeling a bit peckish.'

Her father didn't drive her home. He dropped her off at the Tube station because it was the night for his navigation class. Elizabeth and her mother had dinner in silence in front of the television.

When her father returned, he heated up the leftovers in the kitchen, stirring the pot with one hand while holding up the course textbook, *Introduction to the Principles of Navigation*, in the other. Later, Elizabeth came down to get a glass of water before bed and he was still there, pondering over the diagrams in his *Beginner's Book of Knots*. He had a piece of garden twine and was practising the double hitch and the difficult bowline. He hadn't eaten his dinner.

Elizabeth was worried. She would be leaving home soon. There had to be someone left to look after her mother. Her father had begun to do nothing after work except tie knots.

A month before Elizabeth was due to leave for America, the three of them went to the seaside for a few days. Early summer, but after a few brief sunny days, it had become unseasonably cold. As they drove south, it rained continually, and wraiths of mist drifted over the fields. The B&B was a white-painted farmhouse with patches of moss growing on the roof, and darker spots where tiles had fallen off in winter storms. They usually stayed in hotels when they went on holiday, but her mother had spoken in a dark tone of having to make 'cutbacks'. Her father's business was not doing as well as it had.

Inside, the rooms had tiny, deep-set windows that did not let in much light. There were large fireplaces and uneven floors, and the house was cluttered with bric-a-brac: Victorian warming pans and chamber pots, murderous old farming tools and ancient magazines with their covers frilled with damp. And there were little mice peeping out at you everywhere you looked, dressed in embroidered frocks. The owner made them herself, she said. She was a heavy woman in a man's jersey and green wellington boots, and she liked to talk. She brought them tea and home-made currant cake, and pointed out the features of the old house. 'That's the coffin door,' she said, gesturing at a trapdoor in the ceiling. 'The staircase was too narrow for them to get the bodies down, once they got stiff, so they just stood them up and dropped them through.'

'What a bright idea,' said Elizabeth's father. Her mother frowned at him. When she stayed in B&Bs, she was always on her best behaviour, like a child sent to stay with distant relatives.

'So this used to be a farm?' her mother asked.

'Well, yes. Actually, there's rather a grisly story.'

'Do tell,' said Elizabeth's father. He rolled his eyes at Elizabeth over his teacup.

'Well, there was a couple living here, and one day, they had a terrible fight. He took to his bed and never got up again. They did that in those days: took to their beds. He simply refused to do another stroke of work, and so she had to look after the farm on her own, poor thing.'

'So what did he do all day?' asked Elizabeth.

'He had a view of the sea. And he made model ships in bottles. I've got some of them upstairs as a matter of fact.'

'What did he live on?' said her father.

'Horlick's Luncheon Tablets,' the woman replied. 'I found all the bottles underneath his window when I was digging up the garden.'

'And what happened to him in the end?'

'Well,' the woman answered. 'It's not a pretty ending. She almost never went into his room, but one day she heard giggling, and when she opened the door, he was in bed stark naked with a girl from the next farm over. She was half his age. When the girl saw the wife, she picked up her clothes and scooted out the window. The wife took one look and ran downstairs. And for the first time in ten years, he got out of bed and started to follow her, but he never got downstairs. His wife met him on her way back up with the scythe and stuck it right in his chest.'

'She loved him,' said Elizabeth. The woman nodded.

'They say that you can sometimes see him. Sitting on the stairs, all covered in blood and crying. They call him the Red Man.'

Elizabeth's mother had gone white, her cake crumbled into rubble on her plate. She hardly said anything for the rest of the afternoon.

After they had unpacked, they drove out again for dinner. The sea air was heavy with dampness, and as they got into the car, an owl called from a hedgerow. 'Did you know that male owls go "Too-wit", and female owls go "Too-woo"?' asked her father.

'It's a ghastly sound,' said her mother.

'You know, I think the chamber pots in our room might be haunted.' Her father was trying to cheer her mother up with one of his little jokes. 'When I was waiting for you two to get ready, I heard an eerie trickling sound. Then it stopped. Then it started again.'

'It was the hot-water pipes,' said Elizabeth, laughing. A nervous ghost with its trousers down. For her father, the Other Side was not that different from this one. Her mother didn't laugh. Elizabeth knew that she was thinking about the Red Man. She hated ghost stories, she got frightened easily. Unlike the rest of the family, she couldn't be flippant about death. That was why she never joined in with the Funeral Game.

They stopped in a little town and walked along the shore, admiring the boats. Some fishermen in yellow slickers were unloading their catch, and her father watched them longingly. He had only had *The Black Pig* for a couple of months, and he missed it. 'The wine-dark sea,' he murmured, and his eyes glazed over. Elizabeth could only imagine having such an expression when she thought about sex. She trailed behind her parents and fantasised about Spencer. She wasn't hungry, and when she ate, she could hardly taste the food. Spencer was all she wanted. Eating, walking, talking – they were all interruptions to her shameless reveries. In the college bathroom she had listened to him sing from the other side of the wall for several nights. Then she had told him the hot tap on her side wouldn't turn off and asked him in to fix it.

'What about fish and chips?' said her father.

'Yes, fish and chips!' said Elizabeth. She did not particularly want them, but they were cheap. Her parents liked long dinners where no expense was spared. There was always wine, and dessert, and coffee. Elizabeth shrank from the cost. They were worried about money anyway, and she did not want them to spend any more of it on her. But her mother sighed.

'Don't you want that, darling?' said her father.

'No restaurants around here are any good, anyway. We might as well.'

'But you used to like fish and chips when we met,' said her father.

'It was just because that was all we could afford then,' said her mother nastily.

'Well, why don't we get Elizabeth her fish and chips, then we can have a nice pub dinner?'

'That's silly, darling. We'll have fish and chips. I don't

mind,' said her mother. Elizabeth protested, but her mother stopped her. 'My evening's ruined now, anyway. I don't like it when things are difficult.' Elizabeth should have realised, she thought, that her mother would hate the idea of fried fish. It probably reminded her of the Catholic Women's Home she had lived in during college.

'Let's not go,' Elizabeth said. 'Let's go and find a pub.' But her mother stopped stubbornly outside a fish bar, whose sign read *The Cod Almighty*. It had a drawing of a fish with a fat-lipped grin, standing on its tail and bowing. Behind the counter inside, a woman was plunging a wire basket of chips into boiling fat. A blackboard held a scrawled list of fish and underneath the steamy glass of the counter there were unidentifiable objects coated in golden batter.

They stood inside the door uncertainly, then her father marched up to the counter. 'Can I *plaice* an order?' he said. The woman's eyes crinkled up. She was thin and pale, but she was pretty when she smiled, and Elizabeth saw that the woman was younger than she had thought. She had a great shock of dark red hair that tumbled down her back, although, reflected Elizabeth, given that she worked in a place that sold food, it should probably have been tied up. Despite her greasy place of work, she had good skin too, freckles like cinnamon sprinkled on cream.

'I don't know,' the woman said to Elizabeth's father. 'Cod any money?' She paused and wiped her hands on her apron. 'What can I get you?' He grinned.

'I've got to think turbot it,' he countered. 'Let me look at the whiting on the board.' The woman groaned.

'You're a right scream,' she said sarcastically, but she was still smiling.

Elizabeth's mother wandered away from the counter and stood looking at a small aquarium set in the window in front of a couple of Formica tables. Elizabeth followed. At the bottom of the aquarium, crabs were squatting around a mock-wooden sign that read *This Way to the Topless Beach*. A plastic mermaid sat disconsolate on top of a rock. She was bare-breasted, with long red hair. 'They don't have cod,' said her mother. 'I looked. I was going to have cod.'

'What's the matter, darling?' said her father. He came over from the counter too, his smile fading.

'Nothing's the matter.' Her mother was on the verge of tears. 'I'm just not hungry.'

And so they did not eat. Her mother could quell her appetite, withdraw from her body so easily. Denial of the flesh. Maybe she had learned it from Granny, who was so proud of her ability to fast for the full twenty-four hours before Mass. They left the Cod and walked along the street in silence.

'Maybe we'll see the Red Man tonight,' said her father, relentlessly cheerful. 'Too-whoooo!' His fingers spidered on her mother's neck, and she started violently. Her father looked at her mother.

'Why does everything always have to be *fucking* perfect?' he said. He turned on his heel and walked away. Elizabeth's mother did not go after him, she refused even to wait. She said he could catch a taxi back if he wanted, she had had enough for one night.

Back at the B&B, Elizabeth couldn't sleep. She was used to the city's diluted skies, and it was too dark. And once the heating clanked off, she couldn't get warm. Then through the thin walls, she heard crying. It was past midnight. When she pushed open her mother's door, the crying stopped. Her mother was alone, lying stiffly on her back. In the dark, Elizabeth couldn't tell whether her eyes were open or closed. But she knew what her mother was thinking about. The Red Man. Elizabeth blinked and a red spot danced across her vision. For a moment, she tensed up, but it was just the eyelid's aurora borealis. Nevertheless, she was afraid. She shivered in her pyjamas, then she climbed into the bed. The last time she had slept with her mother must have been twenty years ago.

But the feather mattress was lumpy in odd places and the brass bed frame creaked when she moved. They lay rigid as a doll couple in the comfortless bed and Elizabeth could feel her mother's fear. She wanted to soothe her, but instead all she could do was be frightened too.

And she was angry with her father. Why had he marched up to the counter in the Cod Almighty? Why hadn't he begged her mother to go elsewhere, soothed her with a glass of white wine and a Dover sole in one of the mock-Elizabethan taverns? It was because he always thought things would be all right, just as her mother was always convinced they wouldn't be. It was because of his dangerous optimism, thought Elizabeth, that he couldn't see that there was something really wrong with her mother, something not even he could fix. But even if he couldn't fix it, it was his duty to stick by her. She wondered where he was and why he had not come back that night. Had he gone back to get his fish and chips, bantered a little more with the woman with the mermaid hair?

When dawn crept red along the horizon, Elizabeth got into her own bed. An hour or so later, the owner woke her up, banging on a little gong for breakfast. She served them duck eggs, sausages, fried bread and home-made marmalade. Her mother didn't speak, and as usual, she only picked at her food. When she speared her sausage, she watched for a minute as it wept grease, then she put her knife and fork down, and turned to look out at the sea. It was, for once, a clear day and the sea was smooth.

'Has he gone for a swim then?' said the owner. She walked over to the window, and continued, as if to herself: 'Lovely day, but then you can fall to your death from those cliffs.' Elizabeth sighed. Was it because the woman's husband was dead that she had such an appetite for violence and death? Fear could replace sex sometimes. Elizabeth knew that. But she had a grudging admiration for the woman. She had her stubborn little business here on the flat fields above the sea, she kept ducks and hens, and she took her dogs to shows. She led a meagre but self-sufficient life. At night she would have toast with her home-made marmalade, and watch *Blind Date* while she stitched clothes for Elizabeth's toy mice. Is that what would happen to her mother in the end? She tried to imagine her mother with a French catering business and friends with whom she had lunch, a carefully tended life of small pleasures. It would never happen. Without her father, her mother would not survive.

'Phew!' said her father, climbing through the window. He was wearing last night's clothes, but they clung to his damp body and his hair was plastered to his brow. 'Just went for a swim! Absolutely bracing! You should try it, Elizabeth. I'm tingling all over!' He sat down and reached for the marmalade.

'Where've you been?' asked Elizabeth.

'For a swim, I told you.'

'All *night*?' said her mother sharply.

'No, darling, not all night.' Her father looked startled, then he seemed to realise that the argument of the previous evening would not follow the usual pattern. In Elizabeth's family, rows never consisted of more than a terrible remark or two, abruptly fired off. Then everything was over, like a duel. But this time, things had not been forgotten. 'Not all night,' he repeated. 'I took a taxi home, then I didn't want to disturb anyone, so I went to sleep in Elizabeth's bed. It felt damp. Everything feels damp here. Sheets, curtains, valances, everything you touch. It's the sea air.'

'But I went back to my bed this morning and it was made,' Elizabeth pointed out.

'That's because I made it.'

'Well, why are you wearing last night's clothes?' she said.

'You two were asleep in my room.' Her father stared at them. His shipwrecked eyes seemed to focus. 'Don't you *believe* me?' The two of them stared back.

'Frankly, darling, I'm not sure if I do,' said her mother. Her father looked at Elizabeth, but she didn't say anything.

On her last night at home, her father insisted on cooking a special dinner. Her mother had been in a bad mood ever since they returned from Cornwall, and now she was in a worse mood because Elizabeth's father had had to spend an extra day on his business trip up North. '*I* don't care what you do,' she had said, 'but it's Elizabeth's last week at home and you could have made a bit of extra effort for her.'

And he hadn't brought anything back with him. When he travelled to Europe, her father had brought back wonderful presents. Chocolate pears from Switzerland filled with liqueur. Honey schnapps from Austria. Once, a *tarte aux framboises* in a box tied with gold ribbon, which he bought the same day in a famous patisserie in Paris. But in the last few months he had stopped going to Europe. Now he just drove up the motorway to chilly industrial towns. They were not the kind of places you could buy exotic delicacies, or where you would want to stay an extra night. He was trying to make up for it with *truite aux amandes* and crêpes Suzette.

Her mother began blanching almonds and rubbing off their skin, meticulously. Her father looked at what she was doing. 'Don't bother with all those fiddly skins,' he said. 'A recipe is like a Platonic form,' he said. 'An impossible ideal. You're not *meant* to get it perfect. Besides,' he went on, 'you should want to perform your own virtuoso variation.' When her father cooked, he did what he called 'interpretations' of dishes he remembered eating and had liked. Monkfish with vodka sauce. Duck with blackberries, cocoa and cinnamon. When Elizabeth was little, he was the one who made her sandwiches to take to school. He enjoyed experimenting with strange combinations: peanut butter and pickle, banana and bacon, and sometimes they were oddly successful. But sometimes they weren't.

'I just want to get dinner on the table,' snapped her mother. 'But suit yourself. You always do.'

'All right,' he agreed. 'Elizabeth will help me. I cook by memory and taste alone. Make way, Monsieur Escoffier!' Her mother walked away, and Elizabeth heard her trudging slowly up the stairs. '*All I want is a tall ship, on the lonely midnight sea,*' sang her father. '*All I want is a case of rum, and some hardtack biscuits . . .*' He trailed off. He was making the words up, and he couldn't make them fit the tune. He started frying bananas in butter and cinnamon in one pan, and poured crêpe batter into another. He had forgotten about the crêpes Suzette and had decided to do something more exotic. 'And now, let's flambé!' he exclaimed. 'I love to flambé!'

Elizabeth stood back and watched. There was nothing for her to do. Her father gave a crêpe an expert flip with one hand and stirred the bananas with the other. 'Elizabeth, have you ever played Haunted House?' he asked her.

'What's that?'

'It's an amusing little diversion I've discovered recently. These fleshless ghouls come at you, but if you press the button at just the right moment, you can zap them with a fireball. Before the turn-off for my meeting, I stop at a motorway café, have a double espresso, drop a pound coin in the slot, and play a game of Haunted House. It gets me in the right aggressive mood for one of my meetings.'

The hot-water pipes clanked and hissed. Her mother was running a bath. Anger was a luxury to be savoured like a fine dessert wine. 'I'm a man who throws what he's got on the table and says take it or leave it!' Her mother would not be down for dinner, and he knew it. He splashed rum into the pan with the bananas and put on his pirate voice. 'That'll warm yer cockles, me hearties! Arrr! That's the last of the rum before we sight land again!' He lit the rum, and it burst into angry flame.

12

Carmageddon

Elizabeth is on her way out to buy her wedding underwear when she nearly trips over a small candy-striped box placed on the front step, labelled 'FRAGILE' in large handwritten capitals. She picks it up wondering if it is for her and Spencer, but a little gold card attached to the box bears the words, *For Duncan*. There is no stamp or postmark – it must have been delivered by hand. Elizabeth decides to forget about transparent white panties and strapless bras. Her heart was never in the errand anyway. She's too worried about her father. Instead, she goes back up to her room and opens the box. She will plunder cupboards, peer under beds, even read diaries in her shameless appetite. It's the only way of ever finding out anything about anybody.

Inside, something is nested in tissue paper. It is a beautiful blown egg. On one side, a blue-eyed girl is smiling, but on the other side there is a sad face. A boy with stubble speckling his eggshell jaw, a boy with one green eye and one fading purple. Copperplate words form curlicues of hair. The words *I'm sorry*. She turns the egg round again and sees that the girl's hair reads *I'm sorry* too, in gold ink. A blonde. Jasmine must have returned from Thailand then. It would be easy to crush it in her hand, hide the box, and never say anything. Why should she help them get back together? She looks at it. The colours are as bright as a medieval illumination, and the egg has been carefully varnished. It is an apology, in Elizabeth's family a strange and marvellous thing. Duncan will be pleased, she thinks. She remembers all those years that she listened through ceilings and at doors, hearing their cries. Skulking about as disgusted as Hamlet. Now she won't try to stop them. She has Spencer now.

Duncan slams the front door and the house quivers. Elizabeth hears him stamping into the sitting room. She hastily swaddles the egg in its wrapping, then puts the box in her pocket. He is lying on the sofa, his arm shielding his forehead. He lifts his arm and gives her a tragic look. The handsome soldier who has seen terrible things.

'Pizza makes me puke,' he says. 'They squirt chemicals into the crust to make it puff up. People think it's just instant yeast, but it's some kind of fucking chemical. It comes in an aerosol can.'

'But shouldn't you be at work still?' Elizabeth says.

'Can't believe I ever ate it,' he adds, spitting into the fireplace.

'What happened?'

'I was dropping off a delivery, and this old lady opens the door. She doesn't say anything, just beckons me and nods, yeah? She was foreign or something. So I followed her into her dining room and there was two old men sitting at a table covered with a lace cloth. She nods at the table and I put the box down. Then they kept on looking at me and I realised: they wanted me to *serve* it to them. Didn't even give me a tip. Who do they think I am?'

'But you didn't do anything to them, did you?'

'Might've broken a couple of plates.'

'And you got the sack, I suppose?'

'Wankers can wank into the pizza crust for all I care!' he shouts.

'I've got something that might cheer you up.' She deposits the little box in his lap.

'Fuck is this?' he mutters, plucking at the tissue paper.

'Be careful!' she says. But it's too late. The egg falls into his lap, broken. The egg boy still has his frown, and the girl still has her smile. But their scalps are cracked.

'It said she was sorry,' says Elizabeth.

'*Jasmine* was sorry?' he repeats.

'About Ally and that,' she tells him helpfully. Duncan picks up the broken egg and looks at it in amazement. Then he puts it on the coffee table, gives a long hawk, and gobs into the grate again. His eyes are bloodshot. She feels a pang about the lovely egg.

'Stop hawking like that,' she says.

'Hawking, I'm not hawking.'

'You are. You just did.'

'Hawking means selling things. As in "No solicitors or hawkers".'

'It means gobbing too.'

'It does not.'

'It does. Go and look in the dictionary.'

'You and your fucking dictionary. You *read* the dictionary.'

'I don't. I just know.'

'Yes you do,' he retorts. 'You sit in your little bed at night and read the fucking dictionary.' He looks at her with hatred, works his cheeks, gathering saliva.

'Don't you dare!' she cries. They have always held back, two superpowers knowing that if hostilities ever escalate, they will both be destroyed. But he does. His spit wets her neck. This time he has gone too far.

'I think this might be a new start,' says her mother. Elizabeth has just told her about Duncan's resignation. They are having coffee after dinner, watching the news. 'He could do a lot better than that place. Where is he now?'

'In his room,' says Elizabeth. 'On the computer.' Her mother nods approvingly. Elizabeth knows what she is thinking. Her mother imagines that he is writing carefully worded cover letters and tinkering with his CV.

'He's not *working*. He's playing Carmageddon.' Carmageddon is a computer game in which the player leads a high-speed car chase, the police on his tail, through a grid of city streets. The player loses points for crashing into a shop window, but gains points for running over a bystander, which produces a pool of blood, and lifelike screams.

'Oh, well,' says her mother. 'He's a boy racer.' Elizabeth wishes her mother would tell Duncan off, just once, instead of letting him do whatever he likes, her mother's pampered prince. Elizabeth scrubbed and scrubbed, but can still feel his saliva. He has made her filthy and humiliated.

'Give me some happy! Give me some happy!' the man cries. Elizabeth is lying on her front on a carpet of clean paper, chin resting on her splayed hands. The photographer's fee includes engagement pictures and since Spencer can't be here, Elizabeth is having them done by herself, in proud solitude like the brides in magazines. The photographer is a plump rosy-faced man in a brown suit who is as energetic as a gym mistress. A cheerful square of orange silk blossoms from his breast pocket. He insists on doing both 'formal' and 'casual' portraits. First in crisp jeans with her hair in a ponytail, and then in lipstick and sequined tube.

Her mother stands and watches, leaning against a backdrop of a bookshelf lined with leather-bound books. Elizabeth is having trouble holding the position and the muscles of her face ache. She dreams again of a wedding in the west. Spencer could wear cowboy boots and she could be barefoot with cactus flowers in her hair.

'Head tilted, head tilted!' the photographer cries. Elizabeth adopts a pensive pose and then rolls over to be photographed on her side, as obedient as a dog.

'Now, I like to create a story with the actual wedding pictures,' he says. 'I start by taking the bride in her boudoir getting ready, having her hair styled and her make-up done. Coming down the stairs with all the oohs and aahs. Then I take her walking up the aisle on her father's arm. Her first great step on the staircase of life.'

'This isn't a photo romance. I'm going to be doing my own hair,' Elizabeth says.

'Oh, I don't think so, darling,' says her mother. 'You'll want to look nice. I'll put it on my list.'

'No,' says Elizabeth. 'There won't be either a coiffeur or a cosmetician. And I'd prefer it if you didn't take photographs of me in my boudoir.'

'I assure you it will be absolutely tasteful,' the photographer retorts. 'I liken my relationship with my clients to that of a Renaissance artist with his patrons.' Elizabeth turns to her mother. She doesn't want to waste all this expensive resplendence on walking down the aisle alone.

'I'm not getting married if Dad isn't there. Why don't you tell me why he left?' He left because he didn't know how to tell her mother that he had lost his money. He was always the one who looked after her, and he left because he couldn't do it any more.

'You bloody well better get married,' says her mother. 'I'm not spending all this money otherwise. You don't seem to care that I've been working my fingers to the bone to make this a nice day for you.' *You complain and complain,* thinks Elizabeth, *but there is nothing wrong with you at all. Your tragedy is imaginary.*

In the Plate Game at children's parties when Elizabeth was young, the best china plates were laid out on the floor, and the victim was blindfolded and told to walk between them. Then they were removed. Elizabeth remembers what it felt like to be that victim, proud of her delicate step, her courageous care, and then the pang of disappointment when the blindfold was removed, and she saw that there was nothing there.

Elizabeth's mother has a late appointment with her hairdresser, so Elizabeth stalks home by herself, intending to clean off her mascara with alcohol wipes, change out of the sequinned top, and then go to see Granny. But when she opens the front door, she knows something is not right. She puts her keys down on the hall table and sees the blood. Blood is spattered up the stairs and on the walls, and on the parquet floor beneath her feet. Rich large drops like summer rain. Then she hears a bellow. 'Elizabeth!'

'Where are you?' she shouts back. 'I'm coming!'

'Elizabeth! Elizabeth! Elizabeth!' She runs to the kitchen, but there's no one there. She flings open the cellar door and peers inside, then rushes out into the garden. 'Elizabeth! Elizabeth!' She looks up at Duncan's attic window and sees someone moving, a gleam of white flesh like the underbelly of a shark. Then the bellowing stops. She runs up the up the stairs, two at a time, past the festive drops.

Duncan is in his room, bare-chested, his black T-shirt pressed against his side. For a moment she thinks it's another of his tricks, no wound at all. Then she sees the shirt's sticky gleam. She feels all the blood drain from her own body, as if sympathetically, leaping to his wound. Her heart shrinks. 'Oh my God,' she says. 'What's happened to you?'

'What do you think?' He lifts the shirt a moment and looks underneath, then gives a cry, his man's voice cracking so that he sounds like a boy again. 'Fucking do something! I'm bleeding to death!' She moves towards him, but he shies coltishly away. She steadies him with one hand on his stomach, dabs the wound with his shirt. He holds still, quivering, sweat on his chest.

'Can you see my intestines?'

'No.' She pauses. 'I think you're going to live. But I'm going to call an ambulance.'

'Fuck that,' he says, suddenly cheering up. 'Let's take my car.'

Elizabeth gets him a towel to stop the blood, and he drapes his leather jacket over his shoulders. As they leave, she notices Duncan glance back with fascination. The cat is licking up the blood.

She starts the car and pulls out. Then she says, 'Tell me what happened.' Duncan scowls.

'Flick knife came open in my jacket pocket, and I didn't realise. Stuck into my side when I lay down.'

'Oh.' Somehow she had been expecting something more dramatic. But it occurs to her that she is not sure if she believes him. Did he stab himself, in a melodramatic suicide attempt? It would be like him to do it that way, the hero's way, a Roman emperor falling on his sword. She glances at him quickly, hunched over his wound and frowning. She had thought he was only capable of anger. Not self-loathing and despair.

In the emergency room, the two of them are ushered to a curtained bed. Duncan sits and removes his jacket, winces when the doctor peels away the towel. Elizabeth looks on while the wound is examined. Duncan has somehow acquired the body of a man, his shoulders have broadened, his biceps have swelled, and there's fine, dark hair on his chest. She hasn't seen him without a shirt since he was a child. They should have painted Jesus this way, not as a fey adolescent, the way he was in the pictures in Granny's house. They should have painted him as a man suffering like a man.

'It's a surface wound,' says the doctor.

'*What*?' says Elizabeth. 'He scared the living daylights out of me.'

'He will need quite a few stitches. And I'll keep him here tonight, just for observation. Make sure it doesn't get infected.' She pauses for a moment and looks at Duncan. 'How did you say this happened again?'

'Fell on a knife,' mutters Duncan. The doctor frowns and shakes her head. It irritates Elizabeth that she clearly thinks Duncan is manfully covering up for someone. The doctor thinks he got his stab wound in a fight, a battle sprung from jealousy and passion and long-nurtured hatreds. But the truth is, it was probably an accident, and now he is revelling in the attention. He is revelling in having made Elizabeth show her love, in how her hands shook when she touched his side. She hates him for making her his foolish Florence Nightingale.

'I'm going,' she says. 'I said I'd go and see Granny. You can phone Mum and explain about the blood. She won't be home until later though.'

'How am I meant to get back?' says Duncan.

'Get a bloody cab.'

'But it's my car!' she hears him wail as she walks away.

13

Black and Blue

'I MAY BE LATE, but I've got a bit of a treat for you this afternoon, Granny.' Elizabeth bears two cups of tea on a tray. She made a point of fetching the tea herself, because she doesn't want the nurse to come in and interrupt the treat. Granny smacks her lips.

'Is it something to eat?' She is dressed in a cheerful turquoise suit with shoes to match. Although the other patients favour dressing gowns and pyjamas, Granny is always fully costumed when Elizabeth visits, as if ready to leave the nursing home at a moment's notice.

Elizabeth extracts an aerosol can of whipped cream from her bag, then a paper bag of ground coffee. She sets out a cafetière, and the electric kettle she used in her room at college. 'And finally,' she announces, producing a bottle of Jack Daniel's.

'Irish coffee!' Granny exclaims, beaming. The brightness of her eyes seems to belie her curls and spectacles. She looks like the wolf in a grandmother's outfit, not dying, but full of ravenous life. Elizabeth tips the tea into the sink and gets to work.

'Whiskey's very good for old people,' Granny tells her. 'The priest told me. He shook my hand and said, "What cold hands you have. You should take a glass of whiskey

176

to warm you up." "Oh no, Father," I said. "That doesn't do me any good." And then he said, "Have two glasses then." ' Granny pauses. 'I was wearing a yellow dress with black trimmings, and he said, "You should be singing with the canaries." That was a lovely compliment.'

Elizabeth pours the flame-coloured whiskey into the teacups, sees the priest's large warm hand enfolding Granny's cold one, skin on skin.

'Why did you never marry again?' she asks. When her husband died, Granny continued to manage the corner shop they owned. Her hair turned white in a year or two, and she did not, as far as Elizabeth knows, ever have a date again. Granny makes a sour face.

'I didn't see what the point would be.' Granny unfolds a tissue in her lap to protect her Sunday best. She sips her drink and doesn't speak. For once, conversation is a reluctant tapeworm that has to be coaxed forth.

'You must have had some admirers,' Elizabeth says.

'Well, I had one suitor. Bob, his name was. He gave me a bunch of orchids.' Granny's blue eyes shine and Elizabeth thinks of Sir Andrew Aguecheek. *I was adored once too.*

'And then what happened?'

'He asked me to marry him. He came into the shop one day and said, "You're so beautiful and you have such a lovely figure and you're so intelligent. Do you mind if I ask you a question?" "Not at all," I said, very polite. "Do you promise not to laugh?" "I promise." "Well then, will you marry me?" I couldn't help it. I laughed my head off. "You promised not to do that," he said, and I said, "I didn't know you were going to ask me such a silly question." '

'Why was it such a silly question?' asks Elizabeth.

'I knew what it was like to be married. Why would I want to go back to that?'

'Oh.'

'But things will be different for you, of course,' Granny

adds hastily. 'We got married in the church up the road with me in an old dress and a borrowed hat, then we moved straight in behind the shop.'

'Didn't you love him?'

'Of course.' Granny gazes into her cup. 'He was no oil painting, but I loved him.' And she begins to talk, slowly at first, then faster, until her murmur is as ceaseless as a spider's thread.

'My husband was a fiddle player by trade. He had a wonderful ear for a tune, he could play anything after hearing it once. But he was no good at business. He wanted to turn our corner shop into some fancy London boutique. He kept on ordering posh products like Gentleman's Relish and lily of the valley shampoo, but of course they didn't sell. People in our neighbourhood had no money for things like that. I had to stick all that stuff in the cellar, where we kept odds and ends. He went back to playing his fiddle then, down at the pub, and as often as not he came home drunk. I'd hide behind the counter when he came in. He'd shout out for me but I wouldn't answer. It was like a game.

'I took over ordering the new stock and started keeping the account books, and after a while, your grandfather let me take care of everything. I took a real pride in it. I even hauled in the deliveries. I had such strong arms in those days from carrying your mother around. When she was a baby she would cry if I ever put her down.'

Granny chuckles a little. 'And I knew how to please the customers without putting myself out of pocket. I was terribly clever at it. I cut the cheese wheel up and divided it into two bins. I labelled one "Mild", and the other "Mature". The customers took some of each, never knew they were the same. Thought they were so à la posh. And I got so good at cutting the ham thin with the guillotine that you could see through though the slices. They were like pink tissues.'

The nurse comes in, and Granny shoves her cup under her chair with her foot, rummages in her handbag and pops a mint in her mouth. She rolls her eyes at Elizabeth, and Elizabeth quickly drains her coffee, glad that she remembered to return the whiskey to her backpack. 'Time to change that bandage then,' says the nurse.

'Should I go outside?' offers Elizabeth.

'Oh no, won't be a minute,' says the nurse. 'You sit tight.' She helps Granny off with the turquoise jacket, then rolls up the sleeve of her blouse above the elbow. When the nurse unwinds the bandage, Granny's veins show blue under the freckled skin and her wrist is soft and yellow as a toad's throat. She usually wears so many layers, feels the cold. Elizabeth has never seen this much of her before. A raised pink scar cuts across her forearm. Elizabeth leans closer. It's ridged with little lines, like a ladder in a pair of tights. She puts her finger out and touches it. Something crumples in her and she knows.

'This isn't from your fall, is it?' she asks.

'Oh no,' says the nurse. 'She got that years ago.' Elizabeth waits for the nurse to put on a new bandage, while Granny winces.

When the nurse has gone, Elizabeth says, 'Tell me where you got that.' Granny cradles her wrist in her lap, murmuring to herself. 'Tell me where you got that scar,' repeats Elizabeth sharply. Something in her tone makes Granny sit up.

'We had to make our own entertainment in those days,' she says. 'People used to come into the shop just to watch us. They said it was better than the radio.' Her head droops on to her chest and she murmurs something to herself.

'What was that, Granny?' says Elizabeth. Granny's voice is almost too low to hear.

'It was that cash register. That ffff . . .' For a moment, Elizabeth thinks she is going to swear, then Granny says, 'That flipping cash register.' Then it occurs to her that for

Granny, 'flip' *is* daring, a sally into the forbidden, a tongue stuck out to the Lord. 'It was an old-fashioned one, pinged when the metal drawer opened. Didn't have a digital display. The numbers popped up at the top like bingo cards to show you what the total was.' She sighs. 'He didn't mean to do it.'

'I know, Granny,' says Elizabeth.

'It was when the drawer was open. He threw me against the counter and that drawer opened my arm up.' She smiles ruefully, and Elizabeth wonders if she is even bothered. She seems to regard it as a joke, comic-book violence, *bam!* and *pow!* Or perhaps it's to preserve her dignity that she frames this confession as a humorous anecdote.

'Did Mum know about this?' Elizabeth asks.

'Oh no, not a thing. Bandaged it up with a rag, said I was going out for a breath of air, and slipped down to the hospital. Didn't know a thing.' Granny frowns, plucks at the dressing-table for her inhaler, and sucks at it for a moment. 'Just my angina,' she says. 'I learned my lesson. I stopped eating dripping on my toast after he died. But I ended up getting the same thing he had, more or less.'

Elizabeth pulls the cup out from under Granny's chair, rinses it in the bathroom, and pours her a whiskey, neat. 'Oh, I couldn't,' says Granny. Then, as Elizabeth keeps pouring, Granny acquiesces, coyly murmuring, 'Just a dash, just a dash.' Elizabeth hands Granny the cup and she takes a delicate sip. 'He beat us black and blue,' she goes on. 'But I never blamed him.' She smiles, the old smug smile of the Catholic on the rack. Then Elizabeth realises. *Us.* A wrong syllable, a loose thread, the power to unravel everything.

'What do you mean, "us"?' she asks, trying to keep her voice as light as possible.

Granny's cheeks are flushed from the whiskey and from the drug she has inhaled. 'It was your mother who started it,' she says. 'Always playing her Mozart and whatnot on that piano. She knew he didn't like it, he liked something with a bit of a tune. He slammed the lid down on her fingers once, she couldn't play for a month. But sometimes they got on so well. I heard them all the time, when I was out front in the shop, playing away together, happy as two buzzing bees. Irish jigs, that was what he liked. Him on his fiddle and her on that piano. They stopped a lot, arguing over the music, who'd played a wrong note, who was going too slow.

'I thought it wasn't right for her to spend so much time with him. But he had his weak heart and he was getting his vertigo attacks, and I knew he might not be long on this earth. And she loved her music. I'd go back and the two of them would be banging and sawing away, making an awful racket, bright-eyed and rosy-cheeked and grinning at each other.' Granny sighs. 'Then when he died, your mother never played again.' She sniffs. 'Despite all the money I'd spent on her lessons.'

Something in Granny will not let her think about what went on in the back room. Perhaps she even chatted to the customers and banged the cash register open with particular vigour, so that if a sound came from behind her, something that might have been crying or begging, she wouldn't have to hear it.

Elizabeth sees the back room where her own family has eaten so many Sunday lunches. The table with its cloth embroidered with blue birds and green vines, always set for the next meal. Antimacassars on the yellow velour armchairs, the Virgin standing on the sideboard with bent head, the cheap upright piano. Maybe it was nothing more than harsh words and bruised fingers. Or maybe it was more. Only her mother knows what went on in there, whether the statue of the Virgin had any cause to weep. Elizabeth thinks of a school blouse flung over a chair, a hiked-up pleated skirt. Pleading, breathing with a sob in it, a man's exhalation of relief.

Sadness makes Elizabeth want to curl up. Not just because of what happened in the back room, but because of what it has made her mother: a woman who has been only occasionally present in the world, her senses dull and her passions muted. A woman who barely weighs seven stone. Timid and almost incapable of happiness.

'Time,' says the nurse. She has padded in quietly in her sensible rubber-soled shoes. 'What have you two been gossiping about?'

'Just a few more minutes,' says Elizabeth. 'I promise.' The nurse gives a suspicious sniff, but pads away. Granny keeps on talking, telling more and more. She casts out her secrets like precious things from a burning house.

'I thought he was going to cut it off,' she says. 'They'd stopped playing, must have been for an hour or more. It was just before she was due to go to college, and they hadn't been getting along so well. She had been busy getting herself ready and saying goodbye to her friends. And he moped around and wouldn't even go out to the pub. But that day they were together. Then I heard it. That little Mozart air she liked.

'Next thing, I heard her screaming, and he was in the back passage with her finger in the guillotine. *I'll bloody chop it off*, he said. *I will. I warned you. I'll bloody chop it off*. I crept back to the counter and I picked up the cash register. Heavy great thing, but I was a strong woman in those days. Then I whacked it on his head. He fell down on the stone floor and his face went grey. *I wasn't going to hurt her*, he said. And the Lord took him.

'Your mother fell on top of him and started screaming and crying. I had to slap her in the face. I had to prise her fingers off him. But I ordered her to pack a bag and sent her upstairs. Then I gathered up all the coins that had fallen out of the drawer and I put the cash register back with the money in the right slots. And I took your mother straight up to London the same day. I knew she'd tell if I didn't, she wasn't strong enough to keep it in. She cried all the way up there without making a sound, and she wouldn't let me kiss her goodbye.

'When I got back, they'd found him. I'd left the shop door unlocked so they would. And they didn't suspect a thing. I got him on the back of the head so they thought he'd got the bang on the head from falling on the floor. I said he must have had one of his dizzy spells while he was cutting the ham.

'It turned out that it wasn't the blow that did for him anyway – his heart gave out. And they didn't ask any questions. They knew what kind of man he was. They'd all heard him singing and bawling and roaring on the way back from the pub. Good riddance, they probably thought.' Granny tips back the last drops of liquor in her cup. 'The cash register made a terrible ping when I hit him. Like a pair of cymbals. Still think I hear it sometimes, ringing in my ears. Ping! Ping! Ping!' Elizabeth knows that she is telling the truth. Death is her notary.

'What is going on here!' cries the nurse. 'I can hear you halfway down the hall! Have you been upsetting her?' Granny falls silent at once. Her eyes have faded, the whiskey's fire gone. 'Shoo, now,' the nurse tells Elizabeth. 'Shoo! You should be ashamed of yourself.'

Elizabeth stoops and kisses Granny's cheek, cold and withered, a frost-bitten apple. Granny doesn't move, just stares ahead raptly, her head raised high, listening.

It begins to drizzle as Elizabeth walks home, and by the time she reaches the house, it's pouring. The evening has fallen early because of the storm, and in the light from the street lamps, the rain glitters like razor blades. Elizabeth is not looking forward to the confrontation with her mother. But afterwards everything will be lovely. They will weep and embrace and drink sweet tea. Her mother will beg Elizabeth's forgiveness for years of strangled love, and then

Elizabeth will start talking about a therapist, a support group, self-help books. She will comfort her mother and lead her from her dungeon.

But the house is still empty, except for the cat, sitting on the stairs with its eyes half-closed and a dreamy expression on its face. Her mother has not yet returned from the hairdresser's. Elizabeth looks at the stains on the dove-coloured carpet, the creamy walls. She is not sure how she is going to explain her brother's wound to her mother, who has enough to worry about. But if these marks can be erased, she won't have to know. Elizabeth gets a bucket, fills it with scalding water and the harshest soap she can find, and sets to work.

She wonders how long it will take for her mother to change. Spencer always speaks of 'processing' loss and disaster. It means brooding on things until understanding and recovery is achieved. Translating event into packaged and labelled emotion, the conscience as efficient as a factory.

But her mother has had thirty years to process what has happened. Her misery is tenacious, a black mass that has grown denser over time, accreting around her secret and finally exceeding it. Maybe in the beginning her mother was punishing herself, taking the blame for her parents' crimes. But that doesn't seem to explain her continued regime of silence and starvation, despite the loving husband who cooks her *sole bercy*, despite her lavishly appointed home and her son and daughter. Her mother never really wanted to be a grown woman with her own house and family. Elizabeth flinches a little at the callousness of the thought, but other people have recovered from worse things and not held on to them. All her life Elizabeth has suspected some secret, and now it's out she realises that in a way the secret was never the point. Secret or not, she'll never understand her mother and she'll never be able to make her happy.

Elizabeth slops out water and scrubs the carpet savagely, angry with everybody. Why does she bother? Why should she look after other people and clean up their mess? Duncan's blood is dappled everywhere, the house marked like an animal's territory. Since he lost his job, he has hardly left the house, except to juggle in the garden with flaming brands. He never burns himself, even practising in the dark. He has always been good at tasks requiring speed and risk. He could have become a pilot if he wanted to, she thinks, maybe even a racing driver. Instead, he stays at home and wastes his life. As a boy, he used to say he would leave home the day of his sixteenth birthday – after opening his presents, of course. Instead, he sleeps until four in the afternoon, then loafs about the house in his dressing gown with a kind of swagger, like a penniless lord in a debtor's prison.

The water in Elizabeth's bucket is pink. She has almost finished and the trail of blood has led her up to his room. She puts down her scrubbing brush and goes in. The T-shirt he used to stop the wound is balled stiffening in a corner. By the bed there is a cup half full of scummy grey liquid. She recognises the cheery yellow outsize cup. Her mother gave it to him as a Christmas present once, perhaps hoping that the extra caffeine would rouse him, turn him into what job ads refer to as a 'self-starter'. On his desk there is a notepad starred with flecks of blood. She picks it up and reads: 'Notes for my CV.' The scribbled names of his school and university. No mention of the pizza place. Under a sub-heading 'Pastimes', he has put 'Reading?' *Throwing flick knives,* she thinks. *Playing with fire.*

Suddenly, Elizabeth remembers the egg and begins to look for it, brushing papers and small change off his desk. She desperately wants to find it, to know that he is capable of holding on to this little fragment of beauty and love. She pulls out one drawer after another. Finally, she flings open his wardrobe and finds a shoebox on the floor. She opens it and finds a cache of letters. They are from Jasmine, written, presumably, at times when she and Duncan were not speaking. Elizabeth holds the first one in her hand for a minute. But she has the dangerous curiosity of Bluebeard's wife. She begins to read.

Darling Duncan,
How I want you, my Beast and no other girl's, because if you fucked someone else you know I'd kill both of you. My Beast, how I want you to fuck me again. We've fucked in so many places – do you remember that time on the roof outside your window in London? I'm making a list of all the places we've fucked, though *naturellement* that will just make me feel worse. And do you remember how Elizabeth played her violin to drown my screams, my screams of pleasure? I still can't believe she never noticed that we fucked in her bed, silly cunt . . .

Elizabeth crumples the sheet in her hand, dizzy. But she is, as always, compulsively thorough. Now she has begun, she must read every one, though her heart sinks at the task. It's as if Jasmine's hand is gripping hers, forcing Elizabeth to run her hand over every inch of Duncan's body.

I've been doing nothing but thinking of you. I'm sorry I stormed off. How I wish you would come to me and knock me into shape, ha ha. Seriously, I want you to. I've thought about it and I want you to. Just don't leave any marks.

Elizabeth used to think Jasmine so artificial, with her whirl of blonde hair, incapable of real feeling. But her letters are full of passion, twisted but true. As the letters go on, Elizabeth cringes for Jasmine, cringes for her contrition and servility. Sometimes there is a spark of anger, but it fades immediately.

> Nothing hurts more than not seeing you, I'll bear anything if I can see you. You want her to stand by and wave a palm fan as we fuck, then change your stinking sheets afterwards? You want me to pretend to be her so that you can rape me? I don't care. I'm stupid. I love you.

The writer is enslaved.

> Rape me then, as long as I can adore you. Rape me a thousand times and each time I'll answer to your sister's name.

It is the last letter and Elizabeth lets it fall from her hand. The egg, she realises, is gone. Duncan must have thrown it away. He never loved Jasmine. She was nothing more than his voodoo doll, something he could hurt. He is incapable of loving. Elizabeth sits among the scatter of letters. *Beast, Beast, my lovely Beast.* The words throb in her throat and wrists. She breathes to their beat.

Then she hears a heavier breathing. Duncan must have decided not to stay the night at the hospital after all. She can't meet his eyes. If she does, something terrible will happen. All their lives, they have never fully lost their tempers. But she can't help it. She looks.

Duncan wraps his hands in her hair and bangs her forehead to the floor. When he grabs her shoulders, she strains her neck to sink her teeth into his hand. He pulls back for a moment, in surprise as much as pain, and she twists around and shoves his chest. They struggle violently, and somehow she is on top straddling him. He grips her knees and looks her in the eye. She looks at his mouth. His top lip is swollen, wider than the bottom one. He always had the mouth of a Roman emperor nursing secret vices. She cannot bear his gaze, and his touch makes her tingle with shame.

She finds the pressure point on his neck and presses on it as hard as she can. He gags violently, but she pushes down harder, feeling the muscular column of his throat under the skin. She keeps pressing until his eyes close and he stops moving.

A wash of nothingness sweeps over her. He lies with chin tilted up, his dark hair flowing back from his forehead. She realises that she will see this face for ever, as if it was the last thing she saw before dying herself. There will be nothing in her mind but this sight, day and night.

And then Duncan opens his eyes. He must have been out for only thirty seconds or so, but in that time Elizabeth has contemplated his face for all eternity. She starts and steps back. Her brother blinks and curls his fingers. She only bore down hard enough to make him pass out, after all. He looks at her with a questioning face, but then he remembers. Duncan staggers to his feet and as he does so, she runs, down the stairs and out into the night.

After a couple of hours, Elizabeth calls home from a phone box, wet to the skin and shaking. She ran out without a coat and she is so cold that the blood has retreated from her extremities. Her fingertips are numb and she can hardly press the number. A wind has come up and the threshing trees are losing their last leaves. She has been walking the streets, circling the same blocks several times, keeping away from main roads. Her mother answers.

'Oh, it's you, darling! Where is everybody? I bought some treats from Marks and I've got dinner all ready.'

'Isn't Duncan home?'

'No. In fact when I got home the door was wide open and the house was freezing. Not to mention the danger. I had to get one of the neighbours to take a look round before I felt safe.'

'Oh, Mum, I'm sorry, I'm so sorry.' She realises she is about to cry, takes a deep breath, lies. 'I just went to the pub with Jasper. I'll be home in half an hour.'

'I'll see you in a bit then,' says her mother placidly.

When Elizabeth gets back, she pauses outside the house for a minute, checking for Duncan's car, but it's not there. Somehow he must have managed to pick himself up and slink away. She doesn't know whether he is capable of renting a place or holding down a job, doesn't know what will happen to him. But he won't be back. Like a struck bell, she still shudders from his touch.

14

Hotel Infinity

Elizabeth helps her mother heat up the food for dinner and they eat it in front of the news. After they've finished, she's trying to work out how to tell her mother that Duncan won't be coming home when she sees that her mother's face is empty and her eyes are wide. The storm has devastated parts of England. A shot of rescuers lifting a baby in a cradle from the flood. A homeowner looking bemused at his roofless house. Trees and telephone wires down, cars almost beneath the water. Elizabeth is frozen. Then she feels numb and capable. She gets up and pats her mother's shoulder. 'I'll phone the coastguard,' she says.

'We've had a couple of wrecks,' says the coastguard. 'Let me take a look.'

'It's *The Black Pig*,' Elizabeth repeats. There is a long pause.

'Well, the good news is, it hasn't been washed up in pieces. The bad news is, it ain't in the marina.'

'What does that mean? It's not necessarily bad, is it? I mean, he could easily have taken the boat somewhere else.' There is another pause.

'It's possible,' the coastguard says. The storm has swept across the whole of Britain and her father had never sailed

190

outside its perimeter. But he might have done, this once. Perhaps left early enough to miss it altogether and is now far away. For the first time, Elizabeth hopes he is not alone. She hopes he has sailed off with the red-haired fish woman. The fish woman would have made a competent sailor. Maybe at this very minute she is wearing a bikini with anchors embroidered on it and they are drinking piña coladas and making puns in some exotic resort. And right now, Elizabeth wouldn't blame him. Even if he bought the boat with money that wasn't his, even if he ran away on it, leaving his debts behind. After all, who wouldn't choose to escape from her mother? A woman who has spent half her life in a dead man's arms.

Elizabeth and her mother stand on the dock looking at the empty spot where *The Black Pig* was moored. The rain has stopped, but the sky is still bruised. The forecasters are predicting a new pulse of the storm. When the wind blows, the boat masts clatter like knives and forks. The place is almost deserted, except for one or two weather-beaten men in thick jerseys, making sure their sails are lashed down and all their cabin windows tightly closed. The storm has made some of these casual sailors decide that the end of the season has come, and some boats are already standing bottom-up in the shipyard, waiting to be scraped of barnacles, caulked and varnished for next year.

The local pub, the Jolly Tar, is one of the few that have not yet been gentrified or turned into yuppie bars. There are shabby leather seats and ringed oak tables, polished horse brasses hanging on the wall. Amid a cloud of smoke and beer fumes, red-faced men are jostling at the bar. Behind it, a naked cardboard woman reveals a little more of her breasts each time a packet of peanuts is torn away. Elizabeth leaves her mother at a table and elbows her way up to the front.

A man jostles her and says, 'Sorry, love.' She looks up.

'Oh, hello, then,' he says. 'How's your old dad?' It's one of her father's friends, an old one whose number in the address book was out of date. His eyes are very blue in his red face.

'He's away at the moment,' she says.

'Oh yeah, right you are. He left about a month ago.'

She draws in her breath. 'Did you see him go?'

'Sure. Took off by himself this time, left his old mates high and dry. Heard him singing as he motored out the marina.'

'There was no one with him, then?'

'Pretty sure he was on his own.' The man looks at her. 'Everything all right?' She nods, tries to smile. No wisecracking mermaid, then, no shipmate at all. But her relief sours. Her father was too absent-minded to be an expert sailor. He wore a paper crown from his office Christmas party on the train home from work, and didn't understand why people laughed at him. He mislaid his sandwiches only to find them later, half-eaten and squashed inside the photocopier. Alone, he would forget things. Maybe one of them had been essential. Her eyes prick and she takes a deep breath and says, 'Oh well, I'm sure he'll turn up.'

The man's face crinkles in concern and he pats her arm. 'I know your old dad. He'll be back. That's right, stiff upper lip.' Her face trembles.

Her father never really got along with his mates. They wanted to win races, to conquer distant landmarks up the coast, and he wanted to contemplate the sea. But in the evenings, when the boat was moored and they sat together in the pub, he struggled to be like the others. 'I've found this male-bonding thing quite challenging,' he said to Elizabeth, after one trip. 'But I think I'm getting there. You stare into your pint. Then after a bit, you say, "Shall I get another round then?" That's all. Anything more is fatal. Fatal.' He shook his head.

'It doesn't sound like much fun,' she replied.

'Oh no,' he protested. 'It's a profound bond. When we gaze into our pints, we're thinking about the mystery of the sea, the enigmatic deeps. Look at the Scandinavians. Nothing to look at but the fjords, and they gave us Strindberg and Ibsen. There's something about a body of water,' he concluded, 'that makes you contemplate your own mortality.' He didn't even know the man overboard drill, he had never bothered to learn it. He always wanted to voyage around the world like his heroes, but he was a philosopher, a romantic, not a real sailor.

In his office, the coastguard doesn't look at Elizabeth or her mother. He keeps glancing out his grimy window at the sea. There is a calendar on the wall with a picture of a white-and-grey bird on it. A mug of cooling tea. A desk piled with nautical manuals, scribbled forms weighted down with a lady made out of shells, a clamshell for a skirt and two pearly sea-snail shells for breasts. A map of the coastline is tacked to the wall, pale blue and green, with coloured pins stuck in it. A radio crackles with news from rescue teams.

Elizabeth stares at the calendar. The caption reads: *In the far north, Arctic terns nest on bare rocky islands and fish in ice-filled bays.* The coastguard follows her eyes. 'Are you interested in birds?' he asks. 'That tern winters in the Antarctic, making one of the lengthiest migrations of any bird. It takes the long route, no one knows why. It's actually shorter to go via Africa.' Elizabeth gives a small smile. It is one of those bits of illogic her father liked, indications that things don't quite make sense, proof that there is a joke in the universe's sleeve. Then she realises that the coastguard is trying to avoid the subject.

'Is there anything you can do?' she asks. 'Anything at all you can think of?' He coughs and fiddles with the base of the clamshell woman. A single sequin is glued modestly to the centre of each breast.

'Can't really help you two ladies,' he says. 'Haven't had any radio reports from him. Didn't sign out. Dunno where he went.' He turns back towards them and at last looks Elizabeth in the eye. 'Mystery to me,' he says. *Dad, Dad, Dad*, thinks Elizabeth. She has seen it in the coastguard's eyes. He thinks her father is dead. Her father tried to sail off on some great voyage, and is drowned, lost. And it wasn't the storm. It was something small, some little thing he would have missed. He tried to trail his hand in the water and a wave pitched him in, or he forgot that he had left the gas in the cabin on.

On the way back to the car, her mother shivers. 'I hate that horrible clattering,' she says, as the masts rattle in the wind. As they get in, they feel the first rain on their faces. Elizabeth fiddles with the radio, tunes it to a station playing country and western music.

> *Bye bye baby that's the last I'll see of you.*
> *Shoebox full of old love letters,*
> *I'll tear each one till I feel better,*
> *And I won't look back 'cause I don't like the view.*
> *What my heart needs now is rest,*
> *So I'm packin' up and headed West.*

Her mother winces. 'Do we have to listen to this?'
'I like it.'
'Oh, Elizabeth.' Her mother looks reproachful. 'You can't really like it.'
'I do! Sometimes there's skilful wordplay, and there's real passion. It's about broken hearts and the home you left behind and the call of the road.'
'It's easy emotion. Not like opera.'
'Opera! Opera is the primary colours of emotion! It's about the easiest emotion there is!' After Elizabeth has spoken, her mother falls silent. Elizabeth stares out the

window and watches the wind blow the rain into ellipses on the glass. *Is he dead?* What is wrong with easy emotion, anyway, thinks Elizabeth. Why does it have to be difficult? *Is he dead?*

Her father was the only one her mother would have listened to. If only he had spoken sharp words for once, then perhaps she might have ceased to act the invalid, perhaps he would have stayed. But he didn't understand. He thought her problem was something he could fix with a little lubrication and soldering, like a dripping tap, or a loose hinge. Just a matter of tea and sympathy. But nothing he did worked. He didn't understand that she needed *help*.

If Spencer knew about this, he would take it briskly in hand. He would arrange a confrontation, as with a wayward alcoholic. For him, the world can be understood. He can look inside a body and fish in its intestines for a tumour. Things make sense, and there aren't any mysteries. There would be treatment and cure.

But her mother does not want to let go of her misery. That is *easy emotion* if there ever was any. She huddles under its soft black wing. She is looked after, she does not have to try. She has never tasted life, except for a few short years in her youth. Her mother refuses to swim in the sea, she will not walk barefoot on grass. Like Elizabeth Barrett Browning, she has led a life small and circumscribed. Elizabeth wants to take her by the shoulders and shake her, shout, like the photographer: 'Come on! Give me some happy now!'

And what about Elizabeth herself? Has she loved her mother's tragedy too, even before she knew what it was? Has she proudly borne that cross? She should have done something about her mother years ago.

'Have you thought of taking some medication?' For a moment, Elizabeth can't believe she's spoken aloud. Her mother knows at once what she is talking about.

'I'm not putting chemicals in my body,' she says.

'Why not? They've done research, they've run tests. It's perfectly safe.'

'It's too easy. Easy to say you're mad and get some pills to cure it.'

'Well, maybe you should try talking to someone.' Having got this far, Elizabeth does not dare say the word *therapist*.

'It's not about talking to someone or taking a pill. It's about whether you can grow up or not. Growing up, as you may not have realised yet, Elizabeth, means learning to grin and bear it. The world's not a very nice place, and sooner or later, you just have to accept that.'

'Yeah, yeah,' says Elizabeth. Spencer has broken her open, so that love and anger and indifference run from her and she can no longer hold them in. She doesn't shy from confrontation, or feel ashamed of weeping. 'Soldier on with your stiff upper lip. The world's a vale of tears. That's just not *true*! You don't have to accept it!' She is shouting. She wants, she realises, something operatic, weeping and screaming. She wants them to keen together, like women in a Greek tragedy. But her mother won't. Then she speaks, in a small voice.

'Don't you leave me too.'

'I won't, Mum.' Elizabeth's voice breaks in a sob.

'Yes, you will. Children always do.'

'I won't!' She knows what her mother is saying. Someone must remain and look after her. *Don't get married, stay with me always. A life is the only payment that matches a daughter's debt.* Her mother, she realises, will never change. There will be no pills, no therapy, no confession, no catharsis. She has her lovely moods of generosity and rapture. But they always fade.

Elizabeth decides not to think about what her promise means. Her mother and her in the creaking house, two places at the table where five of them once sat. 'I won't leave you,' she insists. And her father, a new guest at Hotel Infinity.

15

The Electric Ballroom

FOR THREE DAYS, ELIZABETH does nothing but tie up sugared almonds in coloured twists of tissue paper and watch daytime television. Each twist is a wish, a petal cast upon the waves, a flower to appease the gods. She doesn't know where else to look for him now. His boat and his business have both vanished without a trace, without a single hook on which to pull.

She imagines that her father is lining up the pink plastic elephants from successive cocktails and making them march in a line to drink from the mermaid woman's gin-filled navel. She imagines that they are eating fried potatoes huddled under the same blanket, waking to the snort of whales among icebergs lit with chemical blue.

Her mother sleeps until late, wanders around in her bathrobe with her unwashed hair straggling on her shoulders. She forgets her slippers and her feet turn violet. She has stopped tinkering with the wedding menu or contemplating appropriate wines, but she still looks at bridal magazines. She hunches over them almost as if the wedding has become all hers and is nothing to do with Elizabeth. She would probably go ahead with it, thinks Elizabeth, even if she herself refused to be present, her mother a stubborn child pouring tea for guests of air.

Elizabeth thinks of phoning Jasper and asking him to walk her down the aisle instead. She thinks of calling Spencer and telling him the wedding is off. Instead, she doesn't do anything. She doesn't even tell her mother that her son is gone, and her mother doesn't ask where he is. She and her mother are in denial. Spencer never realised that denial could be a good thing, hard comfort to suck on, rock on which to clamp.

The phone rings on the afternoon of the third day. Her father has been gone for at least thirteen days now, the wedding is in three. Elizabeth feels first disappointment then relief when she realises that it is the upstairs phone.

'Is Jazz there?' Elizabeth hangs up. The phone rings again immediately. She snatches it up. Why must Jasmine always intrude on her loves and griefs?

'What?' she shouts.

'Elizabeth? Is that you, my dear girl?' She recognises the voice. The affected style and lilting tones of an opera singer doing recitative.

'Mr Silk,' she says.

'Jasmine wanted me to phone and ask if she stashed any pills there before she went on her travels. She can't find her drugs and is in a flutter.'

'In a flap,' Elizabeth corrects him. 'Anyway, I can't help you. My brother might be able to, but he doesn't live here any more.'

'I know,' Valentino says. 'The two of you look quite alike.'

'Have you seen Duncan?'

'He was round here asking for somebody. The boy on the front door.'

'Ally?' she asks breathlessly.

'That's right. He said he had something to tell Ally.'

'And where's Jasmine?'

'With Ally. That's where she's staying.'

'Did you tell my brother that?'

'I may have mentioned it,' says Valentino airily. 'Why, should I not have done?'

Duncan will go straight there. It doesn't matter that he crushed Jasmine's egg and doesn't love her. He won't allow her to be with the man who slept with her and then punched him. She sees Jasmine and Ally walking home in the pill-spangled small hours, Duncan standing in the shadows with a flick knife in his sleeve.

'You low-life pimp,' Elizabeth says. 'You mother-fucker. Do you realise what you've done?'

'Hey!' says Valentino. 'I thought you were a nice girl and I always liked you. I don't know where you picked up this street talk. But let me tell you something. I did your brother a big favour. You should be thanking me. In any case, this must be goodbye.'

'What?' Elizabeth is not really listening. She is wondering what the favour was.

'I am leaving this damp little island.'

'Why?' He has got her attention now.

'Oh,' he says vaguely. 'For a more temperate climate. To pursue some of my other interests. My establishment can do quite well without me. It's very different. Hip. Funky. It's called the Electric Ballroom now. We do videos. Jasmine's been very good, ever since she got back from Thailand. She just went on stage, as a matter of fact.'

Elizabeth sees Jasmine with heavily made-up Egyptian eyes and bejewelled navel, contorting into impossible poses, and groped by men twice her age. For the first time in her life, she feels sorry for Jasmine. All at once, Elizabeth resolves to help her escape Duncan. She will get to Jasmine first. She will fling a coat over her and the two of them will escape in a taxi. She will give Jasmine aspirins and hot milk and put her to sleep in the spare room. Here is something she can set to rights, the one person she can bring home.

If Jasmine can forgive Duncan, then Elizabeth can forgive Jasmine.

The blue awning has gone, and so has the photograph of the hotel interior. The door has been hastily painted black, and the varnished wood beneath shows through. A skinny young man with a reddish goatee is standing in front of it, clad in baggy trousers and a hooded sweatshirt and a black fleece with silver trim. He bobs up and down on the balls of his feet as the beat pounds through the doors.

'What happened to the awning and that? Is it different inside?' Elizabeth asks.

'Yeah, it's all gone. Never liked it anyway. Velvet drapes, little red chairs, gilt and shit. All at the bottom of the North Sea with the fucking pollution.' He hops up and down. Acne scars stitch his cheeks.

'Oh. Well, can I go in?'

'What's the password?'

'I know Mr Silk. The manager. The ex-manager.' She hadn't thought to dress up, her mind was full of Jasmine. She is wearing jeans and her winter coat.

'Yeah, yeah, but what's the password?' There is a twinkle in his eye. He blows a few notes into an invisible saxophone.

'Jazz,' she says.

'Open sesame.' He pulls open the black door with a mock bow, and the music blares forth.

The gold walls have been painted a light-absorbing matt black and the hotel trappings have been ripped out. The place seems cavernous, its vast floor crammed with dancers. The pillars that used to sprout from the stage have been shorn off and there is a girl dancing on every lopped top. Each girl gyrates among the rays of light, a magician's assistant in a box of swords. Now a video of the dancers is projected on a white screen behind the stage. One of them is Jasmine. She raises her arms and jerks her hips. She is wearing a crop top and her hair is long again. Perhaps it's some deficiency in the projection that makes her look thin and faded.

Elizabeth peers across the floor, but she can't see the real Jasmine. Still with her coat on, she presses through the crowd. Puckish boys in shrunken T-shirts. Girls with glitter on their eyelids, stars and moons stuck to their cheekbones. Hands trail across her body as she passes, languid as seaweed. But no one is groping or kissing or stripping any more.

Then Elizabeth sees long blonde hair and taps a shoulder. But the girl who turns round is not Jasmine. She has a pale, glittering face. As if she is from another planet, she touches Elizabeth's hair with gentle wonder. The room is heady with a safe, chemical love. The Ballroom is nothing but a vast womb, Elizabeth thinks, complete with throbbing beat. Is that why Jasmine stays here? Why can't she grow up? But, Elizabeth realises, neither she nor Duncan have managed to do so either.

Jasmine is elbowing her way through the crowd. Elizabeth looks down at her feet, half-expecting to see the red shoes, but she is wearing scuffed pink trainers. And her hair is yellow and dry as straw. The dye she always used has ruined it. She doesn't look as if she could ever have worn red heels or danced for Duncan.

'Are you all right?' shouts Elizabeth. 'Has Duncan been here?'

'No,' shouts Jasmine. 'Is he coming?' Her eyes light up. Elizabeth feels that somehow things are all wrong. Jasmine should be afraid. She takes Jasmine's elbow and guides her to a corner where three girls are lying on beanbags with beatific expressions on their faces and bottles of Evian water tipping in their hands. It is quiet enough for them to talk.

'He's found out about you and Ally,' Elizabeth says. 'I think he's going to come here and try to do something.'

'What are you talking about? There's nothing between me and Ally. Duncan knows that.'

'Then why did they have a fight?'

'Duncan and I were having a bit of a tiff.' Jasmine looks at her lap. 'It was no big deal. But Ally saw us and came over all macho, trying to protect me. He told Duncan to leave me the fuck alone and Duncan tried to clobber him. Ally gave Duncan a black eye. And Duncan blamed me.'

'But then why are you staying with Ally? Why didn't you go home when you got back from Thailand?' Jasmine wriggles on her beanbag.

'My dad's pissed off because I dropped out of fashion school and went back to dancing. Said I lived only for pleasure. He thinks I'm an airhead. Ally's sweet. He let me have his bed. He makes me boiled eggs with toast soldiers. My friends are my family now.'

'At least it's just dancing, not stripping you're doing these days.'

'I never stripped.'

'Jasmine, I came here and did your job one night. You had to peel off your school uniform, then toss it at leering businessmen.'

Valentino carefully gathered up the uniform afterwards. Elizabeth had forgotten how much she herself enjoyed it. She wonders if anyone clung to her tights or her blouse, burying their faces in her girlish odours.

'Well, if you did that, then you're a sucker,' Jasmine tells her. 'You didn't have to take your clothes off if you didn't want to. Especially not me and my friends. Just the mere fact that we actually were sixteen instead of grown women pretending drove the punters crazy.'

'Valentino told me you did stuff,' says Elizabeth, shifting. The beanbag forces her into a relaxed pose she does not feel.

'Did he? He was just winding you up.'

'But what about Thailand?'

'I went there for my course. Thai massage. It's really interesting. You get to walk on people's spines. It's amazing how all the emotions are concentrated in the back. I'm not going to do this all my life, you know.' Elizabeth stares at Jasmine. Jasmine digs in her pockets and takes out a plastic vial, unscrews it and puts a tiny round white pill on her tongue.

'You found your pills then,' says Elizabeth.

'I can't speak. Got to let it dissolve.' Jasmine flutters her fingers at Elizabeth and blinks. Elizabeth takes the vial from Jasmine's hand and looks at it. It's a homeopathic remedy for stress, the image of a posy of flowers above the dosage instructions. The three girls on the beanbags have formed a circle and begun to plait each other's hair.

'Homeopathy's great,' says Jasmine. 'Hey, I haven't said congratulations. Duncan told Ally you were getting married.' She picks up Elizabeth's hand and examines the ring minutely. 'It's really, really tasteful,' she says. She pauses. 'Did Duncan get my postcard? The box I left? I thought maybe he didn't.'

'Yes,' says Elizabeth.

'Oh.' Jasmine looks down. Her sigh is inaudible but Elizabeth sees her shoulders rise and fall. She always thought that witnessing Jasmine's rejection would be a moment of triumph, but it isn't.

'I don't know where he is,' she tells Jasmine.

'He's house-sitting for Valentino. He was here a few days ago. He didn't come in to see me, he came to apologise to Ally. Ally was just trying to protect me and Duncan really flew off the handle. It was really Duncan who started the fight. But they've sorted it out now. They had a nice chat and Ally promised to get Duncan some weed. He can tell you how to get to Valentino's. He's on the door tonight.'

'That's Ally?' says Elizabeth. That jumpy redhead with pitted skin?

'Do you think I should go and see Duncan?' asks Jasmine, not listening to her.

'No,' says Elizabeth, looking Jasmine in the eye. Then she gets up to go. Jasmine reaches up from the beanbag and clasps Elizabeth's wrist.

'*You're* going to see him, aren't you?'

'Yes. But you're better off without him,' Elizabeth says. She curls her fingers awkwardly around Jasmine's hand for a second and lets go.

'Leaving already?' says the young man at the door. 'Tired of our magic lantern show?'

'I thought you'd look different,' she says. 'I'm Elizabeth. We spoke on the phone. Sorry if I got the wrong end of the stick.'

'You shouldn't judge people,' says Ally. 'It's like branding.'

'What?' She shifts from foot to foot impatiently. It's cold and she's in no mood for Ally's philosophy. But he doesn't seem to notice.

'When Mr Silk rebranded the business, he wanted it to be associated with a couple of keywords: "Modern" and "Hip". That's how branding works. You present things very simply. But what most people don't realise, is that's how we perceive personality too.' Elizabeth rubs her hands together and tries to think of a polite way of interrupting. But Ally warms to his theme. 'Rather than attempt to fathom the mystery of another person, we choose two or three key words to describe him. Look at you and me. You branded me and refused to see who I really am. You decided I was Sleazy and Underhand. You branded Jasmine too. And she's just a sensitive flower.'

'Sorry.' Elizabeth decides that meekness will be the quickest route to escape. Ally seems mollified.

'Your brother's a bit of a psycho, but he's all right. I forgave him. Peace and love. And I've got the stuff he wanted.'

Ally rummages in the pockets of his khaki-coloured trousers, peels off his fleece to grope inside his sweatshirt. A water bottle is strapped to his waist. He is dressed as if the city was an impending nuclear disaster. His copious trousers, with drawstrings at their cuffs, seem designed to become a parachute if necessary. He discovers a small plastic-wrapped bundle inside his boot. He is about to hand it to Elizabeth but then he pauses.

'Listen, did Jasmine talk about me at all?'

'I need to find my brother,' she says.

'But she must've said something.'

'Just give me the address,' Elizabeth says, snatching the little packet. She's not interested in Ally's passions. What matters is that Jasmine has apologised to Duncan and Duncan to Ally. Even if a little crookedly, the important things have been resolved, as in a Shakespearean comedy.

But in the taxi on the way to Valentino's house, Elizabeth trembles, scrunching the little bag between her fingers. So Jasmine's Mirror Face was just the haughty stare she put on for the world. And Jasmine wanted to be Elizabeth just as much as Elizabeth wanted to be her. The way things always have been now seems obvious, enormous but hidden, like lovers mapped in stars. Some ancient saga ending badly.

Elizabeth steps on to a porch tiled with black and white diamonds and a brass lantern clicks on automatically. She stands there, frozen.

'Don't be a fool, Wellington.' Duncan is in the hall, and now he opens the door, then walks back into the house leaving her to follow. She shuts the door and climbs up the stairs after him. Her legs feel heavy and she can hardly breathe.

He takes her into a room with a polished wood floor, white sofas, a Moroccan rug. A glass coffee table holds a crystal ashtray, an African sculpture of curving stone.

Leather-bound books with gold titles line the shelves. *The Iliad. The Odyssey. Paradise Lost. Beowulf.* French windows look out on to a lit balcony, an enclosed garden.

'Valentino had to skip town,' says Duncan. 'Cops found out what was in the Turkish coffee and shit came down. Thanks to you, he set me up.' He nods.

Their eyes meet and Elizabeth realises that he isn't going to say anything, neither kill her nor embrace her. He isn't going to apologise. And neither is she. Their honour has been satisfied.

'I had a job interview,' he says. 'A job designing computer games.'

'How did you manage that? So quickly, I mean?' Too late, she realises her incredulity isn't flattering.

'Thanks a lot.' Duncan frowns. 'Don't you think I'll get it?'

Elizabeth remembers what she used to say to herself when they were young. *He's the good-looking child, but I'm the clever one.* And her parents thought it too. Elizabeth thinks of the weather couple in old barometers, the man came out when it was raining and the woman came out when it was sunny. But they never could come out together. It is as if Duncan had to stay simply because Elizabeth left, and when she returned, he was free to go. He was shaped by her as surely as she was shaped by him. Forced to conform to the dichotomy that had been set up long ago. *The good daughter and the wayward son.* It wasn't even their parents' fault. They always wanted to be opposites, holding aloof from each other, to be as unique as possible. Elizabeth used to be jealous that Duncan had the better deal, but now she realises that neither of them did. Each one cramped in their chosen role.

'The company said they were impressed by my extensive knowledge.' He gives an awkward grin. The awkwardness gives Elizabeth a pang. She wants to say, *You're clever too. Let's share!*

'And running into Valentino when I went to see Ally. Nice bit of good fortune.' Duncan grins, and Elizabeth thinks of his old luck, of coins tumbling into his hands from the fruities.

He peers out into the night. 'Gonna get a barbie out there in the spring and grill stuff.' He pauses. 'You can come over if you want.' He looks around. 'I'd offer you something if I had anything.'

'I got your dope,' she says, extracting the packet from her coat pocket. Duncan looks at her.

'We could smoke it.'

'Sure, why not?' She prides herself on her American ease. *Yes, I'll hang out for a while. Even though three days ago I tried to kill you.*

Shrugging, he extracts a fake cigarette from his pocket and packs the painted wooden tube with weed. He takes the first drag and the smoke smells of fresh basil and dark chocolate. He pats the couch beside him for her to sit and hands her the trick cigarette. They pass it back and forth.

Elizabeth can't quite believe in Duncan's gruff hospitality, his fragile plans. But he has never been able to hide his moods. Maybe this change is real. Maybe when people change it never quite makes sense, even to them. You wake up one morning with a sense of some subterranean shift. Moved to a new perspective like a piece on a board. And wherever you are moved affects where everyone else is moved. Elizabeth has a sense of many threadlike connections, tantalising analogies, if only she could catch hold of one. 'I feel sleepy,' she says, sliding down on the sofa to rest her head on its arm.

'Look at you, you're wilting all over the place,' says Duncan. 'It's weird, I feel like I don't know you any more. I don't know shit about your life in America.'

'Let's not talk about America,' says Elizabeth, waving the fake cigarette. She doesn't want to talk about Spencer or think about later. 'Dad used to say people are impossible to understand, like irrational numbers. Each time we think we've got each other pegged we see a new stretch going on ahead.'

'Where *is* Dad?' says Duncan. Elizabeth realises that he assumes she knows. She shakes her head. When they played the Funeral Game, her father chose a Viking ceremony, pushed out to sea in a flaming ship. But there isn't any body.

'It's not like you to be so concerned,' she says. 'What have you done with the old Duncan? You're acting like a pod person.' Immediately, she realises she's gone too far. Duncan scowls and stamps out of the room. All she wanted to do was get back their foolish mood. All she wanted was for the precious substance to burn away as slowly as possible.

Elizabeth staggers up to go the bathroom. There's an old-fashioned claw-foot tub and a stained toilet the colour of a decaying tooth. The plumbing is old, a disadvantage that comes with the ornate high ceilings. The medicine cabinet contains nothing but a tub of rose-coloured hair wax, an old toothbrush with splayed hairs, and a medicine vial with a typed label. Elizabeth makes a mental note of the name. *Halperidol*. Then she wets the brush and cleans her teeth with water. Her mouth is dry and her teeth fuzzy.

When she sees Duncan's eyes in the mirror, she freezes with his brush in her mouth. She was too dizzy to close the door, and does not know how long he has been there. He has changed too fast and she doesn't believe in it, doesn't believe that he could simply step from that life to this in three days. He has the uncertain eyes of a boy brought up by wolves. He doesn't move and she begins brushing again, one eye on him. Hate has warmed them for so long, summer fire smouldering under the grass. She leans down and spits pink froth. Her gums have begun to bleed recently. When she stands up again, he's not there any more, and it's cold.

16

The Anchor

It is very early, a little after dawn, and the sky is still clouded the thin white of skimmed milk. The birds are just beginning to sing in the wet trees when Elizabeth and Duncan let themselves in. It was so late when she got up to go that she stayed at Valentino's place in the end, wrapped in her coat on the sofa. By the time they went to bed it was after four, and she is light-headed from too little sleep.

The house is quiet and they take their shoes off and creep down to the kitchen. For some reason, the back door is wide open and the kitchen is cold. The grass outside is misted with frost, and as they look out over the lawn, they see their father and mother standing in the meditation garden. Her father is scraping at the ground with a spade, in the place where the fountain used to be, and her mother is plucking dead leaves from the rose bush that he had tried to train over the arched entrance to his garden. In his absence it has sprawled over the unraked gravel. As they watch, a plume of water shoots up and her father leaps back. The water is nearly the same height as him. Her mother says something. She always got angry with their father for breaking things and leaving them broken, or for not fixing them properly, patching them up with string and tape when he should have used nails and solder. He never cared. He always claimed there was a kink in the universe anyway, you only had to look at the meniscus on a glass of water, or to consider the knobbly awkwardness of pi. In his eyes, the universe cranked onwards like an antique bicycle and a few more scratches and squeakings didn't matter. But her mother has always wept at minor accidents, yearned for perfection. Elizabeth's hopes wither as she looks at her parents walking up the lawn and crossing the terrace. They linger there for a moment, and their conversation can be heard.

'It was meant to be understated and Japanese,' says their father. 'I ruined it. I think I broke off some crucial stopper with the edge of the spade.'

'I never liked it anyway,' says her mother. She pauses. 'It's nicer now.'

'I ruined it,' repeats her father sadly.

'Cheer up, darling. Think of it as Italian instead.'

Their father brightens. 'A temple to Venus and spurting passion!' He squeezes their mother's waist.

'Don't be so silly,' she says, blushing.

'Good God!' says their father, starting when he sees the two of them waiting. He is thin and peeling with sunburn. He hugs Elizabeth.

'Duncan, you're back,' says her mother, patting his shoulder.

'I didn't know you knew he'd gone,' says Elizabeth.

Her father squeezes Duncan's arm.

'All right, Dad,' Duncan says, dodging back and grinning.

'I need some coffee,' says their mother.

Is that it? thinks Elizabeth. *Is that how children and parents greet each other after heart-rending absences?* Is it because her family is not demonstrative like Americans? Or is it because they don't want complete union, prolonged embrace? But perhaps that's how it should be. Absolute love is out of place in the family and should be kept for one's beloved. With a lover, after all, no display of affection is cloying or forbidden. Or maybe it's a self-protective instinct, not to love a sibling or a parent with an unfettered heart. After all, one of you must die far sooner, or one of you must change and leave.

'Who needs coffee?' cries their father. 'Let's crack open the champagne!' He prances out and returns with one of the bottles bought for the wedding. 'I know what would make this little celebration perfect!' he cries, wrestling with the cork. 'There's only one thing that goes with champagne better than oysters, and that's egg and chips.'

'Oh, darling,' says their mother. 'Champagne and egg and chips?'

'An unlikely but perfect match. Like King Edward and Mrs Simpson. Speaking of unconventional marriages,' their father adds, 'where *is* Elizabeth's American?'

'He's flying in today,' says Elizabeth, getting out plates. Her father rolls up his sleeves and starts humming to himself, melting butter in a pan and rummaging in the fridge and everyone begins to bustle about except Duncan, who throws himself into a chair and hunches at the table. When her father offers him the bottle he shrugs it away, although he usually likes the task of opening champagne.

'I need a Bloody Mary,' he says.

'Oh, I forgot, champagne's a girl's drink,' says their father. 'Or maybe you need something a bit stronger to dull the shock of seeing me.' He gives an impish grin, seizes the vodka, unscrews the top. He peers in and gives it a sniff. 'What do you think of that, Elizabeth?' he asks. 'Is it off?' The vodka is plugged with scummy black stuff. The morning after Jasmine and Duncan first kissed, Elizabeth had topped it up with water, and now it smells like a brackish pond.

Duncan sits down at the kitchen table and begins to pick off the gold foil from the top of the champagne bottle with a harassed look in his eyes. He shaved before they came out and it has irritated his skin. She can't imagine him holding down a job that requires rising before noon or taking orders from a boss. But maybe he will. He will fill his games with fire-swallowing assassins and expert knife-throwers, and they, instead of him, will dance with danger. His real life will be safe and predictable. Toasted cheese sandwiches in Valentino's house in front of the satellite football, shy dates with female colleagues. Elizabeth inverts the bottle over the sink and watches the vodka pour away. Once it tasted like lighter fuel, like the pure essence of fire.

Her father raises his glass. 'Here's to Elizabeth and Spencer,' he says. After everyone has drunk the toast, Duncan gets up, pulling out some crumpled pieces of paper from his pocket. He laboriously unfolds them and clears his throat. He stares at the papers for a minute, then he puts them down on the table before him. 'I spent all night trying to think of the right thing to say,' he says. 'I wanted to make a speech at the wedding and I made all these notes. But I couldn't get it quite right, so I'll just say my piece now. It's not good enough for Spencer and all your guests and that anyway.' He picks up his notes and balls them in his fist. For a moment Elizabeth thinks that he's not going to say anything more after all. The wolf boy who never became quite comfortable with words. Then he says, in a rush, 'Well, I just wanted to say that we'll all miss you, Elizabeth, and we hope you'll be very happy.'

'Thanks, Duncan!' says Elizabeth, unable to conceal her surprise.

'That was lovely, Duncan, darling,' says their mother. 'Wasn't that lovely?'

'I didn't get it right,' he says. 'It was terrible. I can't put words together like you two and Elizabeth and her bloke.' Elizabeth smiles at him and is about to protest, but he is looking at his plate, frowning furiously and grinding his teeth.

'Just let him be, darling,' says Elizabeth's mother. 'He doesn't like all the attention.'

'So how did *The Black Pig* hold up to the storms?' asks Elizabeth, trying to change the subject.

'Sold it,' says her father airily, taking a swig of champagne.

'But you loved that boat,' she says.

'Sailed her over to France, and sold my brave little vessel to a millionaire in Dieppe. Hand-laid fibreglass hull. Varnished teak panelling and leather upholstery. Unsurprisingly, I got quite a few doubloons. Took the train back and missed the storms, thank God.'

'You sold it for the money?' says their mother. 'We don't need the money.'

'Oh, no, not for the money,' their father replies quickly. 'It's time for me to settle down on dry land and make an honest living. I've had enough of the cruel sea. Did I mention that I decided to close the business? I was thinking of freelancing. Being at sea gave me lots of time to think. I'd be at home more, darling. I'll put my desk and computer in one of the kids' old rooms and turn it into my headquarters. And then we could have little lunches together.' His eyes are cheerful but evasive, and Elizabeth knows what he has done. He sold the boat to help repay his creditors. And he's only telling half the story. He hasn't said why he didn't tell anyone where he was going, but she knows it's because he was considering not coming back. When he left, all he knew was that he wanted to be by himself at sea. She sees him standing at the tiller and gazing across the waves. She sees him eating spaghetti from a can with his feet propped on the cabin table. What did he discover in those hours of silent contemplation? She hopes it was that the ocean was lonely.

'And I got a tattoo,' adds her father.

'You *what*?' Elizabeth says in chorus with her mother. Duncan smirks and her father rolls up his jumper to show them a grey-blue anchor with a chain coiled loosely about it.

'Is it supposed to symbolise something?' asks Duncan.

'Yes, does it represent sailing off or staying put?' says Elizabeth. Her father looks at her. He has aged in the last few weeks, there is more grey in his hair and the sun has wrinkled him. The blue distance has gone from his eyes, the sailor's sway from his step.

Her mother pats his arm and says, 'I'm glad your final voyage was a brave one.' At that he gives a smile and squeezes her mother's hand and then he murmurs something into her hair. It suddenly doesn't matter that he has to lie to her and slave for her. He loves her. Her mother smiles back delightedly and Elizabeth sees the straight-haired slender girl she was, the girl in the leopard-skin coat that her father rescued from the Catholic Home, the girl who fell in love with the man without a temper.

'I need a little shut-eye,' her father announces. 'And your mum needs to catch up on her beauty sleep too.' And her parents slip away upstairs. Spencer is arriving this evening, and the day after next Elizabeth is marrying him.

The doorbell rings an hour or two later, when her parents are still in bed and Duncan has gone back to Valentino's, mumbling something about needing to catch up on his sleep. She opens the door and it's Spencer, dressed in a cotton lumberjack shirt and jeans, his skin golden even here in rain-darkened London, as if the sun of his native deserts still shines on it. He wraps her in his arms and kisses her.

'I couldn't wait,' he says. 'I insisted on getting an extra half-day from the hospital and changed my flight. Then I took a cab here to surprise you.'

'I am surprised,' she says, kissing him all over his face and neck, pulling back to look at him, then kissing him again. With Dax and Quentin, she wanted them for what they could give her. Dax gave her forgetful pain, and Quentin offered an arid sort of education. But she wants Spencer for himself. He is beautiful and kind and adoring and clever and capable. Family love is inexplicable, like a Catholic's knowledge of God. But her love for Spencer makes sense.

'I thought maybe we could get reacquainted before I meet your folks,' he murmurs, and she leads him up to her room. His body is hot and hard and rough as sun-warmed rock. 'I brought the cuffs,' he says, 'to tie you up. I know that's what you like.'

'No, let's not bother with that,' she replies, pushing him down. 'No time for that.'

Afterwards, they lie in the twisted sheets, whispering. Elizabeth is not ready to bring him downstairs yet. Spencer leans out of bed and gropes in his backpack. 'My father wanted me to get these for you as a wedding present. He's sorry he couldn't make it.' Spencer's father felt that he was too old for the long flight. They are going to his ranch after the wedding for Christmas instead.

The gift is a pair of cowboy boots made from delicately mullioned snakeskin. 'So you can dance with me and not get your toes trod on,' Spencer says, 'just like a real cowgirl.'

'I'll have to learn to follow then,' she replies.

'Only on the dance floor. Off the dance floor, you're your own woman.' *Woman* not *girl*. It is the first time anyone has ever referred to Elizabeth as a woman. They will dance together and she will learn how to fix a roof and change a tyre, and apply for the job teaching music at the high school that she saw advertised in the paper. Maybe she will even write some music of her own. Her head fills with plans.

'What have you been up to all this time?' he says, picking up a lock of her hair and twirling it round his finger. 'Busy getting ready for the wedding?'

'Things,' she says vaguely. 'By the way,' she asks, 'what's haloperidol for?' She memorised the name typed on the vial's label.

'Why do you want to know that?'

'It stuck in my head from some newspaper article I was reading about the NHS,' she replies glibly.

'It's a strong tranquilliser. An anti-psychotic drug. For quelling rage, I guess.'

'Oh.' Is that the key to Duncan's sudden transformation, his muted new self? Elizabeth is disappointed to discover that it was just a chemical that dissolved his rage, not his own doing. But then she realises she is being like her mother, expecting everyone to bear their crosses. If a pill can help Duncan make himself a life, then let him swallow it.

In Spencer's honour, Elizabeth's mother opens a jar of caviar from Fortnum & Mason's, and spreads it on little toast triangles with the crusts cut off. She lights the candles in the silver candlesticks and brings up another bottle of champagne from the cellar. She asks Spencer to open it and the cork comes out with an efficient small pop. A faint wisp rises from the bottle, but there's no gush of foam.

'When you let Duncan open the champagne it always shoots out the top like a fountain at Versailles,' says her father.

'Then when you try to pour it out, there's hardly any left,' Elizabeth says.

'Beginner's luck, I guess,' says Spencer. Silence. Despite the candles and champagne, Elizabeth's mother hasn't put on a dress. She's wearing the grey tracksuit that she probably slept in, as if she couldn't forgo this small sign of her reluctance to celebrate. When she met Spencer, he started forward as if to kiss her, but she clasped his hand in hers for an instant, then dropped it.

The door slams and they hear Duncan's boots in the

hall. He comes in and shakes Spencer's hand, then changes his mind and hugs him. He holds the hug for a moment too long, as if once he has Spencer in his grasp he can't decide what to do with him. He is wearing a maroon silk shirt that Elizabeth suspects may belong to Valentino. He rattles a little when he walks, from something in his pocket.

'Thought I'd do it the American way,' Duncan says. Spencer laughs. Elizabeth feels proud of Duncan. Spencer may even mistake her family for a happy one.

'Have some caviar,' says Elizabeth's mother to Spencer. 'I think you'll find it rather special.' The patronising note in her tone is faint but distinct. To Elizabeth, it tastes like mouthfuls of sea water, except that the little eggs pop on the tongue.

'This is good,' says Spencer determinedly. 'It reminds me a little of Pop Rocks. Do you guys have those over here? You know the sugar candy that crackles on your tongue like Rice Krispies?'

'I know what you mean,' says Elizabeth's father. 'Wasn't there some story about a boy who ate five packets of the stuff and drank a Coke, then his stomach exploded and he died? Very tragicomic.'

'I think that was just an urban myth,' says Spencer.

'Oh, what a pity,' Elizabeth's father replies. Spencer looks into his champagne, and her father goes on: 'I've always been amazed that no one has made savoury Pop Rocks. Chicken'n'Gravy Rocks. Corned Beef Hash Rocks. It would probably be wonderful for fat people, because there's only so many popping sweeties you can eat. And it would train them to really savour their food. Mm.'

'It's true that there is an obesity problem in the US,' says Spencer.

'What are you going to do about it?' asks Duncan. 'You are a doctor, aren't you?' Elizabeth frowns at him. Duncan is sitting on the sofa with his legs spread and his arms draped along the back of it, as if trying to take up as much space as possible. His gestures are exaggerated. He must have started drinking earlier.

'I'd advise an overweight patient to watch his diet and exercise regularly,' Spencer replies. It's not that he doesn't have a sense of humour, thinks Elizabeth. After all, the two of them have kissed and tickled and teased each other for hours. But he's always the straight man to her clown. And he doesn't find amusement in this mild, protracted satire, whether of America's fat people or of him. Elizabeth wonders for a moment whether it comes to this: you have to choose between wit and reliability.

Spencer sits in the one armchair and pulls Elizabeth down on to his knee. She would like to perch decorously, but the armchair gives and plunges her deeper into his lap than she would like.

'You see, I think that's the wrong approach, that dry scientific method,' says Duncan, staring at them.

'Spencer doesn't want to talk about Pop Rocks,' her mother interrupts. Then she turns to him, and says: 'I understand you live in a desert.'

'It's beautiful,' Spencer replies. 'You guys should come visit.' There's warmth in his voice, as if he sees the five of them, maybe even Granny too, driving across the great plains in a beat-up VW van, going on mountain hikes and eating potlucks in the backyard.

'Doesn't it get a bit boring?' says her mother. Elizabeth knows that her parents, her mother at least, are too stubborn ever to visit America.

'The sky is always changing,' Spencer replies. 'I never get tired of looking at it. There's a different sunset every night. I could never get bored there.'

'I suppose you've never been to the opera,' says her mother. She wants Elizabeth to move to one of the coastal cities, which at least would be an easier plane flight.

'That's it!' says Elizabeth's father. 'What you should do

with all that unused land is turn all the fat people out to graze there. They'd have to gather their own food, they'd live on nuts and wild grasses.'

'Yeah, they could be let out as soon as they got down to the government-approved weight,' Duncan adds. He never joins in their banter. But this evening the family's jokes interlock like shields.

'Let out?' says Spencer.

'Well, they'd try to escape of course, so you'd put a twenty-foot-high electrical fence around the perimeter.'

'Oh, oh, oh!' cries her father, like a child eager to be called on. 'And the whole thing would be *filmed* as a reality TV show!' Elizabeth laughs. Spencer smiles, but doesn't laugh. No doubt he thought he would be asked eager questions, about his childhood and his future plans. Instead, no one has asked him anything at all, not even how his flight over was. They expected him simply to take part in their teasing. Her family calls it 'picking'. Like pulling open a frayed hem, or digging a nail under a loosening scab. Starting, then making oneself stop, then starting again. Regretting it when it leads to unplanned pain.

'I don't think Spencer finds our theatre of cruelty very amusing.' Elizabeth squeezes his knee. He smiles and shakes his head with polite ambiguity.

'Let me refill your glass, Spencer,' says her mother. It's only half empty. He sits up as if to demur, but she fills it up to the top anyway. For her mother, the appreciation and consumption of fine wine is the mark of cultured man. For her father, it's conversation. This is civilisation for them, thinks Elizabeth: refreshment and mockery, these mild Roman games.

There is a silence. Duncan tosses his champagne down his throat, blinks, and gives a quiet belch.

'Could you not be uncouth?' says Elizabeth.

'What are you dressed up for?' says their mother,

turning to scrutinise him. 'You look like a gangster.'

'No reason,' Duncan snaps. With him, it's always *no one, nowhere, nothing*, a magician opening his palm to show something vanished and flown. Her mother seems to soften.

'What a pity Spencer didn't get to hear your lovely speech.' She smiles, means it nicely. But since irony is the family habit, Duncan misunderstands her.

'That's it,' he says. He gets up and stamps out.

'Where are you going?' her mother calls after him. 'You haven't had your dinner yet. Why don't you stay and get to know Spencer? They're going back to America soon and then we may never see them again.' Elizabeth flinches at the hyperbole.

'*EastEnders*,' Duncan throws over his shoulder.

'It's not even time for *EastEnders* yet,' says Elizabeth.

'Well, maybe he wants to do a bit of work on his computer or play Carmageddon. This is too much togetherness for him, I suppose,' says her mother placidly.

After dinner, Spencer offers to load the dishwasher, and while he does it, her mother stands next to him, watching. She doesn't quite dare to give him instructions, but when he puts the glasses in the wrong place she takes them out and replaces them in the outer row of the top rack, the place where she believes they are least likely to get smashed. She takes the forks and knives out of the cutlery basket and turns them the other way up. 'They get cleaner right-side up,' she says. He doesn't say anything, but suddenly he turns the tap up too much while rinsing a plate and a spray of water shoots on to the floor.

At that, her mother moves away and begins to get out pudding plates and spoons. As if she's been waiting for him to make a mistake, and now he's done so, she's satisfied. Or maybe she wanted to spark a confrontation but couldn't quite face it when the opportunity arose.

Her mother's eyes glaze over. Is she thinking about it

again? Is she *back there*? A pang of the old frustrated curiosity. Elizabeth used to have a book with a picture in it of a Celtic girl dug up from a bog. Archaeologists argued over whether she killed herself or was a murder victim, but no one ever conclusively established whether there was a struggle, whether she was in pain, or whether she willingly submitted. Her mother has the same expression as the bog queen, closed and far away.

Elizabeth realises that she can't force her mother to speak, to say what was done to her and how much it hurt. She must let her mother be, loving her without labour or sacrifice. She pats her mother's shoulder and for once doesn't mind when she doesn't respond.

'I'm going to go and see if Duncan wants any pudding,' she says.

She goes up the stairs, calling his name softly, climbs the ladder to his attic room. She doesn't hear the screams and screeches of Carmageddon. He's lying on his bed on his back, sleeping off the champagne. 'Duncan?' she says. 'Why don't you come back downstairs and join the party?' The amber medicine vial is empty on his bedside table. So that was why his pocket rattled. Then Elizabeth watches everything from a great distance.

She takes him by the shoulders and shakes him, calling out his name. She grasps his face between her hands, but he doesn't open his eyes. She sits down next to him on his bed, murmuring *please please please please*, shaking her head repeatedly, patting his hand. He lies there in his silk shirt, as if he thought, like Granny, that death is something you have to dress up for. He even screwed the lid of the pill vial neatly back on. Elizabeth plucks at his shoulders and tries to pull him up, then she slaps his face so hard that her palm stings. Duncan doesn't move. A slight smile hovers about his lips. She kisses him and begins to weep with anger.

17

The New Suit

ELIZABETH SLEEPS AND SLEEPS and when she wakes up her head is throbbing and her throat is sore. She remembers everything up until he died and almost nothing of the night and the day afterwards. There were horrible screams, over and over. There was a pill mashed up in jam as when she was little and her mother telling her to take it. The slam of doors, voices downstairs, tramping shoes.

Elizabeth gets up and walks out on to the landing. Spencer and her mother are talking in the hall.

'She's been asleep for nearly twenty-four hours,' says her mother.

'Just let her,' Spencer says. 'She's probably exhausted. She was hysterical.'

'What on earth am I going to say to her when she wakes up? I don't know what to say to her.'

'The only thing you can do is be there. When my mom died, I hated it when people told me everything was going to be all right. But I liked knowing people were thinking about her and about me. I just didn't want them to problem-solve.'

'You're right,' says her mother. 'There's no point trying to console her. No one can be consoled.' She has a tissue crumpled in her hand and her eyes are raw.

'There are a lot of really helpful books on the subject,' Spencer replies. 'I could recommend some if you're interested.' Then they both look up and see Elizabeth peering at them over the banisters.

Spencer arranges her on the sofa in the sitting room with a blanket over her and her mother brings her lemon barley water and digestive biscuits on a tray. Elizabeth doesn't touch the food.

'Where is he?' she asks.

'Everything's taken care of,' says Spencer. He squeezes her arm and she shrinks back. She doesn't want his wordless pats, his smug aphorisms, his grief by the book. She doesn't want it, any of it.

'I'm going back to bed,' she says. 'And I'd like two more of those pills.'

'Oh, darling,' says her mother.

'Let her be,' says Spencer. She feels suddenly enraged, as if this is all his fault.

Elizabeth stays in bed for the next five days. Spencer said she shouldn't take sleeping pills night after night, so instead she has glasses of whiskey. She sleeps or pretends to be sleeping when Spencer comes in. The hospital has given him compassionate leave.

Should she have been more grateful for Duncan's speech or praised his new shirt? It must have been something small that changed everything. She goes over all she said and did like a beaten chess player reviewing his moves, changing each one in his mind, wondering at which point he began to lose. Duncan couldn't have been planning it for long. Otherwise why bother with the borrowed house and the job interview? Maybe it was the sight of Elizabeth on her doctor's knee. Maybe it was adult life he couldn't face, thinking it nothing but hard work and tepid passion.

His motive is an abyss over which he dangles her. His

death was a way of ensuring that he would have their attention always. Let Spencer dress and undress her and feed her dry biscuits. *Do whatever you want with me*, Elizabeth thinks. *I am dead too*.

Spencer and her mother take charge, her mother brisk with grief's adrenalin. They choose the coffin, they buy Duncan a suit. Spencer tells the mortician on what side to part Duncan's hair, how much to make him up. Her mother phones the relatives and arranges to use the wedding flowers and the wedding caterers. She says they might as well. In league with Spencer, she has become as unflinching as a nurse.

Her father does not get properly dressed for five days. He wears an old brown dressing gown, which makes him look as untidy as a rewrapped parcel, and sits at Duncan's desk. The horrible voice starts again when his footsteps sound overhead in Duncan's room. Then the doctor comes and gives Elizabeth an injection and her mother sits on the end of her bed while Spencer holds Elizabeth's hand. As she falls asleep, she hears him agreeing with her mother that it is important to let everyone grieve in their own way. Her mother has bought books on the subject, whose names resemble country and western songs: *Death Without Denial* and *But I Didn't Say Goodbye*. On her mother's bedside table, Elizabeth discovers *How To Go On Living When Someone You Love Dies*. She considers this a tasteless title. Although she does not want to die, how she will go on living does not now seem important. But her mother seems to have been waiting her whole life for this, as if now in grief, in its pomp and circumstance, she has found her vocation.

Death makes Elizabeth mean. The funeral seems all wrong, and she is angry with Spencer and her mother. It isn't what

Duncan would have wanted. For a start, he would never have let it take place in a church. He always said he was an atheist. He would have wanted flame-throwers and joke sweets that dyed your tongue blue, Roman candles stuttering gold and indoor snakes of writhing charcoal. He never joined in the Funeral Game, but these things are what he would have wanted. And the pelican lighter in his breast pocket and the bottle of Finnish vodka by his side. Not this cluttered Catholic church with its effeminate Christ, hair down to his shoulders and a loincloth as voluminous as a dress.

Spencer tries to hold Elizabeth's hand as she walks up to look at Duncan, but she brushes it away. The new suit is too tight across the shoulders, and Spencer has had Duncan's hair parted on the wrong side. The mortician has covered up the last blue marks of the black eye.

'His suit doesn't fit him right,' she whispers, frowning at Spencer. Spencer squeezes her hand.

'Sorry, baby,' he whispers. Elizabeth wonders for a moment if at some point he will stop putting up with her.

But Duncan doesn't seem bothered by the ill-fitting suit or the awkward parting in his hair. He has the suggestion of a smile, as if about to attend an interview for a job he is sure he will get.

Her father is wearing a suit too, but there is a stain on the lapel and one point of his shirt collar is tucked in, the other sticking out. He looks like a child dressed hastily by his mother. When he sees Duncan he stumbles against the coffin and makes an ugly ragged sound. Mean in death, Elizabeth wishes he would be quiet. She understands the need for mutes. Picturesque boys in top hats, paid to attend Victorian funerals and be the public face of grief, trailing their banners of black crêpe. That would be more decorous. You could pay them to weep too, but quietly.

Then Jasmine comes up escorted by Ally. Although Jasmine is wearing a blouse and skirt, Ally is wearing combat trousers and a black T-shirt with a smiley face on it. Jasmine's face is pale and greenish. She takes one look in the coffin, then rushes out with a hand over her mouth. Duncan smiles as if death was a toy he held out of reach.

Granny throws holy water on him in handfuls. She is resplendent in her fuchsia suit and a matching hat adorned with black buttons the shape of watermelon pips. Her lips are the same deep and brilliant pink as her suit and hat. Although she is dying, the funeral seems to have brought about a temporary revival. The home would not release her without a nurse, who is sitting at the back of the church, arms folded on top of her black bag. But even though Granny wears a locket full of pills around her neck, her step is sprightly, and in the end Elizabeth's mother has to whisper, 'That's enough, Mum,' to stop her splashing the holy water.

Duncan played so many tricks that he made it seem as if wounds could close and burns heal, as if death itself could be reversed. When the drops fall, even now, Elizabeth finds herself expecting him to flinch.

After the funeral, Elizabeth goes home and sleeps all afternoon. At five she wakes up, hearing doors banging and the rattle of knives and forks in the kitchen. Her mother is in there overseeing the caterers, who are preparing the food for the evening's wake. Two middle-aged men in toques are squeezing out clumsy choux pastry roses and stirring beurre blanc. Elizabeth blinks, feeling her face creased from the pillow, her hair awry and her black dress buttoned up wrong. Her mother draws her to one side. 'I don't think they know what they're doing,' she whispers. 'I could have done it twice as well. But listen, I wanted to tell you something, before you go back to America.' She squeezes Elizabeth's shoulder. 'Spencer's a good man. And he loves you almost as much as we do. Don't let him go, darling, just because of Duncan.' Elizabeth is so surprised she can't respond. Her mother has never been one for girlish confession or maternal advice. Elizabeth bought her first bra on her own, kept sex with Dax a secret. She stares at her mother, who is wearing a black Chanel suit she got in a sale. And her hair is up, expertly spiralled without a pin showing. She gives Elizabeth a sweet smile. Grief has given her the authority of a business empire.

At the wake that evening, Duncan's mates stand in a knot, awkwardly holding cocktail napkins to catch the crumbs from the caterers' smoked salmon pinwheels. There are only three mates. Somehow Elizabeth thought there would be more of them. Duncan would have wanted them to feel at home. He would have wanted salt-and-vinegar crisps, she thinks, and lamb kebabs and arcade games. She drifts around holding her third gin and tonic, hoping that no one will try to talk to her. She wishes she were invisible. She is a lost soul disgusted with the living.

'You're not how I imagined,' Granny is saying to Spencer. 'Elizabeth said you're a doctor. I could have been a nurse, you know. I always thought of doctors as tall and impressive, especially the American ones. They eat a lot over there, don't they. But you're no Arnold Schwarzenegger. It's like when you hear someone with a lovely voice on the radio and then when you see them on television, they don't look as you imagined.' Spencer is Elizabeth's height, not a hair taller.

'I hope I'm not a disappointment,' he says.

'Oh no, that isn't what I meant at all,' says Granny. Elizabeth tries to drift on but Spencer hooks his arm through hers and draws her towards him. He pretends to nibble her ear and whispers, 'Save me.'

'Spencer's not short, he's just compact,' says Elizabeth.

'Oh yes,' Granny agrees. 'Very, very compact. I prefer him to your other ones, at any rate.' She smiles at him, then raises one leg in the air, clothed in a thick beige stocking and a podiatrist's shoe. 'I'm healthy as a horse. Look at that, doctor, what do you think of that? I could be a go-go dancer.' She does look well, bright-eyed and pink-cheeked, as plump and powdered as a sugared bun. It's as if the blood is leaving her dying brain to flow faster and ever faster round her body.

When the Dover sole and profiteroles have been served in the dining room, her father tries to get everyone's attention by tinkling his fork against his glass. But the guests all carry on drinking and talking and eating, relaxed by the copious champagne. Granny has been drinking one deep draught of it after another. Over the rim of the glass her eyes sparkle flirtatiously. She clinks her fork against her glass helpfully and finally everyone is silent.

'Duncan was a loving brother and son,' says Elizabeth's father. 'He could be prickly sometimes, but underneath he had a sweet and generous nature. His favourite pastimes were magic tricks and computer games, both of which he excelled at. He was a skilled slayer of aliens and skeleton warriors and he feared nothing. His life was short but glorious. Let us all raise a glass to him.'

Granny holds her glass high, turns to Elizabeth and Spencer, and says, 'I wish you love, love, love, and happiness.' *You would never guess*, thinks Elizabeth, *that Granny killed a man*. And as Granny killed her husband, Elizabeth tried to kill Duncan. Which was worse? Granny's crime was an accident, hers a failure. And is this death something to do with that one, some unfathomable quid pro quo?

Elizabeth leans over to clink her glass with Granny's, and says, 'So you approve?'

'You are the very embodiment of romance,' Granny replies grandly. 'And the most beautiful bride I've ever seen.' Somehow Granny has managed to smudge her lipstick so that there is a sticky gash of it down her chin. She looks as if she's been drinking blood, full-fed on young life. Spencer starts and Elizabeth smiles nervously. She wonders if this is what Catholicism does to you in the end. On the threshold of the final paradox when death becomes eternal life, maybe you begin to see everything back to front. But then Granny has always preferred to turn a blind eye on misfortune.

Granny begins to chase the peas around her plate with her fork, giggling to herself. Then she gives up, and says out of nowhere, 'I've got a little bird table in my garden now. In the spring, the blue tweets come and I hear them singing from my kitchen window. Tit, tit, tit, tit. Then when the autumn comes, they just fly away.'

'Oh God,' murmurs Elizabeth's mother. She lays a hand on the server's arm before he can refill Granny's glass. 'Are you all right, Mum?' she asks gently.

'In the pink,' Granny replies. 'But soon I'll fly away too. Tit, tit,' she adds, with a sly look in her eye.

Elizabeth realises that soon it will be too late for those two to forgive each other. And even if they did speak the necessary words, even if they both said, *I'm sorry, I love you,* thirty years have passed and been wasted between them. Elizabeth's mother pats Granny's hand. 'You won't fly away quite yet, though,' she says briskly, although her face is sad.

Elizabeth's mother rose at dawn to decorate the dining room with branches of fir and gold-sprayed pine cones and swags of white silk ribbon. There are white roses and lilies and carnations in vases everywhere. She had to borrow some vases from the neighbours because she didn't have enough. The house looks far more festive than it ever did at Christmas. They will make an effort, the flowers say, observe the occasion with due ceremony, no matter how much death there has been. The house is as magnificent as a general loaded with medals.

In the middle of the plain there is a great open gash. Spencer and Elizabeth stand on the one bridge across it, looking down at the river hundreds of feet below. Stunted juniper and seep willow cling to the steep grey crags on either side of it. Duncan would have liked this bridge. He would have wanted Elizabeth to hold his hand and lean as far out as she dared.

'Are you feeling sad?' Spencer asks. She doesn't say anything. She feels him tense. He believes in perfect sincerity, that each should open their self completely to the other.

'I don't have to tell you everything, you know,' she says, squeezing his arm. 'That way you can keep on getting to know me, plumbing ever new mysteries.'

'But you haven't got any dark secrets, have you?' he asks. 'I mean, apart from what I know about?'

'Not really,' she says. 'No real skeletons in my past.' Her mother's secret isn't hers to tell.

'There must be something,' says Spencer. 'Everyone has something.'

'Nothing very dramatic. I kissed a girl. I took cocaine. I was a strip-dancer for a night in a place called the Silk Academy. And I had a boyfriend who used to slash my arms with a knife.'

Spencer shudders. 'You never told me that.'

'It was just a weird phase. I was dabbling.'

'Don't worry, I still love you,' he says. 'Whatever you did or didn't do.'

Elizabeth decides not to mention the fight with Duncan. After all, it's over now. But is she lying to Spencer? Or just not telling the whole truth? *I killed my brother. And he came back to life.* Elizabeth doesn't want to keep anything back from Spencer, to cramp their intimacy. He believes that the periodic exegesis of the heart is necessary for love to flow. But she's not sure she could make him understand. What has happened to her would take so much explaining.

Elizabeth runs her fingers over the names scratched on the railing of the bridge. Hundreds of couples have written their names there. Something about the chasm below drives them to declare their love, their hold on life.

'What do you want to do about the wedding?' Spencer asks. 'We could even do it over here, now that Granny's had her party.' Elizabeth looks at the rushing water hundreds of feet below. She remembers Duncan calling her name. *Elizabeth, Elizabeth.* Spencer strokes her shoulder.

'Sweetheart?' She steps back from the drop and puts her arm through his.

'I was just thinking that Vegas is right down the road,' she says.

She must have been eight or nine. In those days, she almost believed his tricks were real magic. By the suppressed excitement in his voice, she could tell he had another stunt ready. He was standing at the top of the ladder outside his room and he bent down for a minute. There was the tiny scratch of a lighter and then a ring of flame surrounded him. A delicious shiver ran down her spine. *My brother is the Prince of Darkness,* she thought. They stood there with the line of fire between them until it flickered and went out.